Thirteen
Plus One

The Winnie Years

Thirteen
Plus One

LAUREN MYRACLE

PUFFIN BOOKS
An Imprint of Penguin Group (USA) Inc.

PUFFIN BOOKS

Published by the Penguin Group

Penguin Young Readers Group, 345 Hudson Street, New York, New York 10014, U.S.A.

Penguin Group (Canada), 90 Eglinton Avenue East, Suite 700, Toronto, Ontario, Canada M4P 2Y3
(a division of Pearson Penguin Canada Inc.)

Penguin Books Ltd, 80 Strand, London WC2R 0RL, England

Penguin Ireland, 25 St Stephen's Green, Dublin 2, Ireland (a division of Penguin Books Ltd)

Penguin Group (Australia), 250 Camberwell Road, Camberwell, Victoria 3124, Australia
(a division of Pearson Australia Group Pty Ltd)

Penguin Books India Pvt Ltd, 11 Community Centre,
Panchsheel Park, New Delhi - 110 017, India

Penguin Group (NZ), 67 Apollo Drive, Rosedale, Auckland 0632, New Zealand
(a division of Pearson New Zealand Ltd.)

Penguin Books (South Africa) (Pty) Ltd, 24 Sturdee Avenue,
Rosebank, Johannesburg 2196, South Africa

Registered Offices: Penguin Books Ltd, 80 Strand, London WC2R 0RL, England

First published in the United States of America by Dutton Children's Books,
a division of Penguin Young Readers Group, 2010
Published by Puffin Books, a division of Penguin Young Readers Group, 2011

5 7 9 10 8 6 4

LIBRARY OF CONGRESS CATALOGING-IN-PUBLICATION DATA IS AVAILABLE

Puffin Books ISBN 978-0-14-241901-4

Designed by Irene Vandervoort
Text set in ITC Esprit

Printed in the United States of America

for Ariel,
whose mommy is (usually) a very good girl

Acknowledgments

All of you Dutton-buttons, thank you for being fabulous. Y'all take such good care of me! Special smoochie thanks to the sales and marketing folks who work so hard to get Winnie out into the world, and special smoochie-huggie-kissie-playful-smack-on-the-booty thanks to Allison, Eileen, Emily, Irene, Jennifer, Kim, Lauri, RasShahn, Samantha, Scottie, and Theresa. Rock your sweet selves on!

Rosanne? You deserve more "forgive me" cupcakes than I can ever give you. Thank you for caring enough about the book to keep helping me make it better, long after you should have locked me up in the special jail cell copy editors reserve for meddlesome authors.

Beegee, you bring the girls into living color. Thank you. Your Winnie *is* Winnie, and she's just perfect.

Lisa, you are there for me whenever I need you—and I realize with pink cheeks that I need you a lot, and usually for total nonsense, like a delightful distraction chat when Julie—*ahem*—is "working." Plus, you watched over me while I slept. You are a dear.

High-fives to my Starbucks buddies: Angie, Seth, Scottie, Ian, Aaron, Audrey, Bre, Michelle, Lolo, Christy, Carly, and Kendra. It's not the caffeine I come for. It's y'all.

Barry, your inner thirteen-plus-one-year-old is alive and strong, and I love that about you. Plus, you know, the fact that you're the most amazing agent ever, dude.

Julie? You are the "wuh" of Winnie. Without you, she wouldn't be whole. You are Wonderful Plus Infinity, which equals winninity. ☺

Hugs to my friends, who keep me relatively functional: Julianne, Maggie, Virginia, Jackie, Nina, Emily, Sarah, and Bob.

Kisses to my family, who is just dysfunctional enough (in a good way!) to keep life from ever being boring.

And hugs, kisses, and marshmallow dreams for Jack, Al, Jamie, and Mirabelle. I love you, forever and ever, amen.

Thirteen
Plus One

Say Out Loud
What I Want Out of Life

THE THING ABOUT BIRTHDAYS, at least *fourteenth* birthdays, is that they're more . . . well . . . *complex* than every single birthday that came before. Or maybe the only reason I thought that was because I just this very day turned fourteen. Me me me me me me! Fourteen, fourteen, fourteen, fourteen!!!!

In the cozy warmth of my bed, I pointed my toes and s-t-r-e-t-c-h-e-d my arms above my head. Then in one great *whoosh,* I let my limbs flop down. The mattress jounced beneath me, and I exhaled happily and reflected on my life. *Fourteen years and counting, baby.* That was a lot of birthdays!

The earliest ones, I didn't remember. There'd been cake and me looking adorable with icing in my hair, all the normal stuff. On my third birthday, according to family mythology, I'd tilted my chair so far back that it toppled over—with me in it. Dad said my skull hit the floor with a *thwack.* He also said that my older sister, Sandra, had burst into tears because she was so worried about me. *Aw,* so sweet (and a teeny bit funny).

Other birthday highlights:

 • the extremely beautiful fairy cake Mom made
 me when I turned four;
 • the toolbox Dad gave me when I turned seven,
 because that was what I'd wanted;
 • the (okay, embarrassing, but still *a very good
 memory*) American Girl tea party I'd had when I
 turned nine. My friends and I wore fancy dresses,
 and so did our dolls, and Mom served cucumber
 sandwiches, which nobody ate.

Then I reached the land of double digits. That was
huge—though scary, too—and on my tenth birthday, I left a
secret note of encouragement to myself in the hollow interior
of a way-high piece of molding in our way-old house. I also
left a candy bar. Then one weekend Dad threw himself into
a short-lived let's-spiff-this-place-up frenzy, and he ripped
the molding down. Bye-bye candy bar, bye-bye note of
encouragement. Sad!

On my eleventh birthday, I had a slumber party, and I
remember being so excited I couldn't sit still. I bounced on
the sofa, desperate for my friends to arrive, and chanted *get
here get here get here* in my head.

That was the birthday Amanda gave me my cat, Sweetie-
Pie, who was then just a kitten, with paws too big for her
fuzzy little body. She had the scratchiest, teensiest *mew*. I

named her Sweetie-Pie to be twinsies with Amanda's cat, Sweet Pea, because Amanda and I—back then—were the bestest of best friends. Sweetie-Pie still has a scratchy *mew*, but Amanda and I are no longer best friends. For that matter, we're hardly friends at all.

How did that happen? I mean, I know how it happened. I was there for all the cracks and fissures and seemingly unimportant differences that piled up and turned into no-more-Amanda. But still—how did it happen? *Why* did it happen?

This was an example of the complexity of turning fourteen: looking back at your life and just . . . wondering.

The year I turned twelve, Mom and Dad took me to Benihana for a fancy birthday dinner. I was allowed to invite one friend, and I invited Dinah, who had become my new Amanda. Except, not really. Not because Dinah wasn't as good as Amanda, because she was . . . even though that's a stupid and horrible way to put it, "as good as."

Dinah was wonderful, steady and loyal and true. (And she still is.) She maybe wasn't as exciting as Amanda, but that wasn't Dinah's fault.

At any rate, it hardly mattered, since that fall we started seventh grade—and Cinnamon entered the picture. Cinnamon filled the "exciting" role and more. I met her in PE and realized in the locker room that she wore a thong. Omigosh, I was in shock.

For my thirteenth birthday, Mom let me, Dinah, and

Cinnamon get makeovers at the Bobbi Brown makeup counter at Lenox Mall. I still have the Rockstar glitter dust I picked out.

That was a fun night, yet for some reason looking back on it now made me feel melancholy. Well, melancholy-*ish*. *Ish*ly melancholy, not fully melancholy.

I turned my head and looked at my clock. It was seven-thirty, which meant I should be rolling out of bed and getting ready for school. Instead, I let my head loll back, because I wasn't done thinking yet. Because while all my birthdays mattered, they weren't here anymore. They were in the past. Turning fourteen was happening *right now*, and brought me one step closer to growing up, and my feelings toward *that* were all over the place.

For the most part, I was excited. Growing up meant more privileges, more freedom, one day possibly even a car, *mwahaha*. Possibly even a convertible, although that would have to wait till I was in my twenties and living on my own, since no way would Mom and Dad ever let me drive around without a roof over my head.

At the same time, there were aspects of growing up that made my stomach clench. Like, I worried about becoming boring and *serious* (to be said in a very *serious* voice). I worried about the steady march of month after month after month . . . until one day I'd be dead and in a coffin. *Bang bang bang* would go the nails, and gee, wasn't that a lovely birthday sentiment?

But death was a long, long, *long* time away. At least, I hoped. There was something closer on the horizon that worried me far more . . . and its name was high school.

Today was March eleventh, and the school year ended on May twenty-eighth, which meant I had a little over two months left of junior high. Then would come summer, and then, *bam*. A new school year would start, and I, Winnie Perry, would be a freshman in high school.

It was mind-blowing. Like, seriously mind-blowing, so when I heard my brother and sister singing in the hall outside my room, I was glad for the distraction.

"Do you like Pop-Tarts?" Sandra belted out from the hall.

"Yes, I like Pop-Tarts!" Ty caroled back.

"Do you like OJ?"

"Yes, I like OJ!"

My bedroom door flew open, and I smiled to see that the singing brigade was led by neither Sandra nor Ty, but by my brand-new baby sister, Maggie, who was too little to even crawl.

"Doo dootie doot, can't wait to have breakfast!" Sandra and Ty bellowed, while teensy baby Maggie showed off her dance moves, dangling from Sandra's hands like a well-intentioned bag of flour.

"Did y'all make me breakfast in bed?" I said. "You guys!"

"Ooo, that would have been nice of us," Sandra said,

drawing Maggie close and hitching her into a comfy position. "But alas . . . no."

"I brought you this, though," Ty said. He plopped onto the bed beside me and held out half a stick of gum.

"Hey, thanks."

"And now I'm going to bury my head under your shoulder pit." He smushed his warm seven-year-old body against me, attempting to worm his head up under my arm.

"Armpit, not shoulder pit," I said, giggling. "And quit it."

"Then come downstairs and have your delicious Pop-Tart."

"Okay," I said. "Put it in the toaster for me?"

"Sure," Ty said. He kissed my cheek, then hopped up and headed for the door. Sandra moved to follow him.

"Sandra, wait," I called. I kicked off my covers. "Can I talk to you for a sec?"

She turned back. "What's up?"

"Well, there's something embarrassing I want to tell you. It's stupid, but I need to get it off my chest. And you're my big sister, *soooo* . . ."

Sandra glanced at her watch.

"I'm worried about high school," I blurted.

She looked at me like I was crazy. "What? *Why?*"

I looked at her like *she* was crazy. "Well, because it's *high school.*"

"But you haven't even graduated from junior high. It's only March."

"Yes, but what comes after March? *April*. And what comes after April? *May*. And what comes after—"

"I know my months, Winnie. I've known them since I was four."

I stood and took baby Mags from her, being careful of her wobbly head. I pulled her close and whispered, "I would help *you*, baby Maggie. If you were going through times of trouble."

"Oh, good God," Sandra said.

Maggie made the *pluh* sound she was so good at. She was soft and cuddly.

"You want to know what your problem is, Winnie?" Sandra said. "You need to shift your paradigm."

"Huh?"

"Your *paradigm*. The way you look at the world." She leaned against the door frame. "How do you look at the world, Winnie?"

"Um, with my eyeballs?"

Sandra almost smiled, but managed to suppress it. "Winnie, if high school is scaring you—"

"I never said it was *scaring* me," I interrupted.

"Then stop obsessing about it. Live in the now, little sis."

"Live in the now," I repeated.

"Yeah. Quit focusing on *March* and then *April* and then *May*, on and on until infinity. Quit thinking so linearly. Do you know what 'linearly' means?"

I gave her a look.

She gave me a similar look in return, as if to imply that in that case, she didn't see the problem. "So start asking yourself, 'What can I do *now*? What can I change about my life situation *now*?'"

"You've been reading your self-help books again, haven't you?" I said. With college right around the corner, Sandra had started reading books with titles like *What Color Is Your Parachute?* and *Who Moved My Cheese?* "Next are you going to ask me what color my cheese is?"

"Hey, you're the one who asked for advice." She reclaimed baby Maggie. "Get dressed and come downstairs, birthday girl."

I flopped back onto my bed. "Aw, man. Can't my 'life situation' be staying in bed? For, like, a really long time?"

"Nope. You have to move forward, even if you don't want to, because guess what? The only thing worse than growing up—"

I cradled my head in my hands. "*Ugh*. Is *not* growing up. Omigosh, I can't believe you just said that."

"I didn't. You did." She pushed her hand through her blond hair. "What *I* was going to say is that the only thing worse than growing up is never learning how."

She regarded me archly. I struggled to come up with a response, but came up dry.

Baby Maggie hiccuped, and it came with drool, which dribbled onto Sandra's shirt.

"My sentiments ex*act*ly," I said, laughing. I lifted baby Maggie's little wrist and gave her a high five.

I arrived at school to find my locker decorated with streamers, balloons and, inexplicably, mini-marshmallows, the pastel-colored ones that supposedly have fruit flavors.

Cinnamon and Dinah jumped out from behind a classroom door. "Surprise!" they cried. "Happy birthday!"

I beamed and hugged them and told them they were the best friends ever. Then I plucked off a pale green marshmallow and held it up. "Care to explain?"

"Ah, yes, the marshmallows," Cinnamon said. "Marshmallows make your boobs grow, didn't you know?"

"Oh, please. They do not." I processed her remark further. "*Hey*. What are you saying?"

"You want to keep Lars around, right?"

"Lars doesn't like me for my *boobs*. Don't be gross."

"Of course he doesn't," Dinah said, and because she was Dinah, she meant her remark to be comforting.

But because Cinnamon was Cinnamon, she laughed. As in, *Of course Lars doesn't like you for your boobs, since you don't* have *any*.

Plus, Cinnamon was in a bitter phase. Lars's best friend, Bryce, had broken up with her less than a month ago (on Facebook—ag), and she was so not over it, it wasn't funny.

I placed my hands on her shoulders. "Okay, several things to discuss. A: Lars likes me for *me*, not for my body."

She snorted.

"B: While Lars has the highest respect for my hilariousness, wit, and moral fiber—"

She snorted again, and I dug my fingers into the tender space between her shoulder blades.

"Ahem," I said over her elaborate sounds of pain. I also ignored the way she was shrinking beneath my grip like a melting wicked witch. "While everything I just said is true, I suppose it's possible, since he's a boy, that he is C: Drawn to my incredible hotness as well."

"Full of yourself much?" Cinnamon said from her scrunched-down position. "Is that what happens when you turn fourteen?"

I blushed, because while I could talk the talk—boobs, boobage, hotness—I was actually totally faking it. I *did* hope Lars thought I was hot, but no way would I really prance around saying, "Look at me! Ooo, baby, I am *hot*!"

I released her. "And finally, D: If marshmallows are supposed to make your boobs grow, and you think I need bigger boobs to keep Lars around, then why did you give me *mini*-marshmallows, huh?"

I thought I had her, when actually I'd walked straight into her trap.

"Can't build Rome in a day," she said.

I tugged a pink marshmallow off my locker and lobbed it at her. I pulled off five more in assorted colors and did the same thing. She ducked and squealed.

"You guys," Dinah said, scanning the hall for teachers. Then a yellow marshmallow bounced off Cinnamon and hit Dinah's cheek. She swiveled her head my way.

"Oh, *Win*nie," she said, her tone suggesting I'd made a bad decision.

"Uh-oh," I said.

She slipped off her backpack, caught the strap in the crook of her elbow, and unzipped the bottom pocket.

"Teachers?" I called, adopting her survival strategy. "Oh, friendly *tea*chers!"

"Would you grab her, please?" Dinah asked Cinnamon.

"Certainly," Cinnamon said. She pinned my arms behind me as Dinah tugged free a half-full bag of mini-marshmallows.

"I'm sorry, I'm sorry!" I cried. "I'll never marshmallow you again, I promise!"

By now other girls were staring, but we didn't care. We liked being spazzy. We liked it even though we were eighth graders who should be above such things—and I personally hoped we'd stay spazzy all the way through high school and beyond. In fact, right then and there I charged myself with a mission: *Yes, high school is coming—not that I'm obsessing about it, since I'm living in the now. But stay spazzy anyway!!!*

"Cinnamon?" Dinah said. "Would you join me in singing 'Happy Birthday' to our dear Winnie?"

"Absolutely," Cinnamon said.

"Not necessary," I protested. "Seriously."

Dinah stepped closer, jiggling the bag of marshmallows. "Happy birthday to you . . ."

Cinnamon joined in. She had me in a death grip, and she drove her knee into my spine to keep me from slithering from her grasp. "Happy birthday *to* you . . ."

Dinah undid the twisty tie on the bag of mini-marshmallows. "Happy *birth*day dear *Win*nie,"— she raised the bag and dumped it over my head—"*Hap*py *birth*day to yo-u-u-u-u!!!!"

Some of the marshmallows got caught in my hair. Some went down my shirt. They smelled sweet and left puffs of powdery sugar on my skin.

Cinnamon was snort-giggling so hard that her muscles went limp, and together we sank to the floor. People had to step over us. Malena, snark mistress extraordinaire and *not* my friend, sniffed in disdain.

"You have a *marshmallow* in your braid," she announced.

"I know, right?" I said. "It's, like, all the rage in Paris."

"Also Topeka," Cinnamon said, fully spread-eagled on the floor. No one loved taking up space like Cinnamon did. "I mean, don't quote me on it or anything, but . . . yeah."

Malena's gaze traveled up to my locker, to the streamers and the balloons and the poster Dinah and Cinnamon made.

"Let me guess. Your birthday?" She said it as if it—or I—was a disease.

I widened my eyes and made an "O" out of my mouth, to mean *Omigosh! You are a genius!*

"And I suppose Tweedledum and Tweedledee made you a cake," she continued. "And they'll bring it to you at lunch and make you blow out the candles in front of everybody, and it will be *soooooo* special."

"Me sure hope so," I said happily. "Me love cake."

Dinah and Cinnamon shared a glance—only it wasn't of the *hee-hee-we're-so-sneaky* sort.

"You . . . didn't bring me a cake?" I faltered.

Dinah's eyes flew to Malena, which told me she didn't want to discuss it in public. Which also told me (*and* Malena) what the answer was.

Malena laughed a weird laugh, as if she hadn't expected to make an honest hit. *"Ouch,"* she said, and then she strolled away in her tight white pants.

The homeroom bell rang. I stayed on the floor, marshmallows all around me. One in my bra.

"No cake?" I said. "For real?"

"I wanted to make one," Dinah said. "But we didn't have any eggs!"

Cinnamon pushed herself up onto her elbows. "And I suck at cooking. You know that."

True, but even a burned-on-the-outside, oozy-on-the-inside cake was better than no cake at all.

"Won't we have cake tonight?" Dinah asked. She meant at my birthday-slash-sleepover party. It was going to be a low-key affair, just Dinah and Cinnamon.

I tried to shrug off my disappointment. "Yeah, of course."

"I can't wait to see little Maggie," Dinah said. Tonight would be her very first time to meet little Mags—and Cinnamon's, too—since Mom brought Maggie home from the hospital just yesterday.

I got to my feet. "She might be asleep, and if she's sleeping, we aren't allowed to bother her. Just to warn you."

Cinnamon looked at me funny, like maybe I was punishing them for not making me a cake.

Was I?

I didn't want to be that person. *Yuck.* So I added a second item to my mental To-Do-Before-High-School list. Maybe I'd even write this list down at some point.

Anyway, the second thing on my list was to work on BEING MATURE, even when people let me down. That was a worthwhile goal, right?

Then it occurred to me that I'd challenged myself first to be spazzy, and two seconds later to work on being mature.

Wow, Winnie, said a not-so-nice voice inside of me. *How very inspiring.*

"We *did* bring you marshmallows," Cinnamon pointed out.

"Yes," I acknowledged. "Yes, you did." And the one in my bra was going to require a trip to the girls' room, as my oh-so-subtle twitching was doing nothing to dislodge it.

Or I could leave it in as padding, I suppose. Apparently, marshmallows *did* make your boobs bigger. Even the mini ones.

• • •

All morning long, I kept a hopeful eye out for Lars. Yes, my decorated locker was lovely, and yes, I blushed adorably (or so I hoped) when my French class sang *Bon Anniversaire* to *moi*. But Lars was my boyfriend, my yummy, wonderful boyfriend, and I couldn't wait to find out what kind of birthday surprise he had up his sleeve.

Seeing Lars at school was tricky, however, because Lars was in ninth grade, not eighth. Unlike me, he was already *in* high school. Lars had gone where no man had gone before (not counting the fifty jillion men and women who had), and who did he leave behind? *Me*.

It was a sticky wicket, and since the high school was on a physically separate part of campus, our paths didn't usually cross unless we made a point of making it happen. Like, he'd text me, or I'd text him, and we'd plan a quickie by the stone bench outside Pressley Hall at ten o'clock or whatever.

(By "quickie," I didn't mean anything obscene. Just a smile and a brush of our fingertips, *possibly* a kiss. Lips only, no tongue. Because it's school! *Der!*)

But our texting days came to a screeching halt last week when my cell phone, a cheapo from Best Buy, went *fllllemph* and never worked again. I shared with Mom and Dad my very good idea of how they could get me a new one for my birthday—*like for example an iPhone, *big smile*—and they shared with me their exceedingly unsatisfying opinion that if I wanted an iPhone, I was going to have to save up for it myself.

Sadly, that was unlikely to happen in the next millennium. I barely had enough cash to support my Java Chip Frappuccino habit, which frankly was getting out of hand.

At any rate, being without a cell phone meant that I couldn't text Lars and ask him what was up; I could only gaze longingly across the quad and wish he'd miraculously appear. I suppose I could have called him last night and said, "Hey, since tomorrow's my birthday—and let's be honest, I *know* you want to see me—let's meet at blankety-blank after third period, 'kay?"

But I would have felt weird doing that. I would have felt like I was being needy, and I refused to be needy, because our relationship had only recently normalized after a brief breakup that had to do with that very thing. A quick and sad recap: Lars had been flirting with other girls. *Bad Lars.* He'd been especially flirty with one girl in particular, a *cough-cough* high school girl named *cough-cough* Brianna. *Bad bad superbad Brianna.*

I should have been strong enough to confront Lars and say, "You're being a jerk." But I wasn't. Instead, I cried and cried, until Sandra finally said, "Woman up, little sis! Wake up and smell your ultra-fabulous girl power!"

So—big breath—I worked up every ounce of courage I had and told Lars he had to treat me right if he wanted us to get back together. And happy happy joy joy! *He listened!!!!*

And things got better. *Really* better. Matter of fact, things were pretty darn fab between us these days, and I didn't want to jinx it by turning back into Needy Girl.

Anyway, what was I worried about? Lars knew I was celebrating my b-day with Dinah and Cinnamon tonight. Therefore, he also knew that any quality time he wanted to have with me was going to have to happen here, at school.

For the record, I would have celebrated with him tonight if he'd asked. We could have gone to Sugar Sweet Sunshine for cupcakes, which was my secret birthday fantasy. Or possibly not-so-secret, since I might have mentioned it to Lars one or two times. Possibly three.

But I figured he didn't want to get in the way of my girl time, which was gentlemanly and sweet . . . except for the one small fact that I would have rather spent it with him.

Ag, I told myself, not wanting to go down the road of wishing for things that weren't going to happen. *Stop that right now. Say "no" to needy!*

I wondered what sort of birthday treat he'd planned. A present slipped into my locker? Flowers delivered to the school office? A candle stuck into a cafeteria brownie, which he'd bring me during my lunch period?

Or . . . *I know*! A cake, to make up for the one that Dinah and Cinnamon forgot to bake!!!

Of course, I thought. I was finally putting the pieces together, and I felt foolish for being so slow. As if Dinah and Cinnamon would really forget to bring me, their BFF, a cake on her fourteenth b-day. They might "forget," but they would never *forget*.

Last year, when Sandra turned seventeen, her boyfriend, Bo, threw her a moonlight-picnic surprise party. She never saw it coming. And then—*ta-da*! Turned out he'd orchestrated the perfect romantic evening for her, complete with a lopsided three-layer cake he baked and frosted himself.

I wasn't Sandra, and Lars wasn't Bo. I knew that. And I knew I shouldn't use Sandra's life as a model for my own.

But still . . . *hmmm. Hmmity-hmmity-hum.* Take several loudly issued hints about my cupcake fantasy, add in Dinah and Cinnamon's "forgetfulness," and . . . *squeee*! How sweet and adorable would it be to have my high school boyfriend bring me a cupcake in front of the whole eighth grade?!

I could see it now: I would gasp in delight, then hop up and give Lars a hug. I'd look deep into those gorgeous hazel eyes of his, and he'd tilt my chin and kiss me, right there in the cafeteria. Just a light peck.

It would be the best birthday surprise ever.

"So should we sit at our normal table?" I asked as I headed out of the food line with Cinnamon and Dinah.

Cinnamon gave me the old fish eye, with one eyebrow cocked. "Unless you'd prefer to sit at our abnormal table?"

I giggled. My gaze flitted about the cafeteria.

"You're the birthday girl," Dinah said. "We can sit wherever you want."

"Right. Normal table it is." I walked with breezy confidence to our table by the wall. Except, is it breezy confidence if you're faking both the breeze and the confidence?

Once seated, I smiled (brightly!) and said (brightly!), "So!"

Cinnamon chomped off a bite of her corn dog. She had an excellent poker face.

I turned to Dinah, who did not, in general, have an excellent poker face.

"Oh, Dinah," I said fondly. "You're such a cupcake, did you know that? You're my dearest-ever cupcake of a friend. You really are."

I watched for revealing tics or twitches. She gave away nothing, but said only, "I am?"

"You silly! Of course!"

"Well . . . thanks, my little, um, cherry Twizzler."

"Hey, what am I?" Cinnamon demanded. "If she's your little cupcake, and you're her cherry Twizzler, what am I?"

I gave a slight nod of appreciation. Was she good at diversion or what?

"Hmm. You can be . . . my Dorito!"

"What if I don't want to be a Dorito?"

"Then you can be another cupcake, okay?" My eyeballs darted here, there, and everywhere. Ty had a party trick where he could make his eyeballs vibrate, and that's what it felt like mine were doing. *Lars! O, Lars! Wherefore art thou, Lars?*

At some point during the eyeball-vibrating, a weird-ish silence alerted me to the fact that Cinnamon and Dinah were regarding me quizzically.

"Winnie?" Cinnamon said. "Do we have cupcakes on our brain?"

"I don't know. *Do* we?" I volleyed back. Then, because that was too obvious, I lifted my hair away from my head and said, "No, I do not have cupcakes on my brain. See?"

Dinah wrinkled her brow. "You are odd, Winnie."

"Ha ha. I know. But, okay, that new cupcake store . . . it's so cute, don't you think? Sugar Sweet Sunshine?"

"I've only seen it from the outside," Dinah said. "But it looks cute. And I love cupcakes."

"Me too!" I exclaimed. Now we were getting somewhere!

"I like cupcakes *if* they're good," Cinnamon said. "Sometimes they're all about the frosting, you know? In a bad way, like, *Ooo, let's put a big dollop of frosting on this baby just to make it pretty!* But if the frosting is nasty potato, then what's the point?"

Yes, I thought, giving her a moment of my attention. *What* is *the point? Or rather, what is* your *point?*

I returned to my scan-o-rama. And then I asked the one question I should have known better than to ask. I *did* know better, but I was thinking the words so hard, my lips couldn't hold them back.

"Have y'all seen Lars?" I said.

And then . . . *beat* . . . *beat* . . . the *uh-oh* feeling returned. Dinah and Cinnamon were sharing a look, and it was the same exact look they'd exchanged earlier when I asked if they truly hadn't baked me a cake.

"Never mind," I said.

"Oh man," Cinnamon said.

"Really. Never mind."

"You thought he was going to bring you a cupcake," she said flatly. She wasn't trying to be cruel; she was just being Cinnamon. Plus she was in an anti-boy phase.

No, no, no, I said to the tears pressing against my eyes. *Absolutely not.*

"Winnie . . ." Dinah said, and if Cinnamon was too harsh, Dinah was too kind.

"Don't," I whispered.

There was silence for several seconds. Cinnamon stole a fry.

"I'm sure he's got something really nice planned," Dinah said.

"I'm sure he does, too." I smiled. It felt hard on my face.

"Totally," Cinnamon said. There was a chewed-up French fry in her mouth, and then she swallowed, and it was gone. She swiped her mouth with the back of her hand. "Unless he doesn't."

He didn't.

He gave me—wait for it—a Starbucks card.

"Do you like it?" he said.

"I love it," I lied. It was after our last class. He'd found me in the junior high parking lot, where I was waiting for Sandra to pick me up. It was the same parking lot where many moons ago, he'd first held my hand. Seriously, like *twelve whole moons*, practically to the day.

And for my birthday, he gave me a Starbucks card?! A Starbucks card was not many-moons-worthy. A Starbucks card was for a two-moons girlfriend at best. Any moons after that was stretching it.

"It has a beach scene on it," he said, leaning close and putting his hand over mine to tilt the card. "See?"

"It's pretty," I said. *For a Starbucks card*.

"Because I know you love the beach, and those Frappuccino drinks."

I exhaled. I *did* love the beach and those Frappuccino drinks.

He slipped his arm around my waist and drew me close, not caring that the whole junior high was milling about, chatting and texting and waiting for their rides.

"Wouldn't it be awesome to go to the beach together one day?" he said into my ear. "We could sit on the sand . . . watch the sunset . . ."

"Enjoy a delicious iced beverage from Starbucks . . ."

"Ex*act*ly."

I wiggled free, saying, "There's Sandra. Gotta go."

His arms, now empty, fell to his sides. He drew his eyebrows together, and his expression confused me. Was he . . . *sad*?

"Lars?"

He shook it off with a grin. "So, hey. I want you to have fun with Dinah and Cinnamon tonight, all right?"

He was all charm and confidence, only, I didn't *want* charm and confidence. I wanted to boot-kick his charm and confidence to China. I kinda wanted to boot-kick him to China, too. Where did he get off, instructing me to "have fun"?

"We will have fun," I informed him, drawing myself tall. "I'm sure we'll have a blast, *all right*?"

Again his brow furrowed, and I wanted him to *say* it, to ask what was wrong. Then I could hint that while a Starbucks card was a ducky gift for, say, his aging aunt Frances, if a guy's been going out with a girl for a whole year, he was supposed to get her something nicer.

But he lifted his hand that way guys do, an awkward good-bye that was annoyingly adorable.

The edges of my Starbucks card dug into my palm. I ducked my head and left.

At home, Mom said, "Hi, birthday girl. You have a good day?" She was on the sun porch, sprawled on the love seat. Baby Maggie was asleep in her arms. Baby Maggie was perfect and unspoiled, a drowsing daffodil, and I thought, *Oh, to be young and innocent.*

"Listen, sweetie," Mom went on. Apparently she hadn't really wanted an answer about my day. "I hope you'll forgive me . . . but I never found time to bake a cake."

My mouth fell open. My own *mother* failed to make me a cake? For real?

"Mom," I said. "Please tell me you're kidding."

Mom gestured at baby Maggie. "I forgot to order the model with the 'sleep' button, it seems."

"She's sleeping now."

"Because she's in my arms. The minute I try to put her down, she turns into a red-faced crying machine."

Well, I could be a red-faced crying machine, I thought. *If that's what it takes. If I weren't fourteen and too old to throw fits.*

"Want me to call your dad and have him pick up a cake from Whole Foods?" Mom asked.

No, I wanted Mom to go back in time and bake me one. I wanted Dinah and Cinnamon to go back in time and bake me one. I wanted Lars to go back in time and haul his lame self to Sugar Sweet Sunshine and pick me out a perfect chocolate cupcake and jab a single pink candle in it. Was that really so much to ask?

But if I wanted a cake at all, it looked like a cake from stupid Whole Foods was the only option left.

"Fine," I muttered.

She glanced about. She patted the cushions with her free hand. "I don't have my phone. I must have left it in the kitchen. Will you call him, baby?"

I stomped off. First she forgot my cake, and now she wanted *me* to call Dad and ask him to go buy one? And if he said no, then what? Was I supposed to trudge the five miles to Whole Foods and do it myself?

Blah, blah, blah, mean-me said. *Whine, whine, whine. At least you have a roof over your head. At least you're not starving, or in a prisoner detention center, or missing an eye.*

Note to self (to add to the others I'd racked up): *Stop being so self-centered. Your self-centeredness would make starving blind people throw up a little in their mouths.*

Late afternoon sunlight gave the kitchen a magical glow, not that I was in the mood for magic. I skimmed the table, the counters, the granite island, but Mom's cell phone wasn't there. On the funny half-desk by the back door, however, I spotted a slim black box topped with a red bow.

My breath flew out of me, and then I sucked it back in. I felt ashamed, jittery, and buoyant all at once.

Don't get your hopes up, mean-me said as I hurried over. *Don't get excited over nothing.*

I pulled off the bow. Underneath, etched into the top of the box, was an image of an apple.

Omigosh, omigosh.

I lifted the lid to reveal a sleek, white iPhone. An *iPhone.* I slipped it out of its box and marveled at how smooth it was. How nearly weightless. I turned it over and saw that it had sixteen gigabytes of memory, which was a *ton*—enough to store all my dreams and more. Could dreams be stored?

I found the ON button and held it down, and—*oh, the glory*—the screen came to life, complete with a multitude of fabulous application icons. TEXT, CALENDAR, PHOTOS, WEATHER . . . and that was just the first row. There were four more rows beneath. Holy pickles!

One of the icons was designed to look like a tiny piece of

legal-pad paper. Underneath it was the word NOTES. I tapped it, and up came a screen-size piece of legal-pad paper. I tapped _it_, and a miniature keyboard popped up.

I tapped out, "Hi! I'mvwriting a nitr on my brand mew iPhone!"

Across the piece of paper appeared the sentence, HI! I'MVWRITING A NITR ON MY BRAND MEW IPHONE!

I hugged my phone to my chest and twirled around. _I love you, little iPhone!_ I told it telepathically. _Happy happy happy! Me so happy!_

I stopped short, struck by inspiration. This whole day had been a complete roller coaster. I'd gone from joyful one moment to crestfallen the next. I'd been "fun" Winnie, and I'd also—_ugh_—acted like a spoiled baby. But somehow, I just knew it, all of those ups and downs were part of a bigger picture. I tingled with the awareness of being _this close_ to putting it together.

Sandra's advice had been to live in the now. She said I should move forward while sneakily not _thinking_ about moving forward . . . but I knew myself well enough to realize that, alas, I wasn't going to become an instant Zen master. Maybe I needed to come up with a more Winnie-friendly plan?

I imagined a calendar with its pages flipping, flipping, flipping, the way they do in movies to show the passage of time. Up till now, maybe that had been my . . . whatever Sandra called it. My _paradigm_.

But! Maybe Sandra was right, and I was ready for a

paradigm shift! And hey, I could do it. I was fourteen, after all.

I deleted my "Hi, I'mvwriting a nitr" note and started typing a new note. It would be like the note I wrote myself as a ten-year-old, the one I later lost. Only, this note I'd keep close.

My fingers felt clumsy as I tapped the tiny keys, but slowly, and with lots of corrections, I made a to-do list. Some of the things I put on it were variations on the goals I'd come up with earlier in the day. Others I came up with on further deliberation.

I gave one final tap to my keyboard and read my list from start to finish:

> To Do Before High School
>
> Say out loud what I want out of life
>
> Be spazzy
>
> But also practice being older somehow
>
> Do something to help the world, like that
> > Three Cups of Tea guy
>
> Figure out who I am
>
> Become friends with someone new
>
> Talk to Amanda . . . or do *something* with
> > Amanda
>
> Take charge with Lars!
>
> Have a DEEP MOMENT with Sandra before
> > she goes to college
>
> Do something scary
>
> Admit it when I'm wrong

MAKE A PREDICTION, AND . . .
HAVE IT COME TRUE!
DON'T DIE
PEACE OUT!

My list wasn't perfect. So? *I* wasn't perfect. But I was fourteen, and I had a plan.

Have a Deep Moment
with Sandra

a COUPLE OF WEEKS AFTER MY BIRTHDAY, my English
teacher and Cinnamon's English teacher brought
both our classes together and had us watch an old movie
called *Black Widow*. I didn't know why. Nobody knew why.
But every so often, Ms. Kozinski and Ms. Adler did this sort
of thing, and the two of them would whisper and giggle in
the back of the room while we watched the film.

They were good friends, Ms. Kozinski and Ms. Adler.
They went shopping together and had margaritas together
and gossiped about guys together. How did we know? Because
they told us. Cinnamon and I especially loved it when Ms.
K and Ms. Adler went on double dates. They always came
back with ridiculous, horrible things to say about the guys
in question, like that Ms. Adler's date smelled like cheese or
Ms. K's date brought up NPR every third sentence.

"Well, I heard on NPR . . ." Ms. Adler might say in a
pompous voice, and the students clustered around her desk
would giggle and egg her on.

Ms. Adler wasn't the greatest teacher in terms of actually
teaching us academic, English-y stuff, but I liked the fact

that she was a grown-up and still had fun. I liked the fact that she still had a BFF, and that they tried on shoes together instead of playing bridge or doing frozen meal swaps.

I expected Cinnamon and Dinah and me to stay BFFs forever. I imagined the three of us having crazy weekends and then sharing the details with each other during Sunday brunch at some swanky restaurant. Or maybe not a swanky restaurant. Ms. Adler and Ms. K were swanky-restaurant types, but maybe Cinnamon, Dinah, and I would have brunch at a pub, or a truck stop.

Anyway, the tagline for *Black Widow* was "She Mates and She Kills. No Man Can Resist Her." It was about a woman who married one rich man after another, murdering them all and inheriting their money. When class ended, Cinnamon leaned over and said in my ear, "Dude, that black widow lady is my role model."

"Cinnamon," I scolded. "She is not your role model. She *killed* people."

"Not 'people.' Just guys."

I gathered my books and stood up. "Ha ha."

"The lady in the movie used guys the way guys use us," Cinnamon argued. "And that's what I'm going to do from now on."

I headed into the hall. "Cinn, you are going to end up a dried-out, wrinkled pill if you don't get over this I-hate-guys kick."

"But I do hate guys," she said.

"No, you hate Bryce."

"Same diff."

I twisted sideways to avoid being rammed by a seventh grader. "I think you need to go out with someone else," I told her. "Someone who's not a player."

"Okay, great idea," Cinnamon said with over-the-top chirpiness. "Make him for me, will ya? Snap your fingers and make him materialize?"

I shot her a look and considered pulling out my hair . . . or hers. Today she was wearing it in a topknot, held in place with a fork.

"I can't 'make' you a boy," I said. "There's no such thing as the Boy Factory."

"There should be," Cinnamon said.

"You just have to . . . be nicer. Lose your attitude." My gaze traveled up. "And maybe not jab weapons of mass destruction in your hair."

"A fork isn't a weapon of mass destruction," Cinnamon informed me. "A fork is a weapon of minor destruction. Like for stabbing the hearts of cheating, lying exes."

"Uh-huh, doing great," I told her. "You'll have a new boyfriend in no time."

I spotted Dinah by her locker, deep in conversation with a girl named Mary. Mary was doing most of the talking, while Dinah listened intently and gnawed on her bottom lip. I frowned, because what could Mary be saying to make Dinah look so . . . involved?

I didn't mean that in a weird possessive way. Dinah was allowed to have friends other than me and Cinnamon. She was even allowed to have intense conversations with other people. But we hardly knew Mary, and anyway, Mary was . . . strange. Sometimes she was overly fawning, complimenting girls' outfits or teeth or skinniness with an enthusiasm that seemed fake. Other times, she just seemed blank. Checked out.

"Dinah?" I called.

Dinah's eyes widened with relief, or so it seemed to me. Mary looked displeased.

"Don't tell," I heard Mary whisper as Cinnamon and I approached. Then she focused on me and Cinnamon and plugged in her smile.

"Winnie! Cute shirt," she said. "And Cinnamon. *Love* your nails."

Cinnamon glanced at her nails, which she'd painted with her highlighter. They were neon orange.

"Thanks," she said.

Mary laughed—fakily—and took off, though not before giving Dinah a meaningful glance.

When she was out of earshot, I said, "Don't tell what?"

"Nothing," Dinah said, closing her locker. "She . . . um . . ." She shrugged. *"Nothing."*

"Dinah," I said.

"Should we get out of here?" she said. "Want to walk to 7-Eleven and get Slurpees?"

Cinnamon made a *chhh* sound with half her mouth. "Not 7-Eleven. Too likely to see Bryce there."

And Lars, I thought, feeling grumpy. The problem with

having Cinnamon date Lars's best friend, and then get dumped by Lars's best friend, was that I was now in the position of having to choose between my BFF and my boyfriend, since where Lars was, Bryce so often was.

Wait a sec, I thought. Dinah brought up Slurpees instead of answering my Mary question as a distraction technique—and she *almost* got away with it.

"Dinah?" I said. "When someone says 'don't tell,' that means you *do* tell. Maybe not the whole world, but at least your best friends."

"True dat," Cinnamon said.

"What does Mary not want you to tell?" I pressed. "Why was she even *talking* to you?"

Dinah looked wounded. "Gee, thanks."

"Oh, you know what I mean. Do you guys even have any classes together?"

"She's in the hip-hop club with me," Dinah said. "Could we not talk about it? Seriously, it is *so* nothing."

Except it obviously was, or she'd tell us.

"Fine," I said. Deliberately, I fished my iPhone out of my backpack and tapped the Notes application. I pulled up a fresh piece of pretend-paper and typed, FIND OUT WHAT'S UP WITH MARY WOODS!!!

I turned my phone so Dinah could see. She rolled her eyes.

"We could go to the mall," Cinnamon said. "I could get my lip pierced."

"No," I said. Westminster didn't allow facial piercings, and anyway, *please*.

"We could go to a tattoo parlor."

"And that would be another no." I exhaled, like a bull. "You guys are being annoying. *Both* of you."

My phone buzzed, and I glanced down and saw that I'd received a text from Sandra. It said, *"bored!!!! need smoothie!!!! wanna come?"*

"why yes," I typed back, dropping a mask over my delight so that Dinah and Cinnamon wouldn't ask to tag along.

I dropped my phone into my backpack and said, "Sorry, kids. Sandra needs me."

"So I'm getting a tattoo by myself?" Cinnamon asked. "That means no heart with *Winnie* in it, you know."

"I'll try to get over it," I said.

At Smoothie King, I vented about Cinnamon and Dinah. Sandra's typical MO when I complained about things was to imply that my problems were stupid and tell me to go away. But today, remarkably, she listened.

"Here's the thing," Sandra said, keeping her straw in her mouth as she talked. "Remember when you and Amanda quit being friends?"

My cheeks got hot. It was an old wound—the fact of Amanda ditching me to be more popular—and I doubted it would ever fully heal. "She dropped me for Gail Grayson in sixth grade."

"And do you remember what I told you?"

"That sometimes friends outgrow each other," I recited. I shuddered, because it sounded as awful now as it had then. A disturbing question burbled up in my brain, one I hadn't considered back when I was eleven. "Hey . . . did you mean *me* outgrowing Amanda, or *Amanda* outgrowing me?"

She answered immediately, and with a flip of her hand. "Well, Amanda outgrowing you. Duh."

I made an indignant noise.

"But not in a *bad* way," Sandra said. "Wouldn't you rather be you than her?"

"Excuse me?"

"If the two of you could switch identities . . . would you?"

My bottom lip had a chapped spot on it, and my teeth found the flaking bit and tugged. Amanda was prettier than I was, and more popular—or used to be. These days, her status went back and forth. Sometimes she showed up all black-eyeliner-y doom-and-gloom and hung out with slouchy, scowly Aubrey. Other days I saw her in the cafeteria with superstars Gail and Malena, and she'd swish her Alice in Wonderland hair and be effortlessly fabulous in her slinky jeans and outfit-y tops that came from an entirely different planet than, say, my ratty-but-beloved Dr Pepper T-shirt.

On those days, she outshone Gail and Malena without even trying, and I felt perversely proud of her.

But did I want to *be* her?

"She doesn't really seem happy," I confessed.

Sandra tipped her cup so that the mangled end of her straw pointed at me. "See?"

"Uh . . . no."

"Well, don't sweat it. Anyway, I might have been wrong."

"What?!"

"Shocking, I know. But it's *possible* that when I gave you my whole 'outgrowing' advice, I might have been in a weird place personally. Or I might have been just plain wrong. So, um . . . I take it back."

"Sandra!" I exclaimed. "You can't take back *advice*. Not from three years ago. Not when I already followed it!"

"Well, sorry. But now that I'm a senior, now that I'm about to graduate . . . " She turned up her palms. "I can't help it, Win. It makes me realize how little time we have with each other."

"Who? You and me?"

"*Every*body," she said. "Listen. I'm not saying go back and make things work with Amanda. Or *do* if you want to. Unless it's impossible. Sometimes people go their own ways, and there's nothing you can do about it."

"Gee," I said. "How . . . uplifting."

"But if you *can* do something to save a friendship, then you *have* to. Like with Dinah and Cinnamon, because I know how much y'all love each other."

"True dat," I murmured, unthinkingly echoing Cinnamon. Even when they bugged me, I loved them. I loved how Cinnamon was always willing to sacrifice her dignity for

me, like Saturday at the mall when I was having pee issues.
The ladies room was so crowded that when my turn finally
came around, my pee wouldn't come out. I froze, knowing
that so many people were outside waiting . . . and worse, *listening*. Cinnamon knew I was incapable of peeing in front
of an audience. So what did she do? Out of nowhere and
totally randomly, she belted out "All the Single Ladies" at
the top of her voice, all three verses. How could I not love a
friend with that kind of nerve?

And Dinah, I loved how she always always *always* tried
to be a good person. It was part of her very core. That same
day at the mall? We were in Macy's juniors department
checking out swimsuits—summer was coming, after all—
and all of a sudden, Cinnamon and I looked around and
couldn't find Dinah.

"Where'd she go?" Cinnamon had asked, baffled.

Turned out she'd spotted a little old lady in the
accessories section, struggling to get down a purse that was
out of her reach. So Dinah hurried over to help, of course.
After that the little old lady wanted to take a peek at "that
darling purple and green sequined clutch, you sweet girl,"
and after *that*, there were multiple perfumes to be spritzed
and sniffed, and somehow Dinah ended up serving as the
little old lady's personal shopper for the next half hour.

"What?" she said to me and Cinnamon when we finally
marched over and reclaimed her. "She was vertically
challenged! And plus her fingers were like gnarled twigs.
She couldn't push down the perfume thingies. And anyway,

we're going to be old one day. Don't we want people to help us?"

We did. And if we were helped by someone as kind as Dinah, we'd be the luckiest old ladies in the world.

Sandra took a draw of her smoothie. "You shouldn't let yourself outgrow someone unless you absolutely can't help it."

In theory, I agreed with her. But to not "let" yourself outgrow someone, wasn't that like . . . like muzzling a dog so it couldn't bark, or binding a Chinese girl's feet to make them stay small forever?

Sandra trained her blue eyes on me. "Okay, Win?" she said. "I mean it. Don't let your friends slip away."

At that, a great hole of longing opened inside me, because I didn't *want* Cinnamon and Dinah to slip away. I would miss them so much. I wouldn't know who I was without them!

I flopped my forearms on the table and bonked my head on the wood. *Bonk bonk bonk*. The last bonk was harder than I intended. *"Ouch."*

Sandra snort-laughed.

"Don't laugh at me," I told her.

"Don't bonk your head on the table," she said. "Self-bonking will get you nowhere."

I giggled, because "self-bonking" sounded funny. It sounded *dirty*. Sandra giggled, too. We noticed a woman frowning from a nearby table, and our giggling got worse.

"*Self-bonker*," Sandra whispered.

I threw my balled-up straw wrapper at her, and in an amazing, never-to-be-repeated show of skill, she leaped for it and caught it—*in her mouth.*

"Holy pickles," I marveled.

She smiled. She swallowed.

"Yummy," she said.

She was amazing, my sister. And even though she'd made me feel worse—taking back the advice she'd given me three years ago, suggesting that my friends could slip away if I wasn't careful—she somehow made me feel better, too. Such was the mystery of Sandra.

When we left, I gave a small smile and even smaller wave to the frowning woman. Just a hand-raise, really. *We are silly, I know. You might have been silly once. Were you?*

She pursed her lips. Then her scowl loosened, and she smiled back, revealing a smudge of bright red lipstick on her teeth.

On the ride home, we talked some more. Only this time, we didn't look at each other. Sandra kept her eyes on the road, while I leaned back against the headrest, closed my eyes, and let my hair whip around my face. I loved the sensation of wind blowing over me all crazy. Mom hated it, and when she drove, she insisted on having the windows up. But Sandra was a windows-down girl, all the way.

It wasn't a long drive from Smoothie King to our house. Still, we covered a fair amount of territory:

Was Sandra excited to be graduating?

Yup.

Was she scared to be graduating?

Yup again.

Did she ever secretly think about going to Georgia Tech so she could stay in Atlanta and live at home?

"*Hell* no" was her answer to that one. She thwapped my shoulder, making my eyes fly open.

"And don't you, either," she told me. "I know you're only in eighth grade, but next year, you'll be a freshman. And after that, *pfff.*" She sliced her hand through the air. "It goes quick, Winnie. Enjoy it, gobble it up—but when it's time for you to go? *Go.*"

"I will, I will," I said.

She looked at me hard. "I mean it. Atlanta isn't the whole world. And Dinah and Cinnamon—and Lars—they aren't the only people in the world."

"*Ag!* You are so annoying! First you tell me, 'Don't let your friends slip away,' and now you're saying, 'Go! Go! Your friends aren't the only friends in the world!'"

Sandra opened her mouth, then closed it.

"Ha," I said.

"But here is the way you need to put those two ideas together," she said, rallying. She glanced at me. "You ready?"

"I'm ready."

"Okay . . . well . . . they're both true. Don't give away what you have, but don't let what you have be all you *ever* have. Make sense?"

"Like in that Girl Scout song? Make new friends, but keep the old?"

She knew she was being teased. But she went with it.

"Yes," she replied. "One is silver"—she paused, lifted a finger from the steering wheel—"the other, gold."

"You should use that for your senior quote," I said, referring to Westminster's tradition of having all the seniors choose a special quote to go under their name in the yearbook. Sandra made fun of people who picked cheesy quotes, like "If you don't know where you're going, you'll never get there." I made fun of those people, too, mainly to be like her. But sometimes I secretly liked those cheesy quotes.

"Maybe I will," she said.

"Excellent."

We drove up the steep, curvy hill that led to our house.

"I was never planning on letting Dinah and Cinnamon slip away," I said.

"I know," Sandra said.

"I just want to make things better," I went on, my words barely audible over the rush of the wind. Maybe Sandra didn't even hear. "And then they wouldn't be sad. And then *I* wouldn't be sad."

"You can't fix other people's problems," Sandra said.

I faced her. "Why not?"

"It doesn't work that way, that's all."

I turned away. I watched the trees go by, and the big, stately homes, none of them all that different from ours.

Except ours was *ours* . . . and yet in just a few months, Sandra would be moving out. In just a few years, I'd move out, too.

No, I thought fiercely. I wasn't going to dwell on the future when the present was right here in front of me—and when without even meaning to *I was having a deep moment with my sister,* whom I loved so much. That was one of the things on my To-Do list, and here I was doing it.

"Hey, Sandra," I said. "Can I tell you something?"

"Isn't that what you've been doing for the last hour and a half?"

I made a face.

"Kidding." She turned into our driveway, parked, and killed the motor. "You can tell me anything. What?"

All of a sudden, I felt embarrassed. I wanted to break our eye contact, but I didn't let myself.

"I like it when you're nice to me," I said.

She blushed. I did, too.

"You're my little sister," she said.

"I know. But sometimes . . ." I paused. "Well. You know."

Sandra looked away. Not me. She drummed her fingers on the steering wheel. "As soon as September rolls around, I won't be here anymore."

A lump formed in my throat, because there was so much I was feeling. Like how nothing would be the same without her. Like how, when she was gone, *I'd* be the big sister. I'd be the one Ty, and one day Maggie, would come to for advice. The one who would supposedly have all the answers.

Look at me, I willed her with my mind.

She did. And she said, simply, "I'll miss you."

Oh God, I was going to cry. I might *cry*, and crying was so not Sandra, and her expression would grow wary, and—

Oh, who cared.

"Me too," I said, my voice thick with tears. "But I'll come visit you. Tons and tons, wherever you end up going to college. And every weekend, there I'll be! Sleeping in your dorm room, eating everything in your mini-fridge, wearing your clothes." I sniffled. "Won't that be *so great*?"

"Fat chance," said Sandra, her glance so withering that it could turn a plum into an instant prune.

I grinned wobbly. I liked the oddly nice graduating-senior Sandra, but the truth was, I liked sour Sandra, too.

Do Something Scary

O N THE FIRST MONDAY OF APRIL, I found Dinah in the library with weird Mary. I'd gone looking for Dinah specifically, I needed to talk to her, and yet there she was deep in conversation with Mary again. Mary was speaking urgently, just like the other time, while Dinah gnawed on her lip, also like that other time.

"Dinah?" I said.

She jumped and looked guilty.

Mary glared at me—no complimenting my outfit this time—then shoved up from the table and scuttled away like a rat.

"What is going *on* with you two?" I asked Dinah.

Dinah didn't answer. She pulled a piece of her hair to her mouth, and I looked at her, like, *Really? You haven't chewed on your hair since elementary school, and now you're starting back up?*

I reached out to bat her hand away. She twisted to avoid me.

"Quit it," Dinah said. "You don't own me."

"Who said I wanted to own you?" I said. "You just shouldn't chew on your hair. It's gross."

Her eyes flashed. She deliberately brought her hair back to her mouth, and when she drew it out, the individual strands formed a single wet point.

"Gross," I said again.

"You have bad habits, too, you know," she pointed out.

I cocked my head. What was going on here? Was Dinah mad at me?

"Why won't you tell me what Mary's deal is?" I asked.

"Because Mary doesn't have a 'deal.'"

"Um, obviously she does."

"Winnie? Drop it."

Her tone was sharp, and heat rose in my cheeks.

"Fine," I said.

"Fine," she said.

I started to say it again—*Fine!*—then shut my mouth, spun on my heel, and walked away.

Normally in a situation like this, I'd hunt down Cinnamon, who would listen as I vented and then say something funny that would make me feel better, and make me realize I was maybe, possibly overreacting, too.

But hunting down Cinnamon wasn't an option, because Cinnamon was on my bad list—which, ironically, was why I'd come searching for Dinah.

There were many things I loved about Cinnamon. For one, she was extremely amusing. Forks in the hair, deadpan comments to my nemesis, Gail, about Gail's favorite perfume being made from fish oil, that sort of thing. Also, Cinnamon took crap from no one. As she and I headed to choir today, for example, we happened to cross paths with a guy named Chris. Chris was a jock, and arrogant, and today was wearing a camouflage shirt that said, License to Hunt Illegal Immigrants.

I wanted to say something about how obnoxious it was, but Chris has a buzz cut, and he intimidated me, so I kept my mouth shut. Cinnamon, however, marched up, flicked his chest, and said, "That shirt is racist, dude."

Did Chris care? Unlikely, but at least she had the guts to tell him.

Cinnamon wasn't perfect by any stretch, however. Like the "boy hater" phase she simply couldn't let go of, and which I was totally, completely, one hundred percent over.

I did not need Cinnamon dragging me away every time we spotted Lars with Bryce.

I did not need to hear her revenge fantasies, which she'd stolen from *Black Widow* and involved malice-filled utterances like, "She mates, then she kills."

Honestly? It was creating tension between me and Lars, because it made him not want to be around me when I was with her. And with Bryce out of the picture, she was with me A LOT.

That's what I wanted to vent about to Dinah, only I couldn't, as Dinah was off being WEIRD with weird Mary.

Grrrrrrr.

So basically, both of my BFFs were being B-Ps-in-the-B

(big pains in the bottom), and, as Sandra so eloquently pointed out at Smoothie King, I couldn't "fix" either one of them.

And my love life was tanking, *and* today was fish sticks day, *and* I hadn't finished my French homework, and I just knew Ms. Beauchard was going to call me on it.

And my love life was tanking. Did I mention that? I hadn't spent real time—yes-we-really-do-like-each-other time—with Lars in ages, it seemed. And as easy as it was to blame it on Cinnamon, I secretly knew I was looking for excuses. I also secretly knew—so secretly that I tried not to let my mind go there—that my foul mood might *possibly* have had more to do with Lars than with Dinah or Cinnamon.

Stomping around in a sulk wasn't going to solve anything, however, and I had an icky suspicion that if I wanted things to get better with Lars, I was going to have to take a good, hard look at myself. Unfortunately.

On Thursday night, I decided it was time to take action regarding the sorry state of my love life. It might be scary, but so what? *Do something scary*, that was one of the things on my list, right?

To give myself a jump start, I marched downstairs and asked Dad what he thought about wimpy girls who sat in their rooms all weekend and just, like, read books.

"Good books or bad books?" he said, twisting to see me from his lazy-bum sprawl on the couch.

I perched on the back of the couch. Mom hated when I did this; she thought it smushed the pillows into deformed lumps that could never be replumped. But Dad didn't care.

"Good books," I said. "But still. Is that any life for a fourteen-year-old girl?"

"If the girl's as gorgeous as you are? Definitely."

I rolled my eyes. "Then let's say bad books. Bad books *with bad grammar*. You don't want me reading books like that all weekend, do you?"

Dad lifted the remote and muted *Phineas and Ferb*, which he claimed only to watch for Ty's sake. He claimed it was for daddy-son bonding time. But this wasn't the first time I'd caught him watching it on his own.

He put the remote on his chest. "Hmmm. So you're saying you could lock yourself in your room and read grammatically incorrect books"—he squinted one eye—"or you could go out into the big bad world like Little Red Riding Hood, who got eaten by a wolf?"

"She did not!"

"I like the locking-yourself-in-your-room option. Till you're twenty-one." He reached up and shook my knee. "I'm proud of you, Winnie. I think you're making an excellent choice."

"Ha ha."

He pointed the remote at the TV. "Want to watch *Phineas and Ferb* with me?"

"No. And *Dad*." I slid down the back of the sofa,

squishing the cushion to get to him. I pushed the remote back down so that he had to look at me. "Do you really want me being a dried-up spinster who has zero fun and lives a life of misery?"

He made his funny-Dad hopeful expression, much like the one he used when Mom said, "Joel, you're not planning on eating that *entire* can of Pringles, are you?"

"Da-a-ad," I said.

"Princess, what I want is for you to be happy," he said. He hardly ever called me "princess," thank goodness, as it was horribly embarrassing. But secretly, I liked it when he did.

"Okay, good," I told him. "But you should know: It's going to mean leaving my room."

His sigh was loud and long.

"But c'mon. You don't *really* want a wimpy daughter."

"I *do*, however, want a safe daughter," he said.

"Yeah, yeah, yeah." He put his arm around me, and I soaked in the comfort of his hug for a few seconds. Then I pushed myself up and kissed his forehead. "Thanks for the chat, Dad. You're the best."

Upstairs, before I lost my I-am-confident-and-strong feeling, I called Lars.

Ring, ring, went my phone. *Ring ring ring.*

"Hey, Win," he said. "What's up?"

"Not much. What's up with you?"

"Ah, you know. Thinking about homework. Not

doing homework. Considering chucking homework out of window."

"Blech," I said, giggling. "Hate homework." I tried to stay easygoing. "So are we going to do something this weekend? I feel like we haven't done anything in forever."

"Um, sure," Lars said.

Okay, good start, I thought. "So, what do you want to do?"

"I don't know. What do *you* want to do?"

I felt my easygoing-ness start to slip away. I'd been proactive, and now it was his turn. Only he didn't say anything. Just sat there like a lump, waiting for me to do all the work.

I sighed. "Well, tomorrow night I'm hanging with the girls, so we can't do anything then."

"More movies about how guys suck?" he said. He'd heard all about *Black Widow* from Cinnamon. First he thought it was funny. Later, not so much.

"Possibly," I said, then immediately regretted it. I sat on my bed and drew my knees to my chest. I did not want this conversation to go bad.

"How about Saturday?" I suggested.

"Sorry, told Bryce I'd watch the Hawks game with him. They've got a shot at first in the division. Hey—wanna join?"

Um . . . sure, only Cinnamon would kill me. "Nah. But thanks."

From downstairs, Mom called up a request. "Winnie? Would you *margle-gargle* Ty?"

I pressed my phone to my chest. "*What*? I can't hear you!"

"*Mlarfle mflarfle* bath!" she called. "Please?"

I groaned. "Mom needs me to go make Ty take his bath."

"Okay," Lars said. "I should go anyway. I should finish my lab report."

Depression kicked in, intensified by how little he seemed to care. "But . . . are we . . . ?"

"I *want* to," Lars said. He exhaled, and I realized he was frustrated, too. Which made me feel slightly better, but at the same time more stuck in the mire. How pathetic was it that neither one of us could solve such a seemingly simple problem of wanting to spend time together? "You come up with something, and we'll do it. All right?"

Why me? I thought. *Why do I have to come up with something?*

"Winnie!" Mom called. "Are you *flarfle glargle*?!"

"I hear your mom," Lars said. "I'll let you go."

But I don't want to be "let go," I thought. What I said, flatly, was "Okay, bye." I tapped the END CALL bubble and watched his profile picture be sucked—*whoosh*—back into the phone.

Ty had a phobia about taking a bath alone. Why? Because of the Bathroom Lady. And who was the Bathroom Lady? No one. The Bathroom Lady didn't exist.

So why was Ty afraid of her? Because I was good at inventing stories, and long long *long* ago I'd told Ty that a witch named the Bathroom Lady lived in the sewer system and slurped up tasty children through the pipes. I made the story good, too, giving the Bathroom Lady rubbery lips and grasping claws as blue and cold as ice.

Whoops.

I rapped on the door of the bathroom, then twisted the knob and barged in. Ty was squatting fully dressed by the tub. Not *in* the tub, but *by* the tub, just staring at the drain. He whipped his head around at the sound of my arrival.

"Ty," I scolded. "You're seven years old. You're too old to be afraid of taking a bath."

Ty's eyes widened, and he propped his elbows on the edge of the tub and tried to form a wall with his scrawny upper body. "I'm sorry, Ty is unavailable," he said. "*Beep.* Please leave a message."

What was he hiding? I attempted to peek past him. He moved his body in tandem with mine.

"Ty, what's going on?"

"Nothing! *Beep!* Leave a message!"

I spotted his backpack on the bathroom floor. His open, *empty* backpack. He scrambled to his feet and drove his hands into my hip bones, attempting to push me backward.

"Not gonna work, bud," I said, lifting him from under his armpits and moving him out of the way. "Whatever you've got in there, I'm sure it's not—"

My throat closed, *because there was a penguin in the bathtub.* A *penguin*, and it was *alive*, and its chest puffed in and out as it breathed. It pitter-pattered from side to side when it saw me, and its penguin feet made slippery sounds on the porcelain.

"*Heheheh,*" Ty said. It was his robot laugh, which he pushed from his lungs in an anxious monotone.

"Ty?" I finally managed. "There is a *penguin* in our bathtub!"

He made his "adorable me" smile, but like his *heheheh*, it was stretched too tight.

A vague memory floated into my mind. Ty went on a field trip today—the details were coming back to me. To the Georgia Aquarium. And apparently he'd acquired a penguin while he was there, a penguin which was now in our bathtub.

"His name is Pingy," Ty whispered. "He's a baby."

Omigod. I knelt by the tub and gulped. I gingerly touched the penguin's feathers. I thought a penguin's skin would be more slippery, like a seal's, but maybe that happened when they got older?

"Holy pickles," I muttered.

Ty dropped to his knees and scooched in beside me. "Isn't he cute?"

"What did you *do*, Ty? Did you steal him and stuff him in your backpack?"

"No!"

"Then what? Buy him at the gift shop? I'm pretty sure—make that *entirely* sure—that baby penguins aren't for sale at the aquarium gift shop."

"*Heheheh,*" Ty said. "Did I tell you his name is Pingy?"

I looked at Ty, then back at the penguin, whose eyes

were dark and as bright as buttons. It—*he?*—did his funny side step pitter-patter and flapped his wings.

Mom clearly didn't know about Pingy, or there would have been yelling going on. Lots. And rightfully so, because Pingy was probably hungry and scared, and anyway, Ty couldn't go around stealing penguins from the Georgia Aquarium. It just wasn't done!

"Holy pickle crap, Ty," I said. I went into lecture mode, informing him he wasn't allowed to steal penguins from the Georgia Aquarium. That he wasn't allowed to steal, period.

He told me he knew, he knew, he knew. He told me other stuff, too, like how he'd seen Pingy at the aquarium and worried he was lonely, and, oh, that Pingy loved peanut butter, and wasn't that funny? But the stealing part *wasn't* funny, and now he felt really scared.

He shifted from foot to foot and said, "What are we going to do?"

"We?" I said incredulously.

His face fell, and I felt terrible. Because who was going to help him if I didn't?

I sighed. "Oh, Ty," I said. "We'll figure something out. I promise."

I thought hard. At last I told Ty to get Pingy out of the tub, and to get *himself* into the tub, because if Mom didn't hear bath-taking sounds soon, the game would be up. Then I went and found Sandra in her room.

"I'm busy," she said. "Go away."

"I need you to come with me to the bathroom," I said. "Oh, and bring your secret stash of peanut butter."

"I don't have a secret stash of peanut butter," she lied. She glanced at me from under a swoop of blond hair, which she was braiding as she watched an episode of *Chuck* on her laptop. "And Winnie, you are *way* too old to need company while you do your private lady business."

"For real, Sandra. Your presence—and your peanut butter—are needed in the bathroom, pronto. Get in there and I'll tell you my plan."

"Hey, Mom, Sandra's taking me to Barnes and Noble," I said ten minutes later as Sandra and I made a beeline through the kitchen. "'Kay? 'Kay."

"Is Ty in the tub?" Mom said. She had Maggie strapped to her chest, and she was swaying and stirring spaghetti sauce. She didn't notice that I was holding Ty's backpack in front of me like a sack of groceries, or that every so often, it wiggled.

"Yep. Shampoo in his hair and everything."

"Really?"

"What can I say?" I tossed off. "I'm just that good." *And* I had excellent blackmail material. It wasn't often a girl could hold penguin-napping over her little brother's dirty head.

Sandra opened the back door. "Bye!" she called. "We'll be back in an hour!"

But at the Georgia Aquarium, things got complicated.

The heavy doors of the main entrance were locked, and there was a freaky red light blinking from a nearby keypad. It was a keypad like the keypad on Cinnamon's home alarm system, only more heavy-duty looking.

"Do you think they have spy cameras?" I whispered, holding Ty's backpack in front of me. "Do you think we're getting our pictures taken?"

"Oh, great, that's *just* what I need," Sandra whispered back, jerking me into the shadows. *"'Westminster Senior Expelled for Busting into Aquarium. Hopes for Future Thoroughly Dashed.'"*

"Well, we've got to get in somehow," I said. "We can't leave Pingy out here—he'd waddle into the street and get hit by a car."

"This is *insane*," Sandra said.

I cradled Ty's backpack with one arm. With my other hand, I unzipped the top and felt inside for Pingy. "Don't worry, little fella," I said, patting him. "I'm not going to let you get run over."

To Sandra, I said, "Let's check the side of the building. Maybe there's another entrance."

"And maybe there's a security guard on a Segway, ready to pop out and arrest us," Sandra groused.

But she followed me as I ducked under the steel railing that lined the sidewalk. The grass was damp with dew. A low humming came from the aquarium, and the temperature of the air dropped as we sidled up close to the building.

"It's dark," I whispered.

"You don't say," Sandra replied.

"*Really* dark. Axe-murderer dark."

"No, shark-attack dark. In the night, they probably let the sharks roam free."

I giggled nervously. While Ty had a phobia about baths, I kinda, well, had a phobia about sharks, and Sandra knew it.

A side entrance failed to present itself, and Pingy was growing agitated. I kept my hand in Ty's backpack and stroked him as best I could, but it was awkward, and my forearm jarred the zipper open like a silver-toothed mouth. Only I did not want to think about teeth *or* mouths, so I shoved that image away and tried to think about . . . about peanut butter instead. Yes, lovely peanut butter, which *had* kept Pingy occupied and quiet while we snuck him out of the house.

If I'd thought about it in time, I would have grabbed one of teensy baby Maggie's pacifiers and swabbed up a big glob of peanut butter with it. How cute would that be, Pingy sucking on one of baby Maggie's pacifiers?

"I wonder if the security guards actually *are* sharks," Sandra mused. "They breathe air, you know."

"Sharks?"

"Yummy, yummy oxygen. They like people better, though—especially yummy yummy girl flesh."

"Shut up, they do not."

"It'd be a lot less expensive than hiring real security guards. *And* they'd do a better job, don't you think?"

"Sandra! Shut *up*!"

"You think a shark could ride a Segway?"

Sharks on Segways were ridiculous, I knew that. And yet my pulse accelerated. It was extremely creepy tromping through the dark with the huge aquarium looming over us, and just say a shark on a Segway *did* appear . . .

Sandra snapped her jaws, and I screamed. It was LOUD, my scream, and I clapped both hands over my mouth and dropped Ty's backpack.

"Smooth," Sandra said.

Pingy *piu*ed and poked his head out.

"Hey, get back in there," I said. I squatted beside him and pushed on his head.

"Piu, piu!" Pingy said. He flapped his wings, and the zipper opened farther. What used to be a small opening was now a medium-sized opening.

"Sandra! *Help!*"

Sandra tried to grab Pingy, but he was like one of those liquid-filled tube toys that slipped and slid through your fingers.

"Crap!" Sandra said. "Get him!"

"I'm *try*ing!"

"Piu! Piu!"

Pingy was a ball of muscle waddling rapidly away. But I could capture him, I *knew* I could, *if I could just—*

I scrambled on my hands and knees through the grass.

If I could just—ouch! A prickly thing, once on the ground, was now embedded in my knee. *Owwie owwie owwie!*

But there was no time for pain. I tensed and sprang and . . . *yes!*

"Aha!" I exclaimed from flat on my belly. "Gotcha now, sucka!"

"Piu?" Pingy said from behind me.

Huh? How was Pingy *behind* me, if . . . ?

"Winnie," Sandra said tightly.

"Piu? Piu, piu?"

I looked over my shoulder, then I wished I hadn't. Because if *Sandra* had Pingy—and sure enough, she did; she had him firmly in her grasp like a flapping baby—then what had *I* caught? What was *I* gripping in this dark and tangled grass . . . and why was it so hard?

Pingy wasn't hard. Pingy was plump and pliable, like a warm Beanie Baby.

I let go and scrambled backward. What *was* that thing in the shadows before me? Was it . . . a *shoe*?

It was. A large suede loafer, to be exact. Or possibly faux suede. Hard to tell. But definitely large, and definitely— *gulp*—attached to an even larger leg.

My gaze traveled upward: legs, torso, shoulders, head. On top of the head, an army green ball cap emblazoned with the word SECURITY.

Uh-oh.

In my penguin rescue efforts, I'd managed to get dirt in my mouth. I used my tongue to work it out, and then I went *pluh*, much as teensy baby Maggie did when she was spitting up splurts of milk. Then, in a faint-ish voice, I said, "Hi?"

The security guard put his hands on his hips.

I glanced behind him. "Wow. You, um, have a Segway. I thought that was just in the movies."

"I also have a gun," he growled, tapping it for proof.

"Lucky," I said, even more faintly.

"You girls want to tell me what's going on?" he demanded.

Was "not really" an acceptable response? Somehow I doubted it.

I got to my feet, brushed myself off, and turned to Sandra. She was codfish pale, and I could practically see the thoughts racing through her brain: *Omigod, so busted. I'm going to have to go to community college. Omigod, I'm going to end up at a community college!*

It was clear it was up to me to get us out of this, so I straightened my shoulders, tilted my head, and smiled.

"I'm Marla," I said. I picked "Marla" because it sounded sweet and old-fashioned.

"I'm Max," the guard said. "Keep talking."

"Well, um . . . nice to meet you, Max." I gestured at Sandra. "And this is my sister, Fanny."

Sandra's mouth dropped open.

"Fanny, say 'hi,'" I prodded. To Max, I said, "She's a little shy."

"She's also holding a penguin," Max pointed out.

Pingy seemed to know he was being discussed. *"Piu?"* he said.

"Hmmm," I said. "Why, yes, she is."

"Are you going to tell me *why*?" Max asked.

God, so nosy, I thought. I almost giggled . . . but Marla was not a giggler, and this was not a giggling situation!

I took a breath. I gave Max another winning smile. "Well, you see, Fanny has . . . a special connection to animals . . . and, um . . ."

I glanced again at Sandra, needing her to pull it together and offer some assistance here. But no, she continued to stand there like a log. A *mute* log.

My eyebrows flew up. *A mute log! Yes!*

"She's a mute," I said rapidly. "She was born that way, it's not her fault, and she's . . . yeah. Always collecting pets. We have a Chihuahua at home, and also a Seeing Eye dog, not that Fanny's blind. She's not *blind, heheheh*."

Oh, great, I'm channeling Ty's robot laugh, I thought. And then, firmly: *Do not think about Ty's robot laugh! Focus!*

"But, like, if Fanny wants to go for a walk?" I said with wide eyes. "My mom can pin a note to Sarge's collar—Sarge is the Seeing Eye dog, he's a German shepherd—that says, 'If my owner and I seem lost, please call 555-3754.'"

Max's expression showed nothing. Nada, zero, impassive-city.

"That's our number," I clarified. "It's clever, don't you think? So that Fanny can always find her way home?"

Max reached to his waist of his uniform pants and unclipped a black cell phone. Hovering his thumb over the buttons, he said, "You want to give that one more time?"

"Ooo, but nobody's home!" I told him. "I mean—*heheheh— duh*, because Fanny and I are *here*"—I gestured at the weeds around us—"and my parents are . . . at a charity ball!"

"For the mute?" Max said drily.

For the *mute*? What was he . . . ? *Oh!*

"Yes! How'd you know?!"

Sandra—or rather, Fanny—let out a moan. I shot her a glare that said, *You are a mute. BE QUIET.*

"Why don't you tell me what's really going on," Max suggested.

My shoulders slumped. I shut one eye and squinted up at him from the other. "Do I have to?"

"Hmmm. I'm going to say . . . *yeah*."

I sighed, like, *Fine, you got me.* Yet some small awareness hinted to me that if I played my cards right, things were going to be okay. I don't know how I knew this, but I did.

"My little brother took the penguin," I confessed. "His second-grade class came here on a field trip."

Max scratched his neck.

"But he knows it was totally wrong, and he's really, really sorry. We just wanted to get Pingy back to his mom."

"Pingy," Max stated.

I scooped Pingy from Sandra's arms. "He's not hurt or anything. And like I said, my little brother is *so* super sorry."

"Is he a mute, too?"

"Um, ha ha. Good one." From deep in my mind came the thought, *Let him have his fun, that's all right. Work with it.* I gazed sheepishly at Max from under my eyelashes.

Max turned to Sandra. "And you? Are *you* mute?"

"No," Sandra said. She plucked at her T-shirt, disgusted. "I'm pretty much covered with penguin poop, though."

Max gave up trying to be stern and belly-laughed. I grinned, because laughing at us was so much better than putting us in jail. Or shooting us.

He took Pingy and held him under his arm like a football.

"Get out of here, girls. I'll take care of this big boy."

"You're not going to report us?" I asked.

"Marla," he said, "I've worked the night shift here for two years, and not once have I been this entertained."

"Awww," I said. On the inside, I was soaring.

"Go home," he said. "Tell your little brother I'm onto him, and that if he ever steals a penguin again, I'll prosecute him to the fullest extent of the law."

"Scare him a little," I said. "Yes, sir."

He turned to Sandra. "And Fanny? Tell him he owes *you* a new shirt."

Sandra gave him the sourest smile possible. He guffawed.

Since things were going so well, I said, "Hey, can I ride your Segway?"

"No," he and Sandra said as one.

"Okay, okay," I said, holding my hands up. "Sheesh."

"Good night, Marla and Fanny."

"Good night, Max." I elbowed Sandra. "Fanny, say good night."

"Good night," Sandra said in the lockjaw manner of Cinnamon's very old, very Southern grandmother.

Max strode to his Segway and climbed on.

"Good night, Pingy!" I said. Pingy squirmed, but no way was he escaping this dude.

Steering with one hand, Max spun the Segway in a semicircle and leaned back. The Segway wobbled. Pingy's bottom was the last thing we saw, his tail feathers fluttering in the breeze.

In the car, Sandra asked me who I was and what I'd done with her sister.

"Hardy-har-har," I said.

"You were fearless back there," she said. "I totally froze, but you were *fearless*. How?!"

"I don't know. I got lucky, I guess."

"No, it wasn't luck. I don't know *what* it was, but . . ." Her sentence trickled off.

"He was nice," I protested. "We amused him."

"*You* amused him." She shook her head. "You should be an actress when you grow up, I am so not kidding."

"Or a sociopath."

She snorted. "Or a sociopath."

Smiling, I watched the passing scenery. After a moment, my smile faded.

"I honestly don't know how I got brave like that," I admitted. "I'm usually so unbrave."

"Please," Sandra said.

"I'm not just saying that." I thought back to how wimpy I was on the phone with Lars, how I couldn't even come up with a way to say "I want to hang out with you this weekend, end of story."

I thumped my chest with my fist and said, "Seriously. This—*me*—is what unbrave looks like, 'kay?"

"Yes, Marla. Whatever you say, Marla."

"I'm *occasionally* brave in certain situations—"

"Security guards named Max?" Sandra said. "Possible threats of incarceration?"

"But when it comes to important stuff, I blow it. Every. Single. Time."

Sandra considered. She glanced at me and said, "Are you by any chance talking about Lars?"

"No!" I said, horrified that my inadequacies were so glaringly obvious. Then I folded my arms over my chest. "Wait a sec. Are you using your superintuitive big sister vibe, or did you overhear my pathetic phone call?"

She laughed. Slowing down for a light, she said, "But, Winnie."

"But, Sandra."

"Didn't we already discuss this?"

"Discuss what?"

"How you can't be a bystander in your own life. How you have to take initiative."

"No," I said, eyeing her. Was she making things up now, my sister the mute? Had she gone crazy?

"Yeah-huh," Sandra said. "A couple of months ago, when Lars broke up with you, or you broke up with him. Whatever."

Oh, that, I thought, sliding down in my seat.

"And when you were in the middle of your little breakup, what did I say? I said, 'Winnie, if you want him back, you've got to *tell* him that. Grab the bull by the horns!'"

"It's mean to say my 'little breakup,' and actually, no. You never once told me to grab the bull by the horns."

"And you did, didn't you?" she said smugly. "You grabbed Lars's horns—"

"I did *not* grab Lars's horns!"

"And you took control." The light turned green, and she pressed down on the accelerator. "You *did*, Winnie."

I drew my thumb to my mouth, wedging my thumbnail into the crack between my front tooth and the tooth beside it. Lars and I *did* have a rough patch a couple of months ago, Sandra was dead right about that. It was around Valentine's Day—the most awful timing ever—and it centered around the whole Brianna thing. How Lars let Brianna flirt with him, and didn't discourage her and how it made me feel like dirt.

So I called him on it, and we broke up.

And in the aftermath, Sandra helped me realize that being broken up *wasn't* what I wanted. What I wanted was just . . . to like him, and have him like me back, and have fun together and be normal together. And not feel nervous about telling him what was on my mind.

Yet what had happened after we got back together? I'd been strong, outspoken Winnie for a second, maybe. But look at me now: I'd totally reverted to wimpy Winnie. *Ugh*.

"Stop the car!" I barked.

Sandra looked sideways at me.

"Okay, don't *stop* the car," I amended. "But would you turn around? Please? And take me to Lars's house for one incredibly quick second?"

"Winnie. Mom's probably got dinner ready. She's probably wondering where we are."

"Just for a microsecond. I *swear*."

She sighed, then eased up on the accelerator. She pulled into a driveway and turned around.

"Thank you thank you *thank* you," I gushed.

"You better remember this when I need one of your kidneys," she growled.

At Lars's house, I lobbed pebbles at the window of his upstairs bedroom, something I'd always wanted to do. It was such a "romantic comedy" moment, not that we were in a romantic comedy.

But if we were in a romantic comedy, the guy would—suddenly appear! *Yes!* There he was, my beautiful sweet Lars, obviously surprised to see me. I gestured for him to come down, and he nodded and disappeared from view.

As I waited, my stomach filled with butterflies. But when Lars slipped through the front door and came over to me, I didn't hesitate. A single moment of fear could do me in. I knew that.

I grabbed his shoulders, rose to my toes, and kissed him. I was light-headed when I finally pulled away. As for Lars, he looked dazed . . . but in a good way.

Sandra honked. "Marla!" she bellowed through the open window. "Get a move on!"

"Marla?" Lars said, confused.

I touched my nose to his. Then I covered his ears with my hands so I wouldn't burst his eardrums.

"Keep your pants on, Fanny!" I hollered.

Lars drew his eyebrows together. He was so adorable.

"Gotta go," I told him. "But we have *got* to figure out a way to hang out this weekend, okay? Maybe Sunday brunch?"

He nodded. "And afterward we could go on a bike ride or something. Um, spend the whole day together."

"That would be *awesome*," I said happily. I kissed him one more time, not afraid at all.

I Stand Corrected

ON APRIL FIFTEENTH, Sandra got her acceptance letter to Middlebury, which was her top choice college. On April sixteenth, Dinah got suspended from Westminster.

Dinah.

Suspended.

The rumors flying through the junior high halls blew my news about Sandra right out of the water.

"Did you hear about Dinah?" Louise said, running up to me between third and fourth periods.

"*Oh*. My *God*," Malena said to Gail, the two of them miraculously materializing by my locker before Louise could elaborate.

"I know," Gail replied. "I mean, we all knew she had issues." She arched her eyebrows. "But a klepto?"

A klepto? My jaw dropped, and Malena smirked. I'd given them just the reaction they'd hoped for.

"Worst thing?" Malena said, supposedly to Gail but really to me. "From all reports, she didn't even steal good stuff." *Snicker snicker*. "All she stole were more of those crap kitty-cat shirts she wears."

"I know," Gail said. "If she's going to steal, she should at least steal Gucci."

"Pathetic," Malena said.

I banged shut my locker. *"No,"* I said, facing them dead on. "What's pathetic is having a pretend conversation just so I'll listen in. If you're so desperate for attention, go make an appointment with the counselor."

Gail and Malena eyed me with twin sets of narrow eyes. Then Gail altered her features to convey fake sympathy at having to be the one to clue me in.

"Um, y-y-yeah," Gail said. "Only, like, the counselor's totally booked? She's too busy telling Dinah's father what a *klepto* his daughter is."

She and Malena flounced off, peals of laughter trailing behind them like sick moths. I turned to Louise.

"What's going on?" I said. "Dinah doesn't *steal*."

Louise fidgeted, which was out of character, as Louise was a gossip and loved a good scandal. On the other hand, she *did* go to elementary school with me and Dinah. The three of us had known each other forever.

She touched my arm. My chest felt fluttery.

"They found all sorts of stuff in her locker," she said. "Not crap. Not Gucci, either. But not kitty-cat shirts."

"So? People *do* keep stuff in their lockers. That's what lockers are for."

"It was makeup, mainly."

"And again . . . *so*? Dinah wears makeup." *Sometimes*, I added silently.

"But this was *lots* of makeup, still in its packaging. Bobbi Brown, MAC, Stila. A supercute bottle of Gwen Stefani perfume called Lil' Angel, which is, um, kind of ironic."

I was having trouble breathing. There were too many people in the hall, and too many of them were looking at me, no doubt thinking all sorts of shocked and gleeful thoughts about how Dinah—*my* best friend—was a makeup hoarder and a shoplifter.

Only, she *wasn't*. I knew my Dinah, and she wasn't either of those things.

"Louise," I said. "Dinah *does* have money. Her dad's not crazy rich, but Dinah has her own credit card that she's authorized to sign for. Why would she steal makeup when she could just buy it?"

"I think it was more like—"

"No," I interrupted. "So Dinah has a lot of unopened makeup; that doesn't make her a thief. Did anyone come right out and say, 'Hey, Dinah, what's up with this?'"

Louise tried to speak. Once more I rode over her.

"Maybe she bought them to give as birthday presents. Or maybe she wants a fresh image. Or maybe she was attacked by a very forceful Sephora salesclerk. You know how hard it is for her to say no!" I set my shoulders. "But if Dinah said the makeup is *hers*, it's hers. Case closed."

Louise nodded. She waited to make sure I was done. And then she said, "Except . . . she didn't."

"Didn't what?"

"When Ms. Perkins called her into her office, Dinah had a breakdown and confessed."

"Confessed *what*?"

"That the makeup was stolen. Winnie, Dinah admitted flat out that she didn't pay for any of it."

My brain operated in slow gear. "But . . . I mean . . ."

The bell rang.

I've got to go to class," Louise said with unsettling gentleness. "I just thought you should know."

Speculation about Dinah ran rampant. Most theories were outlandish: that her father was so furious he was shipping her off to military school. That, in fact, she was already gone. Or that she'd been checked in to Georgia Regional Mental Hospital because she thought she was a vampire, and that's what the makeup was for—so she could disguise her paleness in the light of day. Or, according to Lucy, a girl in my algebra class, the real issue was Dinah's bulimia. Only, make that Dinah's *nonexistent* bulimia.

"A) Dinah's not bulimic," I said flatly. "And B) Just say she was. She's bulimic . . . and so she steals makeup?"

Lucy pulled her algebra book, a binder, and a purple jeweled pen from her messenger bag. She arranged them fastidiously on her desk. "It's a *control issue*," she said. She laid a second pen by the first, lining them up so they were parallel. "Instead of food, she gorges on product."

I'd never bonded with Lucy. Now I knew why.

Yet some of the stories possessed just enough of a *maybe* to worry me. I gnawed at the skin around my thumbnail until a whole chunk peeled free. It was gross.

And, making everything infinitely worse, I couldn't find Dinah *all day*, or get her to answer any of my texts. Maybe she'd lost her cell phone privileges? I called her landline the minute I got home, and my muscles loosened when she finally picked up.

"Winnie, I'm such a bad friend," she said. Her voice was thick from crying.

"No, you're not," I said. Although what did I know?

"I am," she insisted. "I'm a horrible, horrible friend!"

"Oh, *Dinah*," I said. Off the record, I was gratified at her willingness to admit she'd done me wrong by not coming to me earlier. *Way* earlier. But this wasn't about me. This was about her. Anyway, the best way for her to stop being a horrible friend was to simply come clean.

"Why don't you tell me what happened," I suggested.

"What *happened* is that I got Mary *suspended*!" Her voice ratcheted to a new level of frenzy. "Now *she's* suspended instead of *me*!"

"I'm sorry . . . huh?"

"I'm suspended, too, but only for one day, and I get to make up any work I miss. But Mary's suspended for a whole week, *and* it goes on her permanent record!"

I didn't speak.

"See? I *am* a bad friend! A horrible, horrible friend!"

I still didn't speak. I felt cold inside.

"Winnie, say something," she begged. "Mary already hates me. Now you're starting to worry me, too!"

"Yes, but you see, I thought you already *were* worried about me," I said, pinching off the words. "I thought you meant a bad friend to *me*, because you didn't come to me with your shoplifting problem, which I didn't even know you had."

Dinah fell silent. Then she started crying again. I could hear the muffled sounds of it, and I couldn't bear it.

"So *Mary's* behind all this?" I asked. "Mary Woods?"

"Well, yeah, it's her makeup—didn't you know?"

Irritation resurfaced. "How would I? You sure didn't tell me!"

"Don't be mean to me," she whispered.

I tried to smush my anger back. I did. Or at least to redirect it at Mary, with her crafty fox-face. *Cute shirt, Winnie! Cinnamon,* love *your nails. Dinah . . . don't tell.*

"Was she blackmailing you?" I asked.

"What? *No.*"

"But you said it was her makeup. Hers, as in she owned it? Or hers as in she *stole* it?"

Dinah didn't answer.

"Why did she put it in your locker?" I demanded. "Did she do it without your knowing it? Omigod, did she set you up on purpose?"

"Winnie . . ."

"So Mary Woods is a shoplifter," I pronounced. "What a loser."

"She has a problem," Dinah said faintly.

"Omigod, are you defending her?" I should have stopped there, but I didn't. "Are you a shoplifter, too?"

"Winnie!"

Hey, can't blame me for asking, I thought. *Since there's so much else you haven't told me.*

"You're making me feel worse instead of better," Dinah said. "I'm not a shoplifter, and I would *think* you would know that."

"I would think I would, too," I shot back.

"Mary has a *problem*," she repeated, and now her words came out forcefully. "Shoplifting is an ad*dic*tion, and it's really hard for her, and it's not your place to judge her."

"Dinah—"

"And I let her keep her stuff in my locker because . . . well, I don't *know* why." She sniffled. "And I promised I wouldn't tell, but I broke under pressure! I *broke*, all right? Are you happy?!"

I wasn't. I'd started off mad, and I still was. But now a thread of fear moved through me. She was being . . . so not *Dinah*.

"Okay, um . . . wow," I said at last. I sounded flat. "That really sucks. I'm so sorry."

"No, I'm sorry." The fight had gone out of her, and if I sounded flat, she sounded . . . well, a step below that, even.

"I don't know what's wrong with me. I'll, um, talk to you later."

She hung up.

She didn't come to school the next day, since she was serving her suspension. I still couldn't believe it. *Dinah*.

"Well, maybe that's why," Louise said at lunch.

"Maybe what's why?" Cinnamon said.

"Why Dinah did it. Maybe she wanted to prove there's more to her than people think."

"That's ridiculous," I said.

"Is it?" Louise said, taking a bite of her sandwich. She was sitting with Cinnamon and me, and I think she liked being a member of our group, even though it was only for today. "Maybe she was sick of always being the good girl."

"But she *is* a good girl," I said. "*That's who she is*. Weird Mary just corrupted her."

"Personally, I think people are making too big a deal out of it," Louise said. "What she did wasn't even all that bad."

"Are you kidding me?" I said. "She's a shoplifter!"

Other kids glanced over. I blushed, realizing I was being a little loud.

"I'm talking about Dinah," Louise said. She regarded me quizzically. "Dinah didn't shoplift."

"Yeah, well, she was an accomplice!" I was aware that I couldn't have it both ways: *Dinah is bad* right up there next to *Dinah is my sweet, innocent Dinah*. My emotions were all tangled up, though. I'd *known* Mary was bad news. I'd written myself that note on my iPhone application: FIND OUT WHAT'S UP WITH MARY WOODS!

But then I'd ignored it. I'd made progress on my To-Do-Before-High-School list—*whoopee*—but I'd let the Mary Woods issue slide.

Was it too late? Should I add "Kick Mary Woods's Butt" to my To-Do-Before-High-School list, or would that be cheating?

"Gail says it's abandonment issues," Cinnamon said. "Lucy Blare thinks she's got bulimia."

"Lucy Blare is an idiot," I said.

"True dat," Cinnamon said. "I was like, 'Lucy, Dinah's not bulimic. She's *chubby*.'"

I gaped at her. I flung out my hands to say *What?!*

"If she was bulimic, she'd be throwing it all up," Cinnamon explained. "Hence, no calories. Hence, not chubby. Get it?"

"You do know how wrong that is, right?" I stated. "On so many levels?"

Cinnamon pushed a French fry into her mouth as a single piece, from tip to end. She drew out her finger with a *pop*.

"Go see her," Louise suggested.

I looked at her from beneath my bangs.

"I'm not saying cut class," Louise said. "Just, after school. And instead of *you* talking, let *her*."

She made sense. It ticked me off.

"Think Sandra would take us?" Cinnamon asked me.

"Probably," I said reluctantly.

"Can I come?" Louise said. Cinnamon and I shared a glance.

"Maybe it should just be me and Winnie," Cinnamon said. "But, um, we'll tell her 'hey' for you."

Dinah lived in a white brick house with yellow flower boxes. The flower boxes were one of Dinah's favorite projects to care for, and I couldn't count the times I'd basked in the sun on her front steps as she moved from blossom to blossom with her big-spouted watering can.

Dinah hadn't planted this year's flowers yet.

Cinnamon rang the doorbell. "Remember," she instructed me, "be cool."

"I'm always cool," I replied.

"Well, be kind," she elaborated.

I'm always kind, I almost said, but stopped myself.

She rang the bell again, then rapped on the door.

"Coming!" we heard Dinah call. There were thunky footfalls, and she opened the door. She was pale, and her eyes were puffy.

"Oh," she said when she saw it was us.

I hesitated, then stepped forward and hugged her. Cinnamon joined in so that we made a Dinah-sandwich.

"Hey there, troublemaker," Cinnamon said, giving her a noogie. "Got a smoke for your old bud Cinnamon?"

Dinah smiled wanly. "No. I've got Diet Sierra Mist, though."

Cinnamon gagged. She had Sierra Mist issues, and Diet Sierra Mist in particular. But we followed Dinah into her kitchen, where she served us drinks and Veggie Booty, which was like cheese puffs, only not at all, because it was made from spinach and kale.

"You're trying to kill me, aren't you?" said Cinnamon, who had Veggie Booty issues as well.

"No, not trying to kill you," Dinah said listlessly. "You don't have to eat it."

Cinnamon grabbed the bag. "Fine, fine, I'll eat it." She popped a handful into her mouth, leaving the next move to me.

"So, um . . . how're things?" I said.

Dinah's eyes found mine. Her expression made my heart lurch, and I had the sudden and awful feeling that *I* had done something wrong. Me, and not Dinah. But why would I think that?

"Do you guys . . ." She caught her bottom lip between her teeth. "Do y'all ever . . ."

"Do we ever *what*?" I said, my heart pounding.

Tears welled in Dinah's eyes, which made tears spring to *my* eyes. "Do you ever feel *lonely* inside? Like . . . there's a great big gaping hole where your ribs are?"

I *did* know that feeling. I knew it well, though I was startled to hear it described so perfectly.

"And it comes out of nowhere?" I said. "Yes. But it makes no sense, because I have *y'all* . . . so why should I feel lonely?" I shifted uncomfortably, but pressed on. "I mean, what do I have to feel sad about?"

"I get that feeling, too," Cinnamon said. I turned to her in surprise. "But it's not behind my ribs. It's more . . ." She cleared her throat, as if a piece of Veggie Booty, or something else, was clogging the works. "It's more inside my heart. And when it comes, it comes. And all I can do is ride it out."

Dinah reached over to squeeze Cinnamon's hand, but Cinnamon jerked her hand away. She shoved it back in the Veggie Booty bag and grabbed a fresh handful.

"No, don't," Cinnamon said, making a weird laugh sound. "Who said life was easy, right?"

I swallowed. I asked Dinah, "So you've been feeling lonely?"

Silence.

I forced myself to look at her, to honestly and openly look at her . . . and that was all it took. Her chin trembled, and her story came pouring out. Or rather, her confession. Except instead of *I did this and this and this,* it was *I am this and this and this.*

She was weak, she said, for getting sucked into Mary's lies. She was dumb for not telling anyone what was going on, especially me and Cinnamon. She was ashamed that her dad had to be called in to talk to the counselor. And finally, she was really really *really* sorry for making such a mess of things. For being so stupid and needy.

"Dinah, no," I said. "You're not stupid. *Mary's* stupid. It's her fault, not yours."

My response seemed to frustrate her, or maybe deepen

her despair. She rubbed her forehead. "But do y'all accept my apology?"

"For not telling us about the great makeup scandal?" Cinnamon said. "Dude, we're all human."

"I don't mean that," she said. "Do you accept my apology for being *me*?"

"Stop," I said desperately. It was getting harder to shake the feeling that *I* needed to be apologizing, too. For something. I didn't know what. Or maybe I did, but I didn't want to go there?

Admit it when you're wrong. That was one of my goals for myself . . . but it was hard. *So* hard.

"You don't have to apologize for who you are," Cinnamon said with rock-solid certainty. "None of us is perfect."

"But I'm supposed to be the good girl," Dinah said.

"Oh, Dinah," I said. I recalled Louise's analysis of the situation, and I just felt worse. I drove my fingernail repeatedly into the pad of my thumb.

"Only I don't *want* to be," Dinah went on. "Not always." She trained her eyes on me. "I don't want to be the girl who does embarrassing things, or wears the wrong pants, or says things that make you say, 'Oh, *Dinah*.'"

My stomach cramped.

"I don't want to be the girl you pat on the head, Winnie."

This was it. This was why I'd been afraid. And now that it was out in the open, I bore down so hard on the flesh of my thumb that I could feel the bone.

"I'm not trying to make you feel bad," Dinah said. "It's just . . . I don't want to be that person anymore."

I felt myself turn bright red.

"Do you understand what I'm saying?" Dinah pleaded.

Cinnamon glanced from Dinah to me. When I failed to respond, she said, "Uh . . . I sure don't. Will one of you please explain?"

Dinah kept her eyes on me. I could feel the weight of her need. But I dropped my gaze, while inside my rib cage, my heart tried to beat its way out. I wanted to flee, or tell Dinah she was full of crap, or burst into tears so that she and Cinnamon would feel sorry for *me* and worry about *me*. And if doing so kept them from seeing the real me? That would be fine, especially if the real me was someone who patted her friend on the head and said, so condescendingly, "Oh, *Dinah*."

Understanding dawned on Cinnamon's face. Maybe she absorbed it from the air, or, more likely, she finally put the pieces together.

"Oh my god," she said to Dinah. "You went to the Dark Side to prove you weren't Winnie's pet?!"

I shrunk from the ugliness of it. When I peeked to see Dinah's reaction, I saw her shrink, too.

"Never mind, of course not," she said, her resolve crumpling. "I'm so stupid." She thwacked her head. "So! *Stu*pid!"

It cracked the shell inside of me. I got up and went to her, tears rolling down my cheeks, and made her scooch over so I could share her chair. My pulse was racing, because sometimes I was insanely awkward when it came to showing people I cared about them. Especially when that person was mad at me.

But I looped my arms around her anyway and said, "You goof."

Her shoulders shook, and shame engulfed me as I realized I'd done it *again*. She'd shared something big and scary, and I'd patted her on her head *again*.

"*No*," I said. "I mean, *yes*, but . . ."

Cinnamon stared at us, lost all over again. She actually wasn't blameless herself; she and I probably egged each other on with the whole "Oh, *Dinah*" business.

Not probably. Definitely.

I'd been friends with Dinah for longer than I'd been friends with Cinnamon, however. Today, right now, the person who needed to apologize was me.

"I'm sorry," I said.

Dinah's shoulders shook harder. I *hated* how awful I felt, how sunk in the mire, but I pressed on.

"I'll work on it, okay?" I said. "I do know what you mean—and I'll try to do better."

"You don't have to," Dinah said thickly.

"Yes, I do," I said. "I was wrong, and . . . and I stand corrected."

"Okay," Dinah said. She laughed, only with a gulp added in. "Um, thanks."

Cinnamon regarded us like we were nuts. "Y'all are nuts," she said.

This launched a fresh wave of tears for both of us. Happy tears, though.

"No, seriously," Cinnamon said.

We kept right on being mush pots, sniffling and giggling, until Cinnamon thwonked the table with her palm.

"Moving on," she said authoritatively. "Can we talk about Mary, please? Now that y'all are all lovey-dovey again?"

I rested my chin on Dinah's shoulder blade. Her skin was milky white. "I don't know. Dinah, do you *want* to talk about Mary?"

"It's so embarrassing," Dinah said.

"Excellent," Cinnamon said. "I love it when people who aren't me embarrass themselves."

"Oh, fine," Dinah said. She exhaled. "Remember yesterday, when I was so upset about turning Mary in?"

"Yeah," Cinnamon said.

"Well, today Ms. Perkins called and said she wanted to share some stuff. It's private, which means I'm not supposed to tell. So you guys can't, either."

Ms. Perkins was our eighth-grade counselor, which meant that whatever she told Dinah was probably juicy.

"It's not Mary's first time," Dinah said. "To, um, do stuff, and then make someone else take the blame."

"No way," Cinnamon said.

"She's extremely adept at manipulation," Dinah said in the manner of someone repeating a direct quote.

"Like the Black Widow!" Cinnamon said. "Omigod, Mary is my new hero!"

Dinah shoved her. *I* shoved her.

"I still have to take responsibility for what I did," Dinah said. "But Ms. Perkins said to see it as a life lesson."

"So the times I saw you with Mary," I said, "and she was all, 'Don't tell, don't tell,' she was . . . what? Asking if she could put the stuff she'd stolen in your locker?"

"The first time it was because she was late for hip-hop club," Dinah said. "She didn't say *what* she was putting in my locker. She just said, 'Can I?'"

"And of course you said yes," Cinnamon said. She grabbed the bag of Veggie Booty, tilted her chair onto its back legs, and started munching.

"And then when I saw what it was—"

"Which was what?" Cinnamon asked.

"A bunch of Urban Decay eye shadows, obviously new. But I didn't think anything of it."

"Urban Decay," Cinnamon said. "Nice."

"So when did, like, the red flags go up?" I asked.

"When she wouldn't take any of it back. She was like, 'You keep them. They're for you.'"

"Can anyone say 'random'?" Cinnamon said.

"And then she kept putting *more* stuff in my locker. She knew my combination, so—"

"You gave her your combination?" I said. "Dinah!"

"This was before I knew! I told her my combination that very first time, when I thought she just wanted to put her school stuff somewhere until hip-hop was over."

"Why didn't you get a new lock?" I asked.

"Well . . . because that would have been rude."

Oh, Dinah, I almost said. I clamped my mouth shut.

"So when this pile of makeup grew," Cinnamon said. "This *mountain* of expensive products—was *that* when you realized something fishy was going on?"

"She pretty much took over my whole locker," Dinah confessed. "I didn't have room for my books anymore."

Cinnamon's laughter barked out.

"Cinnamon!" I said.

"I did tell Mary that I wasn't happy about what was going on," Dinah said. "I thought about gathering all the makeup and putting it in her locker, but—"

"Let me guess," Cinnamon interrupted. "She wouldn't give you her combination."

Dinah looked sheepish.

I groaned.

"So it turned into this awful, weird mess," she said. "I *wanted* to tell y'all, but Mary begged me not to. She kept saying it would be the last time, that she would get help, that she'd talk to Ms. Perkins . . ."

"But she never did," I finished.

"And then . . . well . . ."

Cinnamon raised her eyebrows.

Dinah's voice grew smaller. "Yesterday she asked if she could copy my humanities homework—"

"Oh, nuh-*uh*," I said. Dinah and I had the same teacher for humanities, though at different periods, so we were both doing the same lessons. "The assignment on Kohlberg's stages of moral development?"

Dinah's cheeks turned pink.

"Too perfect," Cinnamon said, cracking up. "Cheating on the old moral development assignment."

"I didn't want to, but I couldn't say no. So I said, 'Fine, but I don't have it with me.' And she said, 'Well, will you go get it?' Because her ankle hurt. She'd twisted it at the mall."

Cinnamon smirked. "While making her getaway from the MAC counter."

"She always made it sound so urgent that I help her," Dinah said. "When I was *away* from her, I'd tell myself, 'Dinah, stop. Mary is BAD NEWS.' But then she'd corner me, and like"— she twirled her hands in the air—"work her magical *persuasion* skills, and I'd find myself saying *yes* when what I wanted was to say *no*."

"I knew she was evil," I said. "I swear I did."

Dinah looked at me askance.

"What?" I said.

"She's messed up. Yes. But I'm not sure it's fair to say she's *evil*."

"Sure it is," Cinnamon said. She stood up and tossed the bag of Veggie Booty on the table. "But what's over is over. It *is* over, right? Can we move on?"

"Yeah," Dinah agreed. "I'd be really happy to move on."

"Wait," I said hesitantly. They looked at me, and I had

a moment of doubt. Did I really want to dredge up more ickiness, when we'd plowed through so much already?

Then again: If not now, when?

"Do y'all remember that party at the beginning of seventh grade?" I said. "When Amanda supposedly got drunk and fooled around with some eighth grader?"

"Not 'supposedly,'" Cinnamon corrected. "My next-door neighbor was there. She saw Amanda kiss him with her own two eyes."

"Well, with her lips, probably," I said, since the joke was right there in front of me.

"We remember," Dinah said. "What about it?"

I drummed my fingers on the table, unsure how to articulate what I was thinking. Mainly, it had to do with how we'd be graduating from junior high next month, and though I refused to obsess about high school—I'd forbidden myself to, and I was a girl of my word—that didn't mean I wasn't allowed to bring it up *ever*.

It was out there, and huge, and while I was ready for things to change . . . I also wasn't.

"Lars was at that party, too," I said.

"Oh, yeah?" Cinnamon said.

"Yeah. We talked about it afterward, and about Amanda in particular. He was like, 'If she's drinking wine coolers in the seventh grade, what's she going to be like in high school?'"

Cinnamon didn't understand. Dinah did, and color rose in her face.

"I don't mean *you*," I told her. "I don't even mean Mary, necessarily."

"Then who *do* you mean?" Cinnamon asked.

I spread my hands. "I don't know. I guess, maybe . . . all of us?"

It took her a moment, and then Cinnamon got it. I could read it in her eyes.

All the things we knew about each other. All the things we didn't. All the changes coming our way, whether we wanted them to or not.

"Can we make a pledge?" Dinah said at last.

"No," Cinnamon said immediately.

"Yes," I said. "A pledge that we will be there for each other, through thick and thin."

Dinah nodded happily. Cinnamon moaned.

I made a fist and held it up. "Let's do it, ladies."

"Oh my god," Cinnamon said to the ether. "She wants us to give her some knuckles."

Dinah pressed her fist to mine.

"C'mon, Cin-Cin," I said. I made a kiss-kiss dog-calling sound.

Cinnamon sighed mightily. She thrust her fist against ours.

For several seconds we were connected, our arms stretching from our fists like branches from a single root. Cinnamon pushed inward, then pulled away, splaying her fingers.

"*Whoosh,*" she said, giving sound to our fist-bump explosion.

"*Whoosh,*" Dinah repeated.

Looking at them, I felt happy *and* sad—and maybe that was just the way of it.

"Winnie?" Cinnamon prompted.

I imagined a shooting star, burning and twinkling on its journey through the sky. "*Whoosh.*"

Practice Being Older

SOMETIMES, when a friend calls up and says *get-over-here-my-life-is-over*, it turns out to be a missed episode of *The Secret Life of an American Teen*. Other times it's a horrible bathing suit purchase, or the realization that the pair of jeans earmarked for a certain party have suddenly turned stupid, or too tight, and a new outfit needs to be whipped up *pronto*. Or, if it's Dinah making the frantic call, it maybe has to do with a hair ball. Not hers. One of her cats'. In fact, Dinah's emergency calls often had to do with hair balls, so that's the assumption I was working under when I biked to Dinah's one cloudy afternoon in April.

Cinnamon showed up on her longboard right as I was turning into the driveway. She did a fancy power-slide dismount, flipped her board, and caught it under her arm.

"What do you think's going on?" she asked as we approached the front door. "I could hardly understand her when she called me. She sounded like she was hyperventilating."

"Dunno," I said. "Maybe one of her cats is sick?"

Cinnamon laughed, though I hadn't meant it as a joke. Then the front door opened, and Dinah pulled the two of us in. She dragged us down the hall and into her bedroom, which was frilly and purple. The decorating style was mid-elementary school, and I found it reassuringly steady, despite Dinah's apparent inability to speak.

She shoved us toward her computer. She grunted inarticulately.

"What?" Cinnamon said. "*Talk*, girl."

I squinted at the screen. "Strugglin'—" I reared back. "Strugglin' Teens *Boot* Camp? What the heck?"

"Boot camp," Cinnamon said, sounding interested. She squeezed in and read out loud from the web page. She had to go slow because the syntax was crazy. "'Summer camps are having their own instructors or counselors who can detect—'" She broke off. She tried again. "'Who can detect your teen problem?'"

"Dinah?" I said. "Do you have a teen problem?"

"My dad's making me go to leadership camp," Dinah said miserably.

"'Our programs are based on old-fashioned morals that teach discipline, and physical training that will change your unruly child into a good citizen,'" Cinnamon read in a deranged, off-kilter lilt. She switched back to her normal voice. "Who *are* these people?"

"I think they're maybe from Japan," Dinah said. Her chest went up and down. "I'm *not* going to Japan. I'm not! He can't make me!"

"Slow down," I said. I put my hands on her shoulders and got her to look at me, which was no small feat as her eyes were skitting all over town. "Breathe. That's right. In"—I inhaled to show her, and her nostrils flared and she tried to mimic me—"and out. Good!"

"Now explain," Cinnamon demanded. "Your dad's making you go to *boot camp*?"

"Cinnamon!" I chided as Dinah went right back into lack-of-oxygen mode. She swayed, and I guided her to her bed. I sat beside her and rubbed her back. A moment passed, and then another, before she shakily began to talk.

Her dad loved her so much that he wanted the very best for her, she told us, and he'd come up with a great idea to help her achieve her full potential. He knew she wasn't going to like it, his idea, but he hoped she'd come around. Even if she didn't, she was still going to have to do it. Because he loved her. So much.

Eee, I thought as I kept tracing circles on her back. This didn't sound good at all.

"He doesn't want me to be a follower," she said, staring at her purple shag carpet. "He doesn't want me to be the sort of girl people walk on." Her hands found tufts of her floral bedspread and gripped them. "I'm not the sort of girl people walk on, am I?"

"No," I said. "Absolutely not!"

"Mary Wo-oods," Cinnamon said under her breath in an ominous singsong. I shushed her with a glare.

Dinah let out a big sigh. "Well, anyway, I'm starting high school next fall," she said dully.

"Nuh-uh," Cinnamon said. "For reals?"

"*Cinnamon*," I said through gritted teeth.

"Winnie, I am fully aware that Dinah is starting high school next fall," Cinnamon said. "Dinah does not need to tell me that she's starting high school next fall, as I will be starting right there next to her. And so will you. We will all be starting high school together, unless—" She gasped, and it wasn't for effect. It was a true and honest gasp that made me jump and even roused Dinah from her zombie slump.

"Unless what?" I said.

"Is your dad sending you to boarding school?" Cinnamon said. Her expression grew long with horror. "Is he pulling you out of Westminster like weird Mary's parents did?"

I clasped both hands to my mouth. After the makeup hording incident, weird Mary's parents had claimed Mary wasn't being academically challenged at Westminster, and that's why she'd turned to a life of crime. According to a girl named Bella, who eavesdropped from outside the counselor's office, Mary's parents had wished out loud they didn't have to take such drastic measures, but poor Mary was just so *bored*. What other option did they have?

I made a teeny-tiny crack between my fingers, just big enough for my teeny-tiny voice. "Please tell us you're not being pulled out of Westminster. Please!"

"Omigosh, *no*!" Dinah cried. "I would never let him do that! I would . . ." She worked her face muscles in strange contortions as she struggled to come up with an adequate threat. "I would chop all my hair off first!"

"How would *that* stop him?" Cinnamon wanted to know.

I drew my hand to my chest. All I cared about was that she wasn't leaving us. "Thank God. In that case, whatever it is can't be *that* bad."

"Yeah-huh," Dinah said. "Because he's making me spend the summer 'building moral fiber and enhancing my assets.'" Her lower lip trembled. "Only, I don't w-want to enhance my assets!"

"And we don't want you to, either," Cinnamon avowed. "No asset-enhancing on my watch, nossir!"

"Did you try telling him no?" I asked.

"What do you think?" Dinah said. *"Duh."*

"Yeah, *duh*," Cinnamon said. Dinah hardly ever smart-mouthed me, so Cinnamon delighted in the times she did.

"Well, surely we can find something better than Strugglin' Teens Boot Camp," I said. I got off the bed and took a seat on the bouncy ball Dinah used for a computer chair. I did a Google search for summer camps and came up with a neat thirty-five million. "See? Tons to choose from. You're going to be fine."

"Unh," Dinah said.

"Let's see . . ." I scrolled through some obvious no-go's, like Highlands Military Camp, or Alabama Tech Computer Camp, or Handy-Kids Camp for Future Farmers of America.

"Hold on there," Cinnamon said, stopping me from

clicking past that last one. "Why so hasty? It says here that Handy-Kids is all about fun."

"But I'm not handy," Dinah said. "And I don't want to be a farmer."

"So? Talk about learning leadership skills. You could *totally* dominate a bunch of . . . wheat fields . . . or whatever. Think about it!"

Dinah and I shared a look. I removed Cinnamon's hand from the keyboard and moved on.

"This one could be cool," I said, clicking on a new link. "'White-water adventures, hikes through the scenic Rocky Mountains, a nighttime of stars . . . all of this and more at Camp Crested Butte.'"

Cinnamon chortled. "Camp Crusty Butt? You nix Handy-Kids, but you want to send your dear friend to Camp Crusty Butt?"

"Inap*pro*priate," I said.

"But funny," Cinnamon said, giggling.

Dinah sank to her purple shag carpet. She lay all the way back and stared at the ceiling. I just knew she was going to end up with purple fuzz clinging to her hair.

"Maybe y'all could come with me," she said in a too-casual tone.

"To Camp Crusty Butt?" Cinnamon said. "No thanks."

I understood Dinah's pain. If I were forced to go to camp, I'd sure want my buddies with me. I, however, planned to spend the summer with Lars, kissing and swimming and, you know, kissing.

"Ooo, Dinah, I don't think so," I said.

"Why not?" she whined.

"I've kind of got other things going on. I mean, I *wish*, but . . . yeah."

"But if we *all* went . . ."

"I *know*," I said. "And maybe if you'd mentioned it earlier . . ."

"I didn't know earlier! My dad just told me!"

"Maybe Cinnamon can go," I suggested.

Cinnamon lasered me with her eyes. "Sorry, Charlie. I already said no. In fact I was the first to say no, thanks muchly. But *I* will find you something fab, just wait and see."

She plopped down beside me, making Dinah's super ball roll to the left. I jutted out my leg to stabilize us, while Cinnamon flapped her fingers against mine until I relinquished the keyboard. She typed with brisk efficiency.

"Cultural immersion in Costa Rica," she read. "Now *this* sounds awesome. It says you'd build a rural school in a cloud forest, and—hey! You'd be exposed to a rainbow of colorful flowers and birds! While rolling up your sleeves, working hard, and speaking nothing but Spanish!"

"But I don't speak Spanish," Dinah said.

"Bet you would after living in the cloud forest for a month," Cinnamon said.

"No," Dinah said.

Cinnamon moved on. "Ooo! *Ooo*, this is even better. Fire-walking camp!!!" She swiveled and looked at Dinah.

"Dinah, you could liberate your inner spirit. How cool would that be?"

I peered at the screen. "They also offer Thai massage, henna tattooing, and improvisational dancing."

"No," Dinah said.

"In addition, you can learn the ancient art of *ga-ga*," I continued. "What the heck is ga-ga?"

"No."

Cinnamon cocked her head at the computer. "Wow, look at the position that girl's in."

"They list it as a sport," I commented.

"No!" Dinah cried. "Done! Move on!"

Cinnamon and I fought over the mouse.

"Are you interested in sea-kayaking?" I tried.

"No," said Dinah.

"Herding cows?" Cinnamon said.

"I don't think they're cows," I said, cocking my head at the computer. "I think they're water buffalo. And stop clicking back to the Costa Rica one. She already said—"

"No," Dinah said.

"Well, personally, I think you're being a little picky," Cinnamon said. "I think cows are cute."

"Water buffalo," I said, as Dinah bellowed, *"NO!"*

Cinnamon clicked on a new link, and its home page blossomed on the screen.

"Omigod," she said.

My eyes bugged. *"Oh.* Omi*god.*"

"What?" Dinah said. Then, "No, don't tell me. Whatever you're *omigod*-ing, I'm vetoing it *right now*."

"But, *Dinah*," Cinnamon said. Her voice was reverent. "You have got to do this, please please *please*. It's"—she put her hand to her chest—"a *teen nudist camp*."

"Cinnamon," Dinah warned.

"The site has pictures," I mentioned.

Dinah hesitated, still in corpse pose. Then, reluctantly, she got up. She leaned between us, digging an elbow into each of our backs.

Her inhalation cleared the room of all oxygen.

"See?" Cinnamon said.

"That is so wrong," Dinah whispered.

The site was hi-tech, with photos scrolling across the top. Photos of, well, teen nudists. The pictures were waist-up only, but still. The girl campers had breasts! I could *see* their breasts! Breasts and breasts and breasts!

"Check out the nipples on that one," Cinnamon marveled. "They're the size of pepperonis."

"Ew," Dinah said.

A new photo came into resolution. We screamed.

"Ahhhh!" I squealed. "Nekkid boy bottoms!"

"It burns! It burns!" Cinnamon said, covering her eyes. She made a *V* with her fingers and peeked through. "Use some Clearasil, dude!"

"I bet he *hates* that picture," I murmured. "Can he not call the camp directors and ask them to take it down?"

"It says you can do a multitude of activities, dry, wet, and tanned," Cinnamon said.

"Not going to happen," Dinah said. But like me and Cinnamon, she was riveted.

"'Naked step aerobics'?" I read. "Why???"

"The same reason they'd have naked badminton, I guess," Cinnamon said. "Which is to say: because they're ker-*ray*-zee."

There was a link called "Testimonials." I clicked on it. A picture of a (topless) girl appeared, and we learned that her name was Hannah. The caption beneath said she was a Nude Youth Ambassador.

Silently, I read Hannah's testimonial, which was typed in a font meant to look like cursive. I could tell Cinnamon and Dinah were reading it, too. Dinah, because her lips moved, and Cinnamon because of her repeated utterances of horrified delight.

At Camp Buff, I learned to embrace my body, warts and all! wrote Hannah. *Being nude is very comfortable, and life in the nude is more fun than life with clothing. Plus, at Camp Buff there are hot dogs for sale at the nude volleyball tournament and soft drinks, too.*

Now that I'm back home, I go nude in my room almost always. But I can't wait till next summer when I can return to Camp Buff! After all, if you're going to make a lanyard, why not do it in the nude?

Cinnamon guffawed. "Why not, indeed?" she said. "You, guys, this has *got* to be a joke."

"Only, look," I said. "There's a telephone number and an address. They even have T-shirts for sale." I clicked to get to the T-shirt page. "Now call me dumb, but why would a nudist camp have T-shirts?"

"'NUDE' JUST MEANS BAREFOOT ALL OVER," Dinah said weakly, reading one of the slogans.

Cinnamon nudged Dinah. "What do you say, toots? *You* like going barefoot."

"No I don't."

"Talk about Camp Crusty Butt," Cinnamon continued, giggling.

"Gross," I said.

Dinah leaned in between us and jabbed the power button on the computer monitor.

Are you sure you want to shut down your computer? a message asked.

Dinah punched the "you bet your nekkid boy bottoms" button so fiercely that her laptop jumped. "I am *not* going to camp. End. Of. Story."

That night, Lars and I babysat Maggie so that Mom and Dad could go grab a bite with just each other.

"You can't neglect your husband after the birth of a baby," Mom told me as she handed me the squirming cuteness of my sister. Lars had yet to arrive, which was fortunate, because I felt a Mom-inappropriateness coming on.

"And that goes for . . . *romance*, too," she elaborated.

"'Kay, Mom. Great. Bye, now!"

"Even if you aren't"—she lowered her voice, but not nearly enough—"*in the mood*, if you know what I'm saying. And believe me, you won't be. Not with a new baby."

Oh good Lord.

"Ellen!" Dad called from the back door. He jangled his keys.

"Bye, sweetie," Mom said, giving Maggie a peck. She tousled my hair. "Bye, Winnie. You only need to change her if she poops, all right?"

"Uh-huh."

"And you'll *know* if she poops."

"Yes, Mother. Good-bye, Mother."

"And you know the rule: no boys in your room."

"We will stay in the den. We will watch our movie."

"But you'll—"

"Pay *more* attention to baby Mags than to each other, yes yes yes." I paused. "Unless Lars is feeling neglected and needs some"—I lowered my voice—"*romance.*"

First her eyes widened, and then they narrowed. *"Winnie."*

"Kidding! Love you! Have fun!"

I lifted Maggie's arm and made her wave. *"Bye, Mommy!"* I said in a teensy baby voice.

After one last kiss for baby Maggie, and then kisses from Dad for both his girls, Mom and Dad finally left. Twenty minutes later, Lars arrived, and—*ah, bliss.* It was just me, him, and Mags. Sandra was off with Bo, and Ty was being brave and spending the night at his friend Lexi's house. It was kind of like

Lars and me were the mom and dad . . . not that I would ever say that to Lars out loud. But practicing being older was one of the items on my list of things to do, and here I was doing it. *Yay!*

I smiled to cover my thoughts and gave him the most recent Dinah update.

"If she has to go, she might as well make the most of it, right?" I said. "But the problem is, Dinah has *no* desire to see the world."

"Seeing the world can be overrated," Lars said.

"What do you mean?"

"Nothing. Go on."

"I just think she should see it as an opportunity." I snuggled closer to him on the sofa and pressed my jean-clad thigh against his. "Don't you?"

I was being a little sneaky, I admit. Lars's family was big on traveling, and last year they'd spent the whole summer in Prague while his mom did some fellowship thing. It sucked, as I had no secret portal that led from my closet to the Czech Republic.

What that meant in the context of our conversation was that yes, in theory I was in favor of embracing travel and adventure. But I was feeling happy at the thought of him saying, "Yes, Dinah should see it as an opportunity. But *my* opportunity is right here. My opportunity is *you*."

"I can understand why Dinah wouldn't want to go out of town," he said. "That's all."

"Oh yeah?" I said coyly. What he was expressing was nice, if I read between the lines. But I wanted more.

He put his arm around me. "Yeah. What's wrong with Atlanta?"

"Nothing," I said.

"What's wrong with wanting to hang with people you already know?"

I liked this game. "Not a thing."

"Go somewhere new, and you'll experience things you otherwise wouldn't. I'm not saying you won't. But do you have to travel the world to be happy? No. You can be happy anywhere . . . as long as you're with the right person."

A thrill tickled my spine, because what he was saying was that I, Winnie, *was* the right person. *His* right person. As if to prove it, he pulled me closer and kissed the top of my head.

I melted into him like warm butter. Baby Mags was warm and buttery, too. We were a big warm buttery family, and I thought I might dissolve from happiness.

"I wouldn't leave, if I had the choice," he murmured. "I'd stay right here with you, all summer long."

My body stayed where it was. But my muscles contracted. "I'm sorry, what?"

He exhaled.

I pulled away. "Lars?!"

He couldn't meet my gaze. "My mom got offered another fellowship. In Germany this time."

I felt sick. I wanted to say, *So? Just because she got offered another stupid fellowship, that doesn't mean she has to take it, does she? And anyway, what's so great about Germany?*

"Tell her you don't want to go," I said. *Show some spine. Stick up for yourself!*

"Winnie . . ."

I scooted to the far end of the couch with baby Maggie in my arms. She whimpered, perhaps because I was separating her from her cuddly boy-shaped stuffed animal. Well, I was being separated from my cuddly boy-shaped stuffed animal, too.

"You could stay with Bryce," I said.

"My parents would never let me."

I pressed my lips together. I could feel sullenness coming on, and although I didn't like myself when I was sullen, there was nothing I could do to stave it off. Or maybe there was. Maybe I just didn't want to.

"Have you asked?" I said.

He stretched his legs out in front of him and let his head drop onto the sofa cushion. "I thought you didn't like Bryce."

Maybe not, but I liked him better than I liked Germany. My face by this point had hardened into a petulant mask. Especially my jaw. I would probably get TMJ, or whatever that disease was where you had to have your jaw wired shut and live on a liquid diet and use a computer activated voice synthesizer in order to talk, and it would be all Lars's fault. Except actually it would be mine for being so tightly wound that I was unable to say, normally and without accusation, *But I'll miss you.* And *I'm so bummed.* And *Do you really have to go?*

Baby Maggie squirmed and reached for Lars. I looped my arms over hers and straitjacketed them to her pudgy body.

"Winnie, I don't *want* to go to Germany," Lars said. "This isn't something I'm choosing to do."

"But you're not choosing *not* to," I said.

"We don't leave until June fifteenth. We'll have two full weeks of summer, two full weeks to spend with each other after school lets out."

"Two whole weeks! Wh-hoo!"

He massaged his temples. I was making him feel bad, and that made *me* feel bad. Only it also made me feel better, in a bitter pill sort of way.

"Come back and sit by me," he said. "I miss you."

"You can't 'miss' me," I said. "I'm on the other end of the sofa, not in a whole different country."

He reached for me. I resisted at first, then relented, because I missed him, too, despite his upcoming trip to stupid Germany.

He pulled on my arm, and I let my body slump like a felled tree until my cheekbone met Lars's lap. I shuffled baby Maggie so that she lay sideways, too, spooned against me with her head tucked beneath my chin. I was careful of her soft spot.

Lars finger-combed my hair. It felt like heaven, not that I was about to tell him.

I am the mommy and you are the daddy and this is our

baby, I thought despondently. The words hovered at the edge of consciousness.

Then Maggie pooped. It was a long, spluttering, *pttt-pttt-pttt* of a poop.

Lars's hand stilled. "I think . . . um . . ."

I pushed myself up with a groan. "Yeah." I held Maggie a few inches away from my body, because Maggie's diapers sometimes leaked.

"Come on, Stinky," I said to her. "Let's get you changed."

"Hey now," Lars said, pretending to be offended. "Who are you calling Stinky?"

I looked at him—the first full-on look since Germany invaded—and said, "Ha ha."

He was visibly relieved at our eye contact. "I'll e-mail you. Every day."

"Great," I said flatly.

And now he was less relieved. I could tell by the way his Adam's apple jerked up and down. But instead of feeling bad for worrying him, or sad that this was happening, I felt the urge to pull away from him.

"We're good, right?" he said, and if I were in the right mood, I would be touched by his concern. He *didn't* want to go with his family to Germany. I believed him. He would miss me. I believed that, too. But while I could see all that sweet-Lars angst, it didn't exactly . . . make its way to my heart.

"Of course we're good," I said, as if the topic was rather boring. "Things don't always go according to plan. That's just the way it goes." I gave a wry smile and lifted Maggie's smelly bottom for emphasis. "Poop happens."

He laughed too hard. I mean, I was funny, but not *that* funny.

"Maybe I'll go to leadership camp with Dinah after all," I threw out. "I mean, as long as you're going to Germany."

"Really?" Lars said, obviously startled. He smoothed his expression to hide it. "I mean, sure. Why not?"

Sure, why not? Excuse me, but who was he to give me permission?

"As long as it's not fire-walking camp," he said, laughing in a way that, to me, sounded forced.

I regarded him stonily. "I could learn to walk on fire."

"Or teen nudist camp," he said with more hardy-har-hars.

"I don't know. A full-body tan might be nice."

His hardy-har turned into a nervous chuckle, which turned into another up-and-down jerk of his Adam's apple. "Okay, how about this. Just no camp that's coed. Cool?"

I cocked my head.

"Winnie, I'm kidding."

Hmm. I didn't think he was.

In my arms, baby Maggie truly reeked. I shifted her into the crook of my arm and headed out of the room.

"I might be a few minutes," I said over my shoulder.

"No worries," Lars said. But he *sounded* worried. "I'll be right here. Waiting." He cleared his throat. "I'll just, uh . . . yeah."

How pathetic that my "romantic" night was ending in poop and stupid fighting—because even if it didn't look like we were fighting, we were. And to think that I'd started the night feeling so mature, when I wasn't mature at all. I was a baby playing house. A dumb baby at that.

"Hurry back!" he called. His voice cracked, and I felt a remote pity for both of us.

Do Something to Help the World

I N A WEEK, the seniors would graduate. Two weeks later, the school year would end for the rest of us, and two weeks after that? *Bye-bye Lars*.

I didn't like thinking about that: first, *this,* then *this* then *this*, with good-byes every step of the way.

So don't, I told myself. *Focus on today!* It was good advice, because this very today was sunny and perfect, and Dinah and I were relaxing on the steps of Pressley Hall, chatting as we watched the junior guys set up wooden folding chairs on the quad. It was an excellent day to simply . . . absorb.

Only I was constitutionally incapable of simply *absorbing*, it seemed. My brain kept jumping forward, no matter how many times I told it *no no no*. On different days, my thoughts circled around different things. My right-this-moment obsession? THE BEACH.

I'd gotten permission from Mom and Dad to do a camp-enrichment thing with Dinah—which made Dinah all shades of happy—but I was only going to do it if we could find the right one. It needed to be fun, but also cool, in a "this matters" kind of way. It also needed to accept late applicants, since we were coming up fast on summer.

Last night, I found the perfect camp. A camp that would let me do something good for the world, like on my list of goals. My task now was to bring Dinah around.

"How about somewhere at the beach?" I asked Dinah casually.

"Like what?" Dinah said. "And how would it count as *leadership*-ish?"

"Hmm," I said. I pretended to consider. "Lifeguards?"

"Like 'em," Dinah said. "Don't want to be one."

Dinah wasn't a strong swimmer, it was true.

"Swimsuit models? Like, at a surf shop?"

She looked at me like, *Are you on drugs?*

I decided it was time to hit her with the real one. "Well . . . hey, I know. How about something volunteer-ish? Like involving the ecosystem, maybe?"

"The ecosystem?" Dinah echoed. "As in *nature*?"

"Not *nature* nature," I said quickly. "I'm talking about the *beach*, not ticks and bears and water moccasins."

Dinah shuddered. Snakes creeped her out, as did spiders and ticks and basically all insects except "pretty" ones, like ladybugs. I, myself, took pride in not being scared of that stuff, because c'mon. A snake was not going to jump out at you from behind a door and say, "Boo!" As long as you left snakes alone, then snakes would leave you alone. Same with spiders and ticks, for the most part.

The only creepy-crawly thing *I* was afraid of were cockroaches. Cockroaches gave me the heebie-jeebies. They *scuttled*, and they squirted green ooze when you smacked them with a shoe, but smacking them with a shoe was no simple feat given their aforementioned horrible scuttling ability.

Worst of all? The cockroaches we had here in Atlanta were different than run-of-the-mill roaches. They were called German cockroaches, and They. Could. FLY. That's right, *fly*—right into your ear or hair or *mouth*, if, say, your mouth was formed into a horrified *O* like that famous painting "The Scream."

These days I saw German cockroaches as just one more thing to resent about our Germanic neighbors. *Trot on off and frolic with authentic German cockroaches,* I told Lars in my mind. *I'll pass, thanks very much.*

"There are no snakes or cockroaches in South Carolina, I'm pretty sure," I said. I wasn't sure at all, but that was a small point.

"Huh?" Dinah said. "I'm sorry . . . South Carolina?"

"The summer beach program I'm talking about. Keep up, lady. Sheesh!"

She scratched her head and came away with a bit of dandelion, which she examined with confusion.

"It's called DeBordieu," I said. I pronounced it just like the website said to: *Debbie-Doo.* "It's near Pawleys Island, where I went with Amanda once. You probably don't remember. We weren't friends yet."

She shuffled her fingers to get rid of the dandelion fluff. "We weren't? Why weren't we?"

"It was the summer after fifth grade, and you and I didn't get to be friends until sixth grade." In my mind, I saw little me and little Amanda getting sandy and tan and slurping Grape Nehis at the end of the pier. Amanda wore her first-ever bikini, I remembered. It was white with splashy purple flowers.

Would thinking about Amanda always give me a pang, like a small-but-permanent sliver in my heart?

"We almost got eaten by jellyfish," I murmured. I caught Dinah's expression and backpedaled. "Not that there are jellyfish at DeBordieu. I'm sure there aren't jellyfish at DeBordieu."

"I'm *so* convinced," Dinah said.

One of the guys on the quad called out to us. He was old-school Westminster-style preppy, wearing a pink Oxford with the sleeves rolled up. But he pulled it off because of his longish boy-band hair.

"You girls want to grab us some more chairs?" he asked, wiping the sweat off his brow.

His buddy, not nearly so cute and wearing loafers without socks, looked at us expectantly.

"No, thanks!" I told them.

Dinah blushed, because she wasn't used to saying no period, and especially not to junior guys. *"Winnie!"*

"What?"

The pink-shirted junior regarded us disdainfully. I waved. He shook his head and got back to work.

"I'm sorry," I said to Dinah, "but we don't have time to be their slave girls right now. Do you know why?"

She regarded me apprehensively.

"Be*cause*, dearest Dinah, I happen to be busy sitting with my dear friend—that would be *you*—making plans to go to the beach. And the best part about this particular program? Are you ready?"

"Hold on. Were there *never* any lifeguards in this summer beach scenario?"

"I don't know. There might be lifeguards. But *we*"—I widened my eyes and nodded, hoping to get her nodding, too—"*we* will be saving endangered sea turtles."

She narrowed her eyes. She didn't nod.

"I *know*, right? Coolest camp *ever*, right?"

"Sea turtles," Dinah said, rolling the words around in her mouth like a suspicious new food.

I smiled, reminding myself to play it calm. I'd scared her off too many times already with brochures from spelunking camp, Indian cooking camp, and even trapeze artist camp, which had as its slogan, "Be a Circus Star—or Just Fly through the Air Like One!"

"No," Dinah had said to that one, refusing to even hear about the amazing tricks we'd learn. *"No camps with spangles."*

"Sea turtles are endangered," I explained. "Did you know that? So we'd be doing stuff to help them, like, *not* be."

She looked disgruntled, but she didn't say *no*. "How?"

"Well, we'd patrol the shores and look for eggs and stuff. And nests. Sea turtle nests."

She looked at me with one eye. She one-eye squinted at me.

"Seriously, Dinah, it sounds *so* cool." My hopefulness came through my voice. "We might even see hatchlings."

"What are hatchlings?"

"Teensy little, cute little sea turtles, that's what. Like . . . kittens! Only scaly!"

"I like kittens," she said slowly.

"I know you do. See?"

She caught her bottom lip between her teeth. "Are turtles actually scaly? When I think about turtles, I don't think of them as *scaly*."

"Ah. Interesting. Let's find out!" I grabbed her hands and pulled, using our combined leverage to raise us both to our feet.

"Where are we going?" she said.

"Media center. I'll show you the site."

"I'd *rather* go to a kitten rescue camp."

"That would be nice, wouldn't it? Alas, no such thing."

"There might be."

"There isn't. Only sea turtles." I towed her along behind me. "But, Dinah, for real. You're going to *love* it."

Sandra's graduation ceremony was beautiful, and I cried. Mom did, too, and Dad, and even baby Maggie. Not in a bad, disruptive baby way, just soft whimpers that meant she'd rather be chilling in her bouncy seat.

Ty was the only one in our family who didn't cry. He secretly played Pocket God on my iPhone, and Mom let him, because there *was* a lot of boring speech-making going on.

When it was time for the diplomas to be handed out, I reached over and turned it off.

"It's time," I whispered when he protested.

"Oh," he said, sitting up straight and tugging at his tie, which he was exceedingly proud of.

Since Sandra's last name was Perry, she was near the end of the procession line. So was Bo, whose last name was Sanders. When the headmaster called Sandra's name, she blew Bo a kiss before starting across the outdoor stage. My chest rose and fell. My smile wobbled.

Lifting her chin, Sandra accepted her diploma. Her blond hair spilled out from beneath her mortarboard, and she was my *sister*, and I had a sudden vision of her navigating a busy city sidewalk on the way to a snazzy job, wearing heels and a tailored suit and maybe even a wedding ring.

Mom handed me a fresh Kleenex, and I leaned forward to blow my nose. I stayed down there for a while, just sniffling a little and gathering myself, until I felt a papery wisp on the bare skin between the bottom of my blouse and the top of my gray skirt. I glanced over my shoulder to see Ty holding his program over the back part of me.

"What are you *doing*?" I whispered.

"I don't want anyone to see your bottom crack," he whispered back.

I frowned at him, like *what the* . . . ? Yes, I had a few pairs of jeans that sometimes crept down too low, especially if I squatted or leaned over. But the waistband of my skirt didn't do that, I was ninety-nine percent sure.

"Ty," I whispered, "no one *can* see my bottom crack."

He patted my leg with the hand not holding the program. "I know. You're welcome."

Afterward, Sandra began a long day of celebration, because at least ten different seniors were hosting garden parties. I saw in my mind the senior girls in their white dresses and the senior guys in their slacks and dress shirts, their ties loosened or stuffed in their pockets. It made me melancholy, because already Sandra was leaving us. Already her line-up of parties was more tempting than hanging with her family, not that I blamed her.

"Can y'all believe that Sandra is a high school graduate?" I asked Dinah and Cinnamon after I, too, ditched my family. We were hanging out at the Peachtree Battle Baskin-Robbins. I'd changed from my skirt and blouse into cut-offs and a Krispy Kreme T-shirt, though I still smelled fancy from Mom's Chanel Number Five.

"I know," Dinah said. "In four years, that'll be us."

"Unless we die," Cinnamon said grouchily.

"*What*?!" I said.

"Well, unless we die, which odds are we won't." She slurped a sip of her root beer float. "I'm just keeping it real, that's all."

I scrutinized her expression. Dinah and I had filled out our sea turtle paperwork and sent in our deposits, and we were leaving for DeBordieu on June tenth. Cinnamon had been grumpy ever since we told her.

"Speaking of keeping it real," she went on, "check out that girl's cleavage." She jerked her chin to indicate a super-skinny girl at the ice-cream counter. Super-skinny, but with super-big boobs.

"Whoa," I said.

"Is that possible in the natural world?" Cinnamon said, not bothering to lower her voice. "She has to have had a boob job, right?"

"Cinnamon . . . *shhh*," I said.

She met my gaze and scowled. *Uh-oh*.

"*You* have nothing to worry about, though, Winnie. Nobody's ever going to accuse you of having had a boob job."

I didn't take the bait, as I had no desire to discuss my lack of cleavage. I also thought she was being a jerk, and that it wasn't cool, even if she *was* bummed about being left by herself in Atlanta.

"Or maybe I'm wrong," she went on anyway. "Maybe you'll have a freak growth spurt in the next four years."

My face grew hot. "Shut up," I said, pushing at my ice cream with my spoon.

"Cinnamon?" Dinah said. "Do you remember that talk

we had, about how you were going to stop making jokes about things that actually hurt people's feelings?"

"No," Cinnamon said, but she was lying. Before she and Bryce broke up, Dinah and I had had to do an intervention with her because she kept making Dinah the butt of unfunny remarks, just to make Bryce laugh.

Now she was making me the butt of her jokes, but no one was laughing.

"Cinnamon," Dinah said.

"Fine," Cinnamon said. She sighed. "I'm sorry, Winnie, and your boobs are perky and adorable." And then, as if she couldn't help herself, "I'm sure the sea turtles will worship them. They'll think they're like . . . lily pads."

"I *knew* that's what this was about," I said. "Just stop being a baby about it and come with us. Jeez."

"Yeah, only I *can't*," she said, "because I have to stay in Atlanta." She glared at me. "And you said you were staying in Atlanta, too. Traitor."

"Just quit your babysitting job," I said. "If you told your boss right now, she'd have plenty of time to find someone else."

"Blah, blah, blah," Cinnamon said.

"Seriously," Dinah said. "It's going to be so fun—we might even get to see hatchlings, which would be a once-in-a-lifetime experience!"

"I'd appreciate it if you would stop bringing up those stupid hatchlings," Cinnamon said.

I did an internal inventory, trying to decide whether I'd

forgiven the cleavage remark. I hadn't, not quite, but enough to feel sorry for her. It was never fun to be left behind.

"We'll take pictures," I said at last.

She rolled her eyes. "Whoop-dee-doodle-doo."

School ended, and summer started, and for the first week of June, it was one big happy party. I hung out at the pool with Cinnamon and Dinah. I played Ping-Pong with Lars and kicked his Ping-Pong-i-licious booty. In the evenings, there was kissing. Lots.

Still, June tenth crept steadily closer, and Cinnamon wasn't the only one who was grumpy about my leaving. Lars was grumpy, too. I thought he was being unfair, since he'd be leaving five days later anyway. (And to Germany, a whole different country! He had to have a passport!)

But I was leaving first, and part of me said *ha ha ha*.

"I don't want you to go," Lars said the evening of June ninth. We were having a picnic of sorts at Memorial Park, although in reality we were just sitting on a quilt eating cheese puffs from a can. "We've hardly had any summer together."

"That's not my fault," I said. "I wouldn't have made plans if you hadn't. I just didn't want to sit around bored while you were gone."

He looked at me with Eeyore eyes, and I felt a surge of irritation. I tried to hide it, and I think I succeeded, but it made me feel like a jerk.

I offered the canister of cheese puffs to Lars. He stuck his hand in to get some, then couldn't get his hand back out, and that also got on my nerves.

I tugged the canister, and it came off his fist with a *pop*. I pried opened his fingers, plucked out the cheese puffs he'd been incapable of releasing, and flung them far away into the grass.

"Why'd you do that?" he asked.

"Because," I said.

"Because why?"

Arrgh, I thought, because sheesh, every day I found more and more things to be annoyed with him about. The most recent annoyance was the cheese puffs. Before that, there was the whole stupid Germany thing. Before that there was his *I dunno, what do you wanna do?* lumpishness, and oh, let's not forget the time he farted and thought it was funny.

And waaaaay back at the dawn of time was the lameness called my birthday. If I were being honest (which, *to be honest*, wasn't all it was cracked up to be), that was when my growliness began: When Lars gave me that stupid Starbucks card instead of the cupcake of love I'd secretly yearned for. Which I still yearned for, if I were *truly* being honest.

But even if I wanted to come clean about why I flung Lars's cheese puffs to the wind, I could just imagine how such a scene would play out:

Lars: Why'd you throw my cheese puffs away?

Me: Because you didn't give me a cupcake.

Lars: Huh?

Me: Because you didn't give me a cupcake.

Lars, scratching his head: Am I missing something here?

Me: Yes, you lout, and it's called A CUPCAKE. For ME! Is that really so hard to understand?!!!

Y-y-yeah, that would go over well. If I couldn't stand (or *under*stand) my own pathetic-ness, how could I expect Lars to?

So instead of attempting an explanation, I put my hand on his chest and pushed, so that he was lying down on the quilt. He looked surprised. Then I stretched out beside him, and his eyes grew murky in that way that made me feel powerful.

I brushed my lips over his, so lightly-lightly like a feather. Part of me thought, *Ack! What are you doing?! You're at a park, for heaven's sake!* But my hair made a curtain around us, and there wasn't anyone around, anyway.

Images flashed in my mind: the swing set, Sandra smiling at Bo, the color blue.

"I'm going to miss you so much," Lars said hoarsely.

Good, I thought. Then a more aching emotion welled up, and I buried my face in his shirt.

"I'm going to miss you, too," I whispered.

But. I wanted to be strong Winnie, not weak Winnie. So as I packed for DeBordieu, I sang a little song. I sang it to the tune of "Lucy in the Sky with Diamonds," and it went like this: "Winnie at the be-each with sea turrr-tles! Winnie at the be-each with sea turrr-tles!"

Dinah's dad was going to drive us to South Carolina tomorrow. It would take six-and-a-half hours, but I was cool with that. I liked road trips. I liked the mandatory junk food stops they required.

"You should take your pretty sundress," Ty said as I tossed cutoffs and tank tops into my duffel bag. He lay on my bed, his chin propped in his palms.

"I don't think so," I told him, though I found it adorable how the words "your pretty sundress" tripped so naturally from his tongue.

"But in *Camp Rock*, Demi Lovato wore a dress," Ty said. *Camp Rock* was a made-for-TV movie about kids who spent all summer jamming and dancing and keeping juicy secrets from each other.

"That's because Demi Lovato is a movie star," I explained.

"I think Demi looks pretty in her pretty dress," Ty said. Then, as if worried he'd made me feel bad, he added, "But, Winnie, you look pretty, too, when you wear dresses. Like that one with the birds on it."

I considered. I *did* like that dress. It was goldish-yellow with blues and browns swirled in. If you looked close, you could make out two blackbirds, their wings outstretched. It had spaghetti straps.

Only, when would I need a fancy-ish sundress at sea turtle camp?

"But you look pretty no matter what," Ty continued. He *heheheh*-ed. "Unless if you wore my groin cup."

"Gross," I said, lobbing a balled-up pair of socks at him. He'd gotten his groin cup last week for karate, and he loved it. In fact he loved it so much that on the day he got it, he pranced through the house wearing it and nothing else. He rapped repeatedly on the "cup" part and said, "See? Doesn't hurt! Even if someone *kicked* me, it wouldn't hurt!"

My iPhone *mwahaha*-ed, Cinnamon's custom ringtone which she chose and programmed in for herself. I reached for my phone.

"Winnie Perry, at your service," I said. I motioned for Ty to leave. He shifted his chin to his other palm and regarded me with interest.

"*Not* at my service, because you're abandoning me," Cinnamon said.

"Grouse, grouse, grouse, that's all you do these days. And I'm not *abandoning* you." I pressed my phone against my shirt. "Ty, *go*."

"*No, thanks,*" he stage-whispered.

"Well, I *was* calling to tell you big news," Cinnamon said. "But I don't think I'm going to after all."

"Oh, come on. What's your big news?"

"Never mind," Cinnamon said prissily.

"Cinnamon has big news?" Ty said.

I rolled my eyes and went into the hall. "Did you win the lottery?"

"Nope."

"D'you meet an incredibly gorgeous boy at the tanning salon, and you're going to marry him even though he wears a Speedo?"

"Ha ha," Cinnamon said. "And *no*, because I'm the deadly Black Widow, remember?"

"The Black Widow got married. The Black Widow got married *lots*."

"Oh, yeah," Cinnamon mused. "She did, didn't she?"

"I still don't know what your big news is," I said.

"Does that mean you give up?" Cinnamon said. Cinnamon loved making people give up.

"Yes, Cinnamon, I give up. Though I think it indicates a serious mental imbalance that you get such pleasure out of it."

"Uh-oh," she warned. "Better be nice to me, or I'll change my mind."

Since Ty wasn't leaving, I wandered into baby Maggie's room and dropped into the green recliner Mom used when she nursed little Mags. It was like a rocking chair, only instead of wooden rockers, it glided noiselessly on metal links.

"Are you going to tell me or not?"

"*Yes*, I'm going to tell you." She giggled. "Or not."

"Is it good news or bad news?"

"Hmm. I think I'll go with excellent. It's *excellent* news."

"Awesome, let's hear it," I said. I waited, and then I waited some more. "It's actually your turn to talk now, Cin."

"Well," she said, "the news has to do with me."

"Ah."

"And summer."

"Omigosh, tell me, tell me!" I said, sitting upright and making the base of the glider thunk.

"Well . . . I'm still thinking about that, actually. Whether I will or won't."

"What?!"

Ty appeared in baby Maggie's doorway. He was holding my sundress with the blackbirds on it. "I'll put it in your bag," he mouthed.

"Ty, leave," I said. " I mean it. And Cinnamon, you can-*not* call and say, 'I've got big news,' and then not tell me!"

"Is Ty there? Let me talk to him," Cinnamon said.

"Cinnamon!"

Ty got close to the phone. He put his mouth right up near mine and said, "Hi, Cinnamon! I'm helping Winnie pack! Don't you think that's so nice of me?"

I twisted away and made an aggravated sound. "Ignore him. And *no*, you can't talk to him. You can only talk to me."

"She wants to talk to me?" Ty said, trying to get in front of me. "YES YOU CAN TALK TO ME!" he yelled to her. "TELL WINNIE TO GIVE ME HER PHONE!"

"Sounds like you're busy," Cinnamon said sympathetically. "I'll let you go."

"Tell me your news! Tell me your news *right now*, or I'll be forced to . . . do something!"

She laughed. "Bye, babe. Have fun with the sea turtles."

The line went dead.

Later that evening, after hardly eating any dinner because I was too busy watching my family be silly with each other, I got a bad case of second thoughts about my imminent departure. Jaunting off to the Carolina coast meant leaving baby Mags, who'd just started to laugh. Who knew what I'd miss during an entire month of not being with her? And then there was Ty. Who would Ty turn to if he stole another penguin?

On top of all that, Sandra would be leaving for college in September. She was moving to Vermont of all places, which was far away and, according to rumor, got honest-to-goodness snow in the winter. Was I being a bad sister by not sticking around for her last summer?

I hunted her down. "Hey, Sandra," I said. "Am I being a bad sister by not staying in town for your last summer?"

"Exsqueeze me?" she said.

"It's your *last summer.*" I sat crisscross-applesauce on the end of her bed. "Won't you miss me?"

She put down her book. She had on one of Bo's baseball jerseys, which she wore to sleep in, and which she now tugged lower over her thighs. "Maybe," she said, "but so what? You'll be at the *beach.* You shouldn't be worrying about me."

"Well, do you wish you were going somewhere? I feel bad."

"Don't, and I *am* going somewhere. And when I do, I'll be gone a helluva lot longer than you."

"Gee, that's comforting."

"Winnie, get real. You can't let your life revolve around me any more than I can let my life revolve around you—not that I would."

My face grew hot. She saw it, I guess, because she nudged me with her big toe.

"What's going on?" she said. "Don't you *want* to go to Dapper Dan's School for Sea Turtles?"

"DeBordieu," I said, pronouncing it the southern *Debbie-doo* way. "And of course I do."

"Then, great. Just be happy about it."

I sighed. A moment or two passed, and then I voiced the question I really wanted to ask, though I hadn't known it till now.

"Sandra . . . am I obnoxious?"

"Yes," she answered promptly.

"No, really. Do you think I'm . . . well, I guess I'm just wondering . . ."

"Say it slowly," Sandra coached. "One word at a time."

"Sometimes . . . well, *recently* . . ."

She rolled her hand, *go on*.

I blew up on my bangs. "Sometimes I feel . . . not nice inside. Except I *am* nice. Deep down, I am. But sometimes I get . . . growly in my head, and I think snarky thoughts, and I don't like it."

There. I said it. "And I wondered if it shows, that's all."

Sandra looked at me with an *awwww* expression. She swung her legs underneath her, scooched toward me on her knees, and embraced me. "Winners, you poor thing."

Her hug was sloppy and toppled us over.

"Quit," I said, giggling.

"You're *fourteen*," she said. "It's your birthright to be snarky. Own it. Live it. Re*joice* in it."

"Rejoice in being snarky?"

"Abso*lute*ly. Just don't let it poison you."

We lay on our sides on her bed. She had yet to unclasp me, and we were so close that our foreheads touched.

"You look like a Cyclops," I informed her.

"And this, above all," she pontificated. "Stay true, little sister. Even in the snarkiest of times, stay true."

"Now you sound like a graduation speech."

"Oh, and as an aside? You'll find this hard to believe, but I was *occasionally* obnoxious myself when I was fourteen."

"No. *Way.*"

"*Way*," she replied. She breathed a warm, intentional huff of broccoli breath on me from the casserole Mom made for dinner, then grinned when I gagged. "And just look at me now."

Make a Prediction

This must be it," Mr. Devine said, taking a right off the two-lane highway.

"*Eeee!*" Dinah said, bouncing in the front seat. She whipped around. "I'm so excited!"

I perched on my butt and took in the view. Unlike what we'd been seeing for the last several hours—flat, flat, and more flat, all of it shimmering with heat mirages—the private drive we'd turned onto took us into a whole new land. A canopy of foliage arched over us, dappling the sunlight. The silver-barked trees were gnarled and ancient, and moss hung from the branches. The moss was magical looking, like something from a fairy tale. Like troll's hair.

We pulled up to a weathered gatehouse, and Mr. Devine told the aging security guard that we were here for the sea turtle project.

"Ah-right then," the guard said. "What y'all want is the MacKinnon-Karrer house." His South Carolina accent was thicker than grits. His stretched-out vowels *were* grits, taking up so much space in his mouth that there wasn't room for anything else.

He shuffled to his desk and grabbed a map, which he

spread on the ledge of the gatehouse window. "Yer a-gun keep on this here road fer 'bout two miles. You'll pass the clubhouse on yer right. Best she-crab soup you'll evah taste, if you git the chance."

Dinah and I shared a look of delight—not because of the she-crab soup, but because this old man was such a character. I kind of wanted to marry him, only not really. Not at all, actually. But I loved listening to him talk.

"Then you'll cross on over the marsh," he continued. "Be sure to keep an eye out for Old Gran'Pappy Blue Heron. He likes to greet the visitors, so he sits way up high on one of them posts by the bridge."

"Sweet," I said.

The old man jabbed at the map. "After that, you'll take a sharp left, and not too much later, a sharp right. More like an S curve."

Mr. Devine rubbed the spot between his eyebrows.

"Yer not too far now," the man said. "Jess look for the sign that says MacKinnon-Karrer, and if you don't see that, look for a big ol' house with a stained-glass window in the shape of a nautilus."

"What's a nautilus?" I asked.

Dinah spoke up. "I know. It's one of those gym machines they have the infomercials for. I think it's called the Bow-Flex?"

The guard looked at Dinah funny. "Naw, it's a shell. Kinda like a snail shell."

"Oh," Dinah said.

"The Bow-Flex," I said under my breath, flicking her head and making her giggle.

"Well, all righty then," Mr. Devine said. "Reckon we should get going."

"All righty then" and "reckon" weren't words Dinah's dad normally used, and Dinah giggled harder. I giggled, too.

"Reckon so," the old man said as Mr. Devine flushed and lifted his hand to his collar. It was as if he was adjusting a nonexistent tie.

The final leg of our journey was jam-packed with yummy, beach-y things, starting with Old Gran'Pappy Blue Heron, who was indeed perched on a wooden post by the marsh. He had long, spindly legs and a long, curved neck, and as we drove past him, Dinah rolled down her window and called, "Hi!"

Old Gran'Pappy swiveled his head and eyed her with his beady black eyes, as shiny and flat as pebbles. Then he spread his wings—which were enormous—and flapped away.

The marsh itself was interesting, too. Pale green reeds stuck up from the swampy water, and snow-white egrets dipped and darted among them. I didn't know they were egrets until Dinah told me. She'd read up on the Carolina wetlands to prepare for our trip.

One somewhat freaky thing we saw was a wooden sign standing at a tilt at the edge of the marsh. PLEASE DO NOT FEED OR MOLEST THE ALLIGATORS, it said.

"Alligators?" Dinah squeaked.

"Molest?" I squealed. "What does that even mean? And why would anybody want to?"

Dinah blinked at the murky water. "There aren't really alligators, are there, Dad?"

"It's a marsh, so probably," he said. "Did you not come across alligators in your research?"

Dinah gulped, and I suppressed a smile. Knowing Dinah, she probably read up on all the cute South Carolina creatures—egrets, baby turtles, hoppy toads—and selectively blanked out any and all mentions of grinning reptiles with sharp teeth.

"If Cinnamon were here, she'd steal that sign," I said. "She'd take it home with her and put it in her bedroom."

"No, she would not," Dinah said, doing a meaningful head-jerk to remind me that her dad was in the car with us.

"Oh, please," I said, because what was Mr. Devine going to do, bust Cinnamon for a crime she couldn't commit even if she wanted to? And then I thought, *Ooo, it's the "stealing" part Dinah wants me to shut up about, because of Mary Woods and the makeup.*

I changed the subject. "What is up with Cinnamon, anyway?" I said. "Is she ever going to tell us her 'big news'?"

Dinah lifted her shoulders. We'd bombarded Cinnamon with phone calls and texts from the road, but every call went straight to voice mail, and the one text she'd sent back was purposely evasive. *Dear fellow countrymen: I am unable to text right now, as I am . . . well, I can't exactly say. Or rather,*

I *could*, but I choose not to. Pip pip, cheerio, and all that rot!

"I'm trying her again," I announced, pulling out my iPhone. The call went straight to voice mail. *Aargh!*

I punched END CALL. Then, needing to somehow punish her, I went to the SETTINGS function. I would change her incoming ringtone, oh yes I would. I would take away her beloved evil laugh and replace it with . . . *hrmm.*

What to do, what to do?

I scrolled through my options. Perhaps the cheerful chorus of "Walking on Sunshine"?

Heck, no.

Well, what about the melodic "Dolphin Splash"?

And no again. Sorry, Cinnamon. You may not pass go, and you may not swim with the dolphins.

"Jungle Monkey"? Maybe. It was the sound of a chimpanzee screaming its head off, if I remembered correctly. Still, it wasn't obnoxious *enough.*

A ringtone called "Cleanup Johnny" caught my attention. "Cleanup Johnny"? What was this "Cleanup Johnny"? I gave it a tap to make it play, and a rough voice snarled, *"All right, boys, clean up Johnny and send him home."*

It made me jump, and I'd known it was coming. Apparently it startled Mr. Devine even more, as he swerved violently to the right.

"What the . . . ?!" he exclaimed, glancing over his shoulder.

"Sorry!" I punched at my phone to make it shut up. "Sorry, sorry, sorry!"

"Omigosh," Dinah said, giggling. "If an alligator attacks us? Play *that*."

"Ha ha." The ringtone looped back to the beginning. *"All right, boys, clean up Johnny and—"*

Dinah raised her voice. "And then bean him with it. The alligator, with your phone."

"Never," I said indignantly. I finally managed to shut up Mr. Crime Lord, but there was no OFF button for Dinah's giggles.

A drop of sweat trickled down Mr. Devine's face. "All right, girls, time to start looking for the MacKinnon-Karrer house," he said in a strained tone.

"But I haven't seen the ocean yet," Dinah said. "Where's the ocean?"

"I can smell it," I said, inhaling the wonderful scent of salt, sun, and seaweed. "It's got to be out there somewhere."

"There's a sign," Mr. Devine said. He eased up on the gas. "Dinah, can you make out what it says?"

"LOGGERHEAD TURTLE NESTING AREA," Dinah read. "EGGS, HATCHLINGS, ADULTS, AND CARCASSES—" She broke off. "Carcasses?!"

"—ARE PROTECTED BY FEDERAL AND STATE LAWS," I finished. "Loggerhead *turtles*, Dinah! *Loggerhead turtles*!"

I squealed, which made Dinah squeal, which startled Mr. Devine anew. He stomped on the brake, and the car stopped, lurched forward, and then rocked back. Gripping the steering wheel, Mr. Devine pressed his upper body against his seat.

"Sorry, Daddy," Dinah said. "But it's so exciting, don't you think?"

"I think I need a cold drink," he muttered.

Dinah's voice shot back up to screeching-chipmunk level. *"Ooo! Ooo! That's it I know it I know it! Look there's the sign!"*

I hyper-bounced along with her and added my chipmunk screech to the din. It was so fun to ride this wave of manic energy, so fun to be fourteen and at the beach, coming up on a sprawling, weathered house that was all angles and slopes and peeling wood. A deck wrapped around the front, its railing draped with swimsuits and towels. At the tip-top of the house was a small, square room with windows on every side, like the observation room of a lighthouse.

"Turn, Daddy!" Dinah ordered. "Turn!"

Mr. Devine hauled the steering wheel to the right, and gravel popped against the belly of the car. He pulled into the driveway and cut the engine . . . and suddenly it seemed *really* quiet.

"Eeek," Dinah whispered. She twisted around with big eyes. "Winnie . . . we're here!"

I gazed at the house and swallowed, because we were. We really were.

"What do you think we're supposed to do?" I asked. "Do we just . . . go up and knock?"

"I don't think we have to," Dinah said. She nodded at the ramp of the deck, where strolling toward us was a woman about my mom's age, her blond hair streaked with gray. She wore a loose blue dress and no shoes. Also, no makeup.

"Girls, hi!" she said, approaching the station wagon. "Dinah and Winnie?"

"Yes, ma'am," Dinah said.

"Hi," I said. In another situation, I might have felt intimidated—capable-seeming women who didn't wear makeup sometimes intimidated me—but her smile was so sunny that intimidation wasn't possible. Plus, I loved her earrings. They were beautiful silver spirals interspersed with tiny shells.

"I'm so glad you're here," she said. "Come on, let's get you inside. My name's Virginia, by the way."

She and Mr. Devine did the grown-up nice-to-meet-you thing as we climbed out of the car. My tank top stuck to the small of my back, and I pulled the fabric away and fanned myself with it. Dinah had it even worse. She was wearing thin cotton shorts, and they were wrinkled and slightly damp.

I grabbed my duffel bag from the back of the car, along with a baseball cap of Bo's I'd accidentally-on-purpose borrowed from Sandra's dresser. I slapped it on and tugged down the bill.

Virginia led us up the walkway and across the deck.

"No sand inside the house," she said when we reached the front door. She gestured at a mat. "Wipe your feet here. If your shoes are sandy, leave them under the bench."

"Okay," I said, kicking off my flip-flops.

She pushed through a screen door, and we followed her into a large main room with built-in bookshelves. An L-shaped sofa made a comfy looking sitting area, and sprawled on the sofa was a comfy looking boy. A *very* comfy looking boy, who was reading a paperback and not wearing a shirt. I didn't glance at Dinah, and she didn't glance at me. But a message vibrated between us nonetheless. *Hmmm,* was the gist of it. *In-n-nteresting.*

"Girls, meet Alphonse," Virginia said. "Alphonse, meet Winnie and Dinah, the last of our group."

Alphonse put down his book and got to his feet. He was a black guy, medium dark skin, with dreads that grazed his bare shoulders. Caribbean, maybe? Jamaican? He was our age(ish) and extremely cute—as in, he-should-star-in-a-movie cute. As in, Dinah-was-no-longer-breathing cute.

He wasn't as cute as Lars, of course, but that still left plenty of cuteness to be gobbled up and enjoyed. Not that I planned on doing any gobbling!

But. Yes.

Cute.

"Hey," he said, holding out his hand. I gave it a firm shake and said "hey" back. Dinah, whose cheeks had grown pink, did a little wave with her elbow tight by her side.

"Alphonse is from Louisiana," Virginia said. "He came last week. Tomorrow, he'll show you how to patrol the beach for crawls."

"What's a crawl?" I asked. I put down my duffel bag, and Dinah copied me by plunking down her suitcase. She'd started to breathe again, which I knew only because her chest was rising and falling far too rapidly.

"Sea turtle tracks," Alphonse said. He had an easy way of holding himself. He also had a completely smooth and hairless chest. "They look like small tractor trails."

"Huh?" I said, jerking my gaze back to his face. *Omigosh*, had I been staring? Great, now I was blushing just like Dinah. I could feel it. She and I were the staring twins—I mean the *blushing* twins. Oh god. Both.

"The turtles come on shore to nest," Virginia explained. "They push themselves up with their flippers, and their tracks look like tractor trails. One of the things you'll do is keep a record of where you spot those tracks, which means getting out to the beach in time to beat the early morning walkers."

"What are the early morning walkers?" I asked.

Alphonse shared a look with Virginia, who smiled. To me, Alphonse said, "People who take walks early in the morning."

I blushed harder. "*Oh*. I thought maybe they were . . . um. . . ."

Ah, fudge. I giggled. I couldn't help it. And actually, it made things better, because it helped my chest loosen up.

"People like to get out early if they're searching for starfish," Alphonse said. "Some just want to enjoy the sunrise."

Dinah found her voice. "Um, does that mean we'll be getting up *before* sunrise?"

Alphonse furrowed his brow.

"Dinah isn't a morning person," I said. "She has been known, I am sorry to report, to fall asleep while eating her strawberry Pop-Tart—*after* her dad has already steered her out of bed and into the kitchen."

"So untrue!" Dinah protested. "Dad, *tell* them."

"Sometimes in her waffles," Mr. Devine said. "Makes an awful mess."

"Dad!"

"Nice one, Mr. D," I said. I held up my hand, and he slapped it, looking pleased.

"There are plenty of jobs to go around," Virginia said. "We'll find a good fit for everyone. For now, let me show you the house."

"Virginia, before you go," Alphonse said. "More plastic netting?"

"Right," Virginia said. "I'll call in the order after I get the girls settled. And when Erica gets back, find out how Myrtle's doing."

"Will do," Alphonse said, saluting.

"Myrtle has a skull fracture," Virginia told us.

"Oh no," I said, wondering who Myrtle was.

"We think she was hit by a boat propeller. Her jaw took a blow, too. She might pull through, might not."

I cringed, thinking that Virginia seemed awfully casual about Myrtle's chances of recovery.

"She's got size on her side, that's one good thing," Virginia went on. "Old girl's as big as a kitchen table."

I opened my mouth, then shut it, realizing in the nick of time that this was another early morning walker moment.

"Is Myrtle . . . a turtle?" Dinah asked.

"What else would she be?" Virginia said, surprised. "She washed up two weeks ago on Myrtle Beach. She's still carrying a full clutch of eggs, so we're crossing our fingers she survives."

Myrtle from Myrtle Beach, I thought. *Got it.*

"I've heard of Myrtle Beach," I contributed. "That's where college kids go for spring break, right?"

"Mmm," Virginia said disapprovingly. "The beach is for everyone, but the creatures that inhabit the ocean were here first. All those hotels? All those bright lights? Why do you *think* the turtles no longer nest on its shores?"

I was fairly sure she wasn't really asking, but I tried nonetheless to muddle it out. The hotel part was easy: If there were hotels everywhere, that meant less space for the turtles. But I didn't know what bright lights had to do with anything.

"*Well*," Virginia said, as if ridding herself of a bad taste. "Enough of that. Let's give you the tour."

She led us across the living room to a stairwell. "This is the blue staircase," she said. She paused. "Because it's blue."

Sure enough, the wooden stairs were painted bright blue, with gaps of air between each one. One flight led up from the main level, another led down.

"Below are the crew's quarters," Virginia said, gesturing.

I peered through the slatted steps and saw a room with a partly open door. "Alphonse sleeps down there, along with Milo and James. Nice guys. Milo can be pretty quiet, but nothing wrong with that."

I nudged Dinah, who could also be "pretty quiet." She gave me a *shush* look. But so many guys—it was exciting! Not for *me*, but for Dinah, who had yet to have her first kiss.

Dinah is going to kiss a boy at the beach, I decided right then and there. Or maybe it was a premonition? Either way, this was my prediction, which meant I could cross yet another item off my To-Do list. *Dinah's first kiss will happen with the sound of the waves in her ears and a salty breeze lifting her hair.*

Hopefully I'd get to cross off the ". . . and have it come true" part before our time at the beach ended, too. *Eeee!*

Virginia climbed the flight of stairs and extended her hand toward a room on her left. "Master bedroom. Where I sleep. Also, the supply closet, if you need more toilet paper or lightbulbs or sunscreen."

"And girls, *always* wear sunscreen," Mr. Devine interjected.

"Yes, Dad," Dinah said, sounding pained.

Virginia went up another flight of stairs and reached a landing, where she took a right. The staircase itself went higher, leading to an attic room with a closed door. Right as I was looking at it, it creaked open, and a sliver of face appeared. Someone's eye locked with mine. The eye widened, and the door slammed shut.

Oka-a-a-ay, I thought. *Creepy recluse in the attic. That's . . . atmospheric.*

I grabbed Dinah's forearm and whispered, "Dinah, there's someone up there. In the attic."

She shook me off. Virginia had opened the door to a different room, and Dinah stepped closer to hear.

". . . the red room," Virginia was saying. Past her shoulder, I saw two twin beds, each with a red bedspread.

Blood red, a voice inside me said. To which I replied silently and fiercely, *Shut up, you've read too much Stephen King.*

But somebody *had* peered out at me. I knew what I saw.

"Brooklyn and Erika share this room," Virginia told us. "You'll meet them at dinner." She pulled the door shut, saying, "Oh, and do please keep the windows and doors closed during the heat of the day. This old house doesn't have air-conditioning."

No AC? In the summer? In South Carolina?!

Virginia looked at me, and I quickly fixed my expression, which I hadn't intended to make.

"It's part of its charm," she said.

Past the red room was a bathroom, with a rolled-up tube of Colgate on the counter. After that, the hall opened into a den. The walls were lined with shelves, which held paperbacks, board games, and old VHS videotapes. Against the far wall sat a TV with rabbit ears antennae.

"There's no reception," Virginia said, following my gaze, "but the VCR works. Sometimes we have movie nights. Do you like movies, Winnie?"

I was about to answer when Dinah squealed.

"The ocean!" she exclaimed. "There it is! Winnie, look!"

I turned to see her scrambling onto a long, cushioned window seat. She tucked her knees beneath her and her pressed her forehead to the glass, sighing rapturously. Outside, beyond a line of trees and another row of houses, stretched a shimmering expanse of blue.

The ocean.

I *loved* the ocean, and even the lack of AC and the possible presence of a crazy attic-dweller couldn't take that away.

I joined Dinah on the window seat. Our shoulders touched, which was our bodies' way of saying *yes* and *hi* and *isn't it wonderful?* Sunlight danced on the water. My soul expanded and pressed outward against my ribs.

Even if the crazy attic-dweller does *hack me to death with scissors in the night, I don't care,* I thought. *At least I'll die happy.*

Well, except for the small fact that I'd be being attacked with scissors, which would put a damper on things.

"Let me show you the rest of the house," Virginia said, "and then you two can get out there."

Her voice pulled me back, and I slid off the window seat. I felt slightly embarrassed . . . then decided that was dumb. How could anyone be faulted for loving the ocean?

Im-poe-see-bluh, my French teacher would say in her Frenchy accent.

Virginia led us through the den and gave us a peek at

the blue room, which was identical to the red room, except that the bedspreads on the twin beds were blue.

"Ryan and Mark," Virginia said. She closed the door. To Mr. Devine, she said, "Five boys, five girls. The house can sleep more—the sofa in the den is a pullout, and three people can sleep on the living room sofa if they're willing to scrunch—but ten's a good number."

"Are you the only chaperone?" Mr. Devine asked as she led us to a second stairwell. This stairwell was green, so I wasn't surprised when Virginia told us it was called the green staircase.

"Yes, it's just me," she told Dinah's dad. "I don't think of myself as a chaperone, though. I'm simply the project leader."

Mr. Devine frowned.

"I have some ranger friends from Huntington Beach State Park who stop by every so often. And Jason—he's a naturalist, works for the state—he likes to help mark the turtle nests." The green staircase, like the blue staircase, led both up and down. Virginia took the up route and kept talking. "There's plenty of adult supervision, don't worry."

"Um, yes," Mr. Devine said as he gripped the railing and started carefully after her. "Very good."

Dinah turned to me and rolled her eyes. *Because I'm sooo in need of adult supervision,* her expression said.

But I was thinking about something else. *Five boys, five girls,* Virginia had said. The five boys were Alphonse,

James, Milo, Ryan, and Mark. The girls were me, Dinah, Erika, and Brooklyn—but together, we made four, not five. Who was the fifth?

"Um, Virginia?" I said. This stretch of stairs was supersteep, and Virginia's body disappeared as she went up, swallowed by a small rectangular door in the ceiling.

"Yes?" she called.

"Who's the fifth girl?" *It's not the creepy attic-dweller, is it?*

"She's in the rainbow room getting settled," Virginia said, which didn't answer my question. "You and Dinah will be rooming with her. It's close quarters, but the view is terrific from up there."

I stopped still. *The view is terrific from "up there"?* The only bedroom that could be described as "up there" was the attic room, which meant that . . . *holy crudballs.* Creepy Attic Girl was our roommate!

"The view is terrific from *here*," Dinah said from above. "Omigosh. Winnie, come *see*!"

I climbed the last couple of stairs, emerging in a room made entirely of windows.

"Wow," I breathed. Out of the front window was the ocean, blue and sparkling and forever. To the right was more ocean, plus some houses, and then a stretch of undeveloped shore. To the left was pretty much all houses, and out the back window was the marsh. The sun was beginning to go down, making the reeds glow reddish-gold.

"We call this room the Crow's Nest," Virginia said. "It's the highest point in DeBordieu. In the evenings, if a storm's coming in, we come up here to watch the lightning. If the wind's strong, we sometimes feel the house sway."

Aye-yai-yai, I thought, sharing a glance with Dinah.

"And sometimes we spot—oh, look! *There!*" She pointed toward the ocean. "Those humps coming out of the water . . . do you see? It's a school of porpoises, swimming along the shoreline."

I scanned for humps. *Humps, humps, humps, where are you?*

"Well, I'll be," Mr. Devine said.

"Omigosh, look how *cute* they are!" Dinah cooed.

My ribs constricted. Where were the porpoises? What if they disappeared before I got to see them?

Virginia stepped behind me, placing her hands lightly on my shoulders and rotating me an inch to the left. "About halfway between the horizon and the shore. Look for the curve of their backs."

But I didn't see them. Everybody else saw the porpoises, but all I saw was—

"Ohhhh," I said. *There* they were. A dozen gleaming bodies, maybe more, smooth and muscular as they made their rhythmic crescent dives. They were glorious.

We watched until every last porpoise was out of sight. Then Virginia breathed out big and clasped her hands. Smiling, she said, "Shall we go see your room?"

We descended single-file from the Crow's Nest and backtracked to the blue staircase. I doubted I could have done it on my own, not without getting lost. My thoughts wandered to Cinnamon, who would have adored this maze of a house with all of its nooks and crannies. She would have even dug the gothic possibility of Creepy Attic-Dweller—and if she were here, maybe I'd have felt better equipped to deal with Creepy Attic-Dweller myself.

I wanted to check my cell, to see if Cinnamon had called or texted.

"I'm confused," Dinah whispered, falling behind with me. "Where *is* our room?"

I shrugged. It had to be the attic room I'd glimpsed when we first came to the second level, but I was still clinging to the hope that it wasn't.

"Okey-doke," Virginia said. She extended her arm like a tour guide, and my heart sank. "I've put you girls on the third floor. How does that sound?"

"Just great," I said weakly.

She climbed the stairs. I hesitated, and Dinah nudged my spine to make me proceed.

"Like I said, your roomie's already here," Virginia said.

"Is she nice?" Dinah asked. "What's her name?"

"Does she play well with others?" I said.

Virginia rapped on the door. "People to see you—your new roommates!" To Dinah and me, she said, "I'd say she's nice. Sure. A little strange, but we like strange, right?"

"Depends," I said. "Hacking-with-scissors strange?"

Virginia laughed.

"Winnie, *shush*," Dinah said. "She could hear you!"

"What'd you say her name was?" I asked Virginia.

"Hmm?" Virginia said.

"Her *name*." Why was she avoiding the question? Was it something unspeakable, like Trixie "The Nose" Gaglioni? Bloody Amy? Elvira?!

When our nameless roomie failed to open the door, Virginia twisted the knob and said, "We'll just go on in."

Dinah waited for me to file in behind Virginia, and when I didn't, she made an impatient sound and pushed past me. After a few moments, when no ghastly screams pierced the air, I followed. I skittishly took in three twin beds: all of them made up with rainbow comforters; none of them occupied. The walls were made of wood, and the ceiling was sloped, with two skylights filling the room with buttery light. Best of all? Nowhere in the room did I spot a demented, scissors-wielding sociopath. Not a single one.

Well. I felt silly.

Dinah stood on her tiptoes by the nearest skylight. "We can see the ocean," she said. "Come see!"

"In the nighttime, you can see the stars," Virginia said. "And once the sun goes down, you can crank the skylights open. This room gets pretty hot, but you'll catch a nice breeze in the evenings."

"We can fall asleep to the sound of the waves," Dinah

exclaimed. She let go of the windowsill and gave a series of light claps. "This is my favorite room in the whole house!"

It *was* a pretty awesome room. I admitted it. *But there had been a girl up here* . . . so where was she now? Like I said, none of the three beds had been claimed. I saw no duffel bags or suitcases.

"Where's our roommate?" I asked Virginia.

"What's that?" she said.

I walked apprehensively to the closest of the three beds, ducking as the roof sloped down. The way the room was designed, a person my height—even a grown-up, as long as he or she wasn't six feet tall—could stand up straight in the center of the room. But over by the walls it was Hunchback City. I'd have to remember that when I rolled out of bed in the morning. Otherwise I'd be looking at a nasty bump on the head.

I hesitated, then sat on the edge of the bed. I bounced a little, because it was virtually impossible to sit on a bed for the first time and *not* bounce.

"You want that one?" Dinah said.

"I suppose," I said.

"Try lying down," Virginia suggested. "I wonder if you can see the sky from there."

I swung my feet onto the bed and lay down. At first I held myself stiff, like a corpse, but gradually I let myself relax. I *could* see the sky, which seemed both tangible and intangible at the same time.

"Nice," I said.

Dinah came over and told me to scooch, which I did. The mattress bucked as she climbed on.

"Ahhh," Dinah said. She bent her elbows and slipped her hands beneath her head. "I could get used to this."

"Me too," I said.

"Me too," said the person under the bed.

I bolted upright, and *wham*, banged my head on the ceiling.

"Ow!" I cried.

Dinah's reaction was more of a full-body convulsion, which toppled her off the bed and onto the floor.

"Ow!" she cried, clutching her bum. "Ow ow *ow!*"

I leaned over to check on her, registering as I did that Virginia was holding her hand to her mouth and laughing. *Laughing!*

"Omigod, that was *awesome*," the girl under the bed crowed. She began to worm her way out, denim-clad fanny first, and I stiffened, because *I recognized those jean shorts.* I recognized that *fanny*, and I leaned over the bed and pummeled it, one fist per cheek.

"Cinnamon, you are *so* dead!" I cried.

"Hey!" she said, still half underneath the bed. *"Ow!"*

"Dinah, get her," I commanded. Dinah came out of her stupor and lunged for Cinnamon's ankle. I scrambled off the bed and grabbed the other.

"One, two, three—heave!" I said.

The yowls coming from Cinnamon made it sound as if we were torturing her, but she was laughing, too. "Mercy! I beg for mercy!"

"Not a chance," I said. "Ready, Dinah? One, two, three—*heave*!"

We pulled her out as far as her shoulders. She scrabbled at the carpet, trying to retreat, and I straddled her and dug my knuckles into her armpits.

"Stop for real!" Laughing hysterically, she contracted into a fetal position, which effectively drew her head out from under the bed, ha ha ha.

"You can run, but you can't hide," I said. I kept tickling her, and I bounced up and down on her for good measure. Just like I'd bounced on the mattress, but harder.

"Can't . . . breathe . . ." she panted.

"Pity," I said.

"Was *this* your big news?" Dinah asked. She walked forward on her knees, and together, we rolled Cinnamon over.

"Yes." Cinnamon said in a teensy voice. She was sweaty and strands of hair were plastered on her forehead, and she couldn't wipe the grin from her face.

"You're really here?" Dinah pressed. "For the whole month?"

She nodded.

"Cinnamon! That's *wonderful*!" Dinah hugged her, and I sat back on my haunches.

Eventually, Dinah let Cinnamon up.

"Hi, roomie," I said in a smooth and cheerful voice.

Cinnamon gazed at me warily. "What about you, Winnie? Are *you* glad I'm here?"

"Abso*lute*ly," I said.

"Yeah?"

I tilted my head. "Cinnamon, of course. We are going to have *so. Much. Fun.*"

At first, I didn't think she was going to buy it. I smiled winningly, because we *were* going to have fun. I wasn't lying about that. I was going to get her back for this, absolutely, but even that would be fun.

"Want to help them bring their bags up?" Virginia asked Cinnamon, and the twinkle in Virginia's eyes told me she'd been in on this from the beginning. Cinnamon must have told her about us: how we were all three best friends, and how we didn't know she was going to be here since she deliberately kept us in the dark.

They were both dirty rotten scoundrels, Cinnamon the dirtier and rottener of the two. But again: Why get mad when I could get even?

"I suppose I could give them a hand," Cinnamon said. She groaned as she got to her feet.

Mr. Devine tugged at his collar. Of all of us, he seemed to be having the hardest time processing everything.

"Cinnamon?" he said. "Do you . . . uh . . ."

The three of us regarded him.

His pudgy hand moved from his collar to the back of

his neck, which he massaged. At last, he said, "Do you have anything to say for yourself?"

"*Yes*," Cinnamon said, as if she'd been waiting all day for that very question. She rubbed her fanny. "My boom-boom hurts."

Take Charge with Lars!

WHEN I WAS A LITTLE KID—like, in second grade—I was a total social butterfly. I didn't know that term, and I didn't set out to be one . . . I just *was*. I loved people, especially kids my own age, and I had no problem marching up to someone on the playground and saying, "Hey! Wanna play Candy Store, and we can make up candies and give them names? Like the yummy-coco-puffball, that's my first invention. What's yours?"

I'd be in my ratty shorts and T-shirt, usually, and usually the girl I'd approached would have her hair done all cute and be wearing an actual *outfit*. But back then, those differences didn't matter. Back then, those differences didn't even register. I *now* know that I was rattier than the typical second grader, but only from looking at old school pictures.

Anyway, back then I just smiled and propped my hands on my hips and waited for whoever it was to grasp the glory of the yummy-coco-puffball. And whoever it was usually did, and off we'd go, arm-in-arm, and it was just so easy. And if she didn't, I'd find someone with better taste. No biggie.

I'd long since lost my blind self-confidence, but I still considered myself reasonably adept when it came to social situations. I knew how to smile. I knew the fake-it-till-you-make-it strategy, as well as the trick of holding my body as if I were Miz Total Chill Girl, even if inside, I was a big knot of nervousness.

I planned to use all of those skills and more when I met the rest of the kids who'd be working on the sea turtle project. I wanted to get off on the right foot, and plus I was determined to have a GREAT SUMMER even if Lars was off in stupid Germany.

Over a dinner of fish tacos—sounded really gross, tasted *really* good—I worked my mad charms on the other campers. We ate at a big round table in the kitchen, while out the window we watched the sun set over the marsh. Dinah's dad was gone. We were in a new place with new people and new food. Everybody looked happy and tan, although that was possibly due to the gorgeous russet light flooding through the windowpanes. Even Dinah looked tan, and Dinah didn't *get* tan.

As I smiled and chatted, I took mental notes on the rest of the DeBordieu gang:

Alphonse I'd met already. He was still as cute as ever, the only difference being that now he was wearing a shirt. *Hello, shirt!* I thought. It said ANALOG REASON across the front, and it was so worn out as to be practically falling apart.

Alphonse's roommates were James and Milo. James seemed like a skater-dude kind of guy, with long floppy hair that hid his eyes. He ate *a lot*, even though he was as lanky as a spaghetti noodle and did that stupid thing of letting his jeans hang halfway off his butt. Still, he gave off a vibe that was goofy and sweet. He glanced at Cinnamon all throughout dinner, and at one point, after ducking under the table to retrieve a dropped napkin, he popped back up and told her she had "sweet kicks."

I peeked to see which "kicks" she was wearing, because sometimes guys used the I-like-your-shoes line as a come on. Was James randomly hitting on her, or was he being real?

I felt better when I saw that Cinnamon was wearing her hot orange, flip-flop–style Etnies. James was a skater boy, and he dug Cinnamon's skater girl vibe. *Of course.*

"Why, thank you," Cinnamon said. She reached down, slipped off a flip-flop, and brought it above-table so the others could appreciate it as well. Then she flipped it over and displayed the sole. "Check out what they say."

"I can't see," Dinah said. She grabbed Cinnamon's wrist and pulled the shoe closer. "Omigosh, that is *awesome.*"

"You gonna tell the rest of us?" Ryan asked. Ryan was one of the guys in the blue room. He and his roommate, Mark, were buddies from Chicago—which they pronounced Chi*cah*go—and their accents were hilarious. It was possible, I suppose, that they thought our Southern accents were hilarious. But theirs were far more so.

Cinnamon read aloud: "Preserve the Ocean, Respect the Beach, Don't Litter." She grinned. "It's so I can leave a positive message in the sand."

"Tight," Mark said.

Cinnamon slid her flip-flop back on. She promptly reached for a chip, but the girl named Brooklyn swatted her hand. Brooklyn was bone-skinny with curled blond hair. Not *curly* blond hair, but long, thin hair she'd clearly gone at with a curling iron. She wore short-shorts and a stripey tube top, which I found both impressive and slightly disturbing. I have never ever ever in my life worn a tube top.

"Whoa," Brooklyn told Cinnamon. "You were just touching your shoe."

Cinnamon gazed at her, confused.

"First wash. Then chip."

"Oh, sorry," Cinnamon said, pushing back her chair with a scraping sound.

"What's the plan for tomorrow?" Erika asked. Erika, who was Brooklyn's roomie, wore a white, ribbed wife-beater, green army fatigues cut off below the knee, and combat boots. Hooked on her belt loop was a thick metal chain, the other end of which snaked into her front pocket. I wasn't sure what would be on such a chain. A pocket watch seemed unlikely. A . . . knife? Did people carry knives on chains?

I hadn't formed an opinion about Erika yet, except that she seemed sort of . . . well . . . *butch*. Not that there was anything wrong with being butch! I just didn't run into many butch girls at Westminster. Zero, to be exact.

"Alphonse is going to take Dinah and Winnie out and show them how to patrol for crawls," Virginia said in response to Erika's question. She raised her eyebrows at Dinah. "Unless you'd rather have a different assignment? I want this to be fun for you."

"Patrolling for crawls is fine," Dinah said gamely.

Virginia cocked her head. "Or you could canvass the beach later in the morning, when more people are on the beach. You could help Brooklyn and Ryan distribute bumper stickers."

"I pick that," Dinah said so quickly that everyone laughed. Her cheeks turned pink. "Um, why bumper stickers?"

"To remind people about the light ordinance," Ryan said.

"Huh?" Dinah said.

"The bumper stickers say LIGHTS OUT," Virginia explained. "After ten P.M., property owners and renters are supposed to turn off any beachfront lights. We don't want the sea turtles to come ashore and get confused."

Dinah wrinkled her forehead.

Cinnamon who'd had more time than we had to absorb turtle knowledge, jumped in. "Say I'm a turtle, 'kay?" she said.

"You're a turtle," I said, though I wasn't the one she'd addressed.

Alphonse chuckled. Cinnamon made a face.

"I'm not *really* a turtle," she said, talking s-u-p-e-r s-l-o-w-l-y. "I'm just pre*ten*ding."

"Ohhh," I said.

"So I'm a turtle"—she glared at me—"only not really. And I swim out of the ocean. Swim swim swim, swim swim swim. And it's nighttime, so it's dark. With me so far?"

"Nighttime. Dark." I glanced at Dinah and raised my eyebrows. When she nodded, I turned back to Cinnamon. "Please, go on."

"Well, since it's dark, I can't see," Cinnamon said. "That's good, because that means other people can't see *me*."

"Other animals, mainly," Erika said.

"Right. Other animals, if they saw me, might want to eat me or my eggs. So I come to shore at night, and because I'm clever, I know to always keep the moon at my back."

I turned to Dinah to see if she was following. This time she lifted her shoulders. I turned back to Cinnamon. *"Excusez?"*

Alphonse grabbed the edge of the table and rocked back on the legs of his chair. "The moon rises over the ocean. The sea turtles know this, and they know that if they keep the moon behind them, they'll eventually reach the dunes."

"Which is where they lay their eggs," Brooklyn said.

Dinah's mouth fell open. One of the things I loved about Dinah (but which I didn't want for myself) was the fact that she was constitutionally incapable of hiding her emotions.

"That is *so cool*," she said, her tone full of wonder.

"Isn't it?" Brooklyn said. "And the babies, when they hatch, they use the moon too."

"How?" I said.

"That's how they get to the ocean," Alphonse said. His eyes met mine. "The hatchlings are born knowing to head *toward* the light of the moon. But if a house has its porch lights on, or if light's blazing from the front room . . ."

"The hatchlings could go the wrong way," I finished.

"If they did . . . what would happen to them?" Dinah asked. She searched the faces around the table.

"They wouldn't make it," Virginia said.

"What do you mean, 'wouldn't make it'?"

Virginia took a sip of wine. The rest of us were having Coke, which Ryan and Mark called "pop."

"The baby turtles have to make the trek from the nest to the shore," she said, "and they have to do it on their own. It's how they imprint on the beach— so they can return one day—and it's how they develop the strength to survive once they enter the water."

"Yeah," Ryan said. "So if they head the wrong way, like toward a house, they'll just. . . . you know . . ."

"Die," Cinnamon finished.

Dinah looked at Cinnamon. Then at Ryan. Then around the table at the rest of us. "But . . . no! That's so *sad*!"

"So come with," Ryan said. "Give out bumper stickers with me and Brook."

"Brook*lyn*," Brooklyn said. She gave Ryan a skinny-blond-girl stare, fierce in the way only skinny blond girls can be. "Not Brook."

Ryan held up his hands. "My bad."

"I want to build cages," Erika announced.

"All right, you can build cages with Milo," Virginia said. "And Cinnamon and Mark, why don't you put in some hours at the aquarium? I can drop you off when I go into town for groceries." She scanned our faces. "That's everyone, right? We're all good?"

"All good," we chorused.

She smiled. "In that case, let's get this kitchen cleaned up."

Chairs scraped the floor. Individual conversations broke out, and Ryan reached across the table and snatched the last bit of Cinnamon's fish taco.

"Hey!" she protested.

Ryan grinned. James did, too—but not as convincingly. More like he wished he'd been the rascally taco stealer.

So this is our group, I thought. *I'll be spending the next month with these people.*

Alphonse, gorgeous and exotic. James, skater dude, who maybe had a thing for Cinnamon. Mark and Ryan from Chi*cah*go, Brooklyn with the curled hair, and Erika, who'd probably never used a curling iron in her life. Except possibly as a weapon.

Add Dinah, Cinnamon, and me to the mix, and that was it. That was the ten of us. Except . . . oh, man! I totally spaced Milo!

I studied him surreptitiously and couldn't generate much of an opinion about him . . . except that he was quiet, and that tomorrow he'd be building cages with Erika.

He wasn't bad looking. His posture was hunchy, and patches of acne marred his cheeks. But his eyes were intelligent and kind.

He must have felt me looking at him, because he met my gaze and smiled. It was a quick smile, and shy, and surprisingly sweet.

I smiled back.

On the beach that night, while the others sat in a circle and passed around a two-liter bottle of Mountain Dew, Cinnamon, Dinah, and I snuck off by ourselves. We lay on our backs on the sand, Cinnamon to my right and Dinah to my left. I touched feet with both of them as I gazed at the stars. They were brighter here than in Atlanta, and so plentiful I could lose myself in them.

That was one good thing about living in the olden days, I thought randomly. *Sure, life was tough, and they didn't have washing machines. But they had these glorious stars.*

"So beautiful," Dinah murmured.

I pressed my big toe against hers, the foot equivalent of a hand-squeeze.

"Yay, stars!" cheered Cinnamon, who was in high spirits. "And you know what else I say yay to?"

I turned my head, enjoying the coolness of the sand. "What else do you say yay to, Cin?"

"James." She rolled it off her tongue like a delicious caramel. "Cinnamon gives a *big* yay to James."

"I thought you swore off boys," Dinah said.

"I thought you were the Black Widow," I said.

"Ehh," Cinnamon said. "It's time for me to heal and move on—and did you see how he kept staring at me?"

"He *might* have been staring at you," I said to tease her. "He might have been staring at the wall. Kinda hard to tell with all that hair in his eyes."

"James is adorable," Dinah said. "I figured you'd be more into Ryan, though."

"Ryan?" Cinnamon said. *"Why?"*

"Um . . . because he reminds me of Bryce?"

"Ugh. If you say that ever again, I will be forced to bury you up to your neck and let the seagulls eat you."

"Don't worry," I whispered, swiveling my head her way. "I'd save you."

"I *heard* that," Cinnamon said.

"I think James is cute," I said. "But Cinnamon, for reals, don't you think he's a little . . . ?"

"A little *what*?"

"Hmm, how to put this." I interlaced my fingers and used them as a pillow. "Pure? Trusting? Naïve?"

*"Win*nie!" She pushed me with her foot.

"You'd eat him alive! He's so . . . *sweet*, and you're so . . ."

"I'm so *what*?"

"Um. Um." I giggled. "Burly?"

"Burly?!"

"Okay, bad word choice. I just mean . . . well . . . who do you think would wear the pants in the relationship, you know? There's kinda no doubt who it would be."

"So?" she said. "Lucky him, I say. I'll train him how to be a *good* boyfriend, and *not* like Bryce, and he will be my pet."

"Your pet?" Dinah said.

"Ker-*eep*y," I said.

"And please don't call me fat," she muttered. "You're always all, 'Cinnamon, be nice. Cinnamon, don't tease.' Shouldn't the same rules apply to you?"

I was baffled. When did I call her . . . ?

Ohhh. She thought, when I said "burly," that I was referring to her weight.

"Wait," I said. "I didn't mean 'burly' as in a big, burly football player. I meant like a *burr*, a real live burr."

"Whatever."

"You're not burly, I swear. You're just, you know, strong! You're tough!"

"Winnie? Are you somehow under the impression that you're making things better?"

"Yes?"

"You are sadly mistaken."

I sat bolt upright, craned over, and gave her a loud, wet smooch, making her cringe and go, *"Ewww!"*

"Now are things better?"

She *hmmph*-ed, and I grinned and leaned back on my elbows.

The waves lapped the shore, and a feeling hung in the air that was different from the feeling of being in Atlanta. Maybe it was the sand digging into my skin, or maybe the balmy breeze ruffling my hair. Or . . . was I missing Lars? Was that it?

As if she'd read my mind, Dinah said, "How's Lars, Winnie? Have you talked to him?"

I gazed at the dark water, allowing its ebb and flow to hypnotize me. "He called, but we were cleaning up the kitchen, so I didn't answer. And he's sent about a thousand texts."

"You say it like it's a bad thing," Dinah said.

"What? *No*."

Dinah waited.

"If I did, it was by accident. I'm glad he's texted. I just haven't had time to text him back."

"Are y'all having a fight?" Dinah asked.

I lay back on the sand. I closed my eyes and covered them with lightly clenched fists. "No, not a fight."

"Then what?"

"Yes," Cinnamon said. "Please enlighten us."

"Oh, I don't know. I need to call him back . . . and I *will* . . . but I've got, like, this tangled feeling inside."

"Hmm," Cinnamon said. "Carry on."

"It's nothing. I'm just being stupid. But sometimes I just want—" I broke off.

"Sometimes you just want *what*?" Dinah said.

Oh, fine, I thought. *It's dumb and stupid and embarrassing, but fine.*

"A cupcake," I whispered, barely letting the word slip from my lips.

"Huh?" Cinnamon said. "Couldn't hear ya, pardner."

I opened my eyes, because it wasn't just the cupcake. I was also mad at him for going to Germany, despite the fact that he hadn't even left yet. How ridiculous was that? I blamed him for his mom's travel plans, as if he had the option to say, "No, thanks, I'd rather stay in Atlanta with Winnie."

Anyway, he would have chosen to stay with me if that had been an option. So what *was* my problem? *Ag!* It was just so hard to explain!

"I guess I want that giddy-crush feeling back," I said at last.

"Ah," Cinnamon said. "You don't want to be a sofa cushion."

"I don't want to be a sofa cushion," I agreed. "Though I have no idea what that means."

She rolled onto her side and propped her head in her hand. "You don't want to be the comfy place he comes home to."

"She doesn't?" Dinah said from the darkness.

"Yeah, I don't?"

"Well, according to you," Cinnamon said. "You're the one who agreed."

"No, I just said I don't want to be a sofa cushion." I paused. "Do *you* want to be a sofa cushion?"

"I wouldn't mind being James's sofa cushion," she said in an eyebrow-waggle voice.

"Hey, girls!" one of the guys called out to us from farther up on shore. "Get over here—we're going to play Chubby Bunny!"

Cinnamon twisted her head, aiming her words over her shoulder. "What's Chubby Bunny?"

"Youse guys don't know Chubby Bunny?" either Ryan or Mark said.

Dinah sat up and finger-combed her hair. To us, she whispered, "I don't. Do y'all?"

"Nope, but I'm up for finding out," Cinnamon said. She got to her feet and started over toward the rest of the group. She paused and looked back. "Dudes?"

"I thought we were talking about Lars," I said.

"You don't want to be a fixture," Cinnamon said. "You want to be"—she circled her hand—"the fabulous new Wii game that he's obsessed with, not the couch he plants his butt on."

"Ew, and ew again," I said. "And you're wrong. I don't want to be a Wii game." I wanted to be . . . the girl he adored and brought cupcakes to. The girl he wooed.

Omigosh, was that it? I wanted to be *wooed*?

"Okay, you win," Cinnamon said to me. "Now c'mon, let's go find out about this Chubby Bubby."

"Chubby *Bunny*," yelled either Mark or Ryan.

"That's what I *said*!"

She pulled Dinah up first, then extended her hand toward me. "C'mon, c'mon."

I rocked myself to a sitting position and clasped her hand. She groaned as she heaved me up.

"*You're* the burly one," she said.

"Sorry again about that. I really didn't mean it like you think."

"Then come play Chubby Bubby and let me win so I look good for James."

"Sweetie, how could you not look good for James?"

She grinned. "Now that's the kind of talk I like to hear."

Chubby Bunny turned out to involve shoving as many marshmallows into your mouth as you could, and after each new addition, you had to say "Chubby Bunny." And it had to come out intelligible.

Cinnamon was a natural. With an astounding *thirteen jumbo-size marshmallows* crammed into her cheeks, she was the chubbiest bunny ever.

The instant Ryan lifted her arm in victory, she spit them out rapid-fire like soggy, squishy bullets. One of them hit James in the stomach, and he doubled over.

"Death by marshmallows!" he cried. Cinnamon blew exaggerated kissy sounds at him, and her lips were powdery-white, and it filled me with joy to see her turning on the ol' Cinnamon charm. It had been too long.

And then, *very* eye-popping, I noticed that Dinah was turning on some charm of her own—with quiet Milo!!! I'd turned to her to share a yay-Cinnamon moment, only she didn't see me because she was *waaaay* too busy sharing a moment with Milo. They were smiling at each other with matching shy smiles, and a lump formed in my throat. I looked away and swallowed repeatedly.

"You all right?" Alphonse asked, appearing by my side.

"Me? Yeah." My gaze flitted to his face, and I gave him a wry grin. At least, I was aiming for wry. I wasn't sure why—to impress him? The corner of his mouth curved up, so I guess it worked. Feeling suddenly awkward, I jammed my hands in the pockets of my cutoffs.

"Well . . . good night," he said.

"Good night," I said.

"See you in the morning? Bright and early?"

"Bright and early," I echoed. *Urgh,* I told myself. Stop *repeating him!*

"Right," he said, saluting. Alphonse was a saluter, I was discovering. Some people were.

He loped off to the beach house. The rest of the group broke apart soon after, wandering back in two's and three's. Ryan and Mark joked loudly in their Chicago accents. Brooklyn reached the ramp of the deck, paused, and craned her neck to see the stars. She closed her eyes as if she were making a wish, then opened them and blew a kiss to the sky.

Up in the rainbow room, as Dinah put on her summer PJs and Cinnamon slipped into a long T-shirt, I checked my iPhone for messages.

WINNIE THE POOCH! the first text said. It was from Lars.

WHERE R U, GIRL? *"Pooch" indeed,* I thought. *I am pooch-free, Lars-O, as you well know.*

The next four texts were variations of the same: He wanted me to call, he wondered where I was, he missed me already.

"Aw," Cinnamon said, peeking over my shoulder. "He's in *lurrrrrve.*"

"Shut up," I said, twisting away.

I saw that there were three voice mails from him, too, and while part of me was touched, another part wondered if so many calls were necessary.

But isn't this what you want? an annoying voice said inside my head. *Doesn't this count as wooing?*

I don't know, I said back to that voice. *Does it? Or is he just worried by the idea of me being off with potentially hot beach boys?*

I tapped the VOICE MAIL icon and brought the phone to my ear. His voice was so familiar.

"Hey, Win. Call me."

"Winster! At the beach yet? Call me."

"You must be having fun. Maybe you're riding the back of one of those huge sea turtles, and that's why you're not answering your phone. So, uh . . . right. Call me!"

I sat on my rainbow-quilted bed and called him. As his line rang, I scooched back and leaned against the rickety headboard.

"Winnie!" he answered. "Hey!"

"Hey," I said. "Omigosh, you would not believe how hectic everything's been. I'm *so* sorry I haven't been able to call till now."

"No worries," he said. I'd been afraid he was going to be pissed, but he seemed to be in a great mood. "So how are you? Still popping those wicked Junior Mints?"

"Ha ha, and no, but only because I don't have any. But Lars . . . the beach is so gorgeous! We saw dolphins! I mean, porpoises! And the house we're staying in? A*maz*ing. It's got all these nooks and crannies, and at the way top there's—"

"Guess what?" he interjected. "I'm not going to Germany. My mom lost her funding."

My eyebrows shot up. "For real?" His announcement took me by surprise, and I didn't know how to respond. "Wow. I'm sorry."

"Don't be. I'm stoked."

"Oh," I said, still trying to figure out how *I* felt. Mainly, I was confused, but also a little miffed that he cared more about his big news than my own.

"O-*kay*," he said, chuckling in a way that suggested my reaction wasn't good enough. "Don't jump up and down with joy or anything."

Well, you cut me off, I wanted to say. *I was all excited to tell you about the Crow's Nest, and you totally cut me off.*

"Win, you're not getting it," he explained. "You don't have to stay in South Carolina. You can come home."

"What?!"

Cinnamon glanced over. I twisted my upper body toward the wall.

"You just got there, I know. But you never really wanted to go in the first place, right?"

"What are you talking about? Yes, I did."

"You only decided to go after I told you about Germany," he said. "And now Germany's off."

"Lars . . ." I felt a whirlwind of emotions. It was strange and wrong for my boyfriend to expect me to come trotting home just because his plans had changed. Wasn't it? It verged on slightly psycho, like Edward from *Twilight* and how he watched Bella sleep. The guy sat in her room by her bed and *watched her sleep*—and since she was *asleep*, she didn't even know it.

Plus, Edward was so . . . pale! And he was always *smelling* Bella! Sorry, but I found that unsettling.

Bella: "Hello, Edward! I'm home!"

Edward closes his eyes, flares his nostrils, and inhales deeply. "Ah, Bella. Yessssss." He inhales even more deeply, shudders uncontrollably, and pierces Bella with his stare. "You look tired, my darling. You should rest. And please, don't worry: I'll be right here . . . smelling you for all of eternity . . ."

"Winnie? You there?" Lars said.

"Oh. Sorry." I drew my knees to my chest. "But Lars . . . I'm having fun here."

"At Camp Sea Turtle?" He laughed. "Ah, Win. You're a good friend to Dinah to not want to abandon her. But she'll understand. Anyway, Cinnamon's there to take care of her."

Oh no you dih-un't, I thought, my confusion transforming into anger. Anger was easier and gave me the courage to say, "Okay, first of all, Dinah doesn't need 'taking care of.'" My mattress dipped, and a sideways glance told me that Cinnamon and Dinah were perched on the side of my bed. "And secondly: How did you know Cinnamon was here?"

"I told him," Cinnamon whispered.

"She told me," Lars said. "She wanted me to download my Spearhead CD."

Cinnamon, who apparently could hear Lars through the tiny speaker, nodded. "*Love* Michael Franti," she said in rasta-speak. "Perfect for da beach, yah?"

I gestured for her to get off my bed. Dinah, too. They smiled with pretend confusion and stayed where they were.

"And *C*," I said, "I don't want to go home."

"Go *home*?" Cinnamon said, her voice rising. She grabbed my phone. "Lars. *Dude*. What kind of crazy pills are you taking?!"

"Cinnamon!" I said.

She kept my phone out of my grasp. "Uh-huh . . . uh-huh . . . so?"

"You're not helping," I said through a clenched jaw.

"You? Hush," she said, pointing at me as she rose from my bed. "And *you*"—this time, to Lars—"I don't know *what* to say to you, except we're at the beach, dude. The *beach*.

And we're in a house full of hotness monsters—"

I groaned and covered my face.

"—and we're having the time of our lives—"

"Yeah," Dinah said.

"—and I have nothing more to add, other than . . . well . . ." She worked her forehead, and then smoothed her expression and threw back her shoulders. "*Nobody* puts Baby in the corner. Dig?"

Oh. My. God. I got off the bed, strode to Cinnamon, and held out my hand.

She spoke quickly into the phone. "I believe I've made my point. And now, farewell."

"Sorry, Lars," I said. "She's got sun poisoning."

"Do not," Cinnamon muttered.

Lars cleared his throat. "Hotness monsters?"

"That's just Cinnamon," I said. "You know Cinnamon."

"I thought she swore off guys."

"Yeah, well . . ." I shrugged, not that he could see it.

There was silence. I walked to the far end of the room, leaned against the wall, and slid down.

"So you don't want to come home?" Lars said.

"My parents have already paid for me to be here," I said. "How would I, anyway? Mr. Devine *just* dropped us off. It's a six-hour car ride from here to Atlanta."

"My brother could come pick you up. I'd come with him."

"Lars . . ."

"All right, fine," he said, abruptly backing off. "I get it."

"I made a commitment."

"I said I get it." There was another silence, and it was tense. When he next spoke, his voice was tense, too. "So, it's good? You're having fun?"

"Yeah, I guess. So far." I glanced at Cinnamon and Dinah and lowered my voice. "That doesn't mean I don't miss you."

"I miss you, too," he said stiffly. "But if you're having fun—hey, that's all that matters."

"Um . . . thanks." I felt itchy with the pressure of not living up to his expectations. It was awful, and the thought of caving crossed my mind. *But, no. No way.*

"So, talk to you tomorrow?" he said.

"Absolutely," I replied. "Only, it might possibly be slightly complicated, because we've, like, got this whole schedule, and—"

"Not a problem," he interrupted. "Say no more."

"I *want* to call you. It just might be hard."

"Like I said, I got it."

"Lars . . . now I'm worried I'm making you feel bad," I said anxiously. He *sounded* solid, but in a way that wasn't exactly *him*.

"Well, don't," he said, shifting his tone to give the slightest tint of, *Hey, babe, you're kind of exaggerating your own importance here.*

Subtle, but a cold splash of water nonetheless.

"Call when you can," he said coolly. "Or text. What-ever."

"Ok-a-a-y," I said. "I probably *can* call every night. I'm just not positive."

"Whatever."

We said our good-byes. We were very cordial. And then I hung up and let my head fall back against the wall.

"Is everything okay?" Dinah asked.

"You got me," I said, staring up at the skylight. We'd cranked it open since it was nighttime, but the inky, starry sky seemed millions of heartbeats away.

Make Friends with Someone New

OVER THE COURSE OF MY LIFE, I have spent a fair amount of time considering what it would be like to be a boy instead of a girl. Some things would be great: Sitting all sprawled and casual and taking up all the room you wanted, without even a whisper of needing to keep your legs together or be "ladylike." Belching with impunity. Being a smart aleck in school and having teachers (well, female teachers) find you delightful.

Other things would be interesting, like peeing while standing up, or not having to wear a shirt if you weren't in the mood.

Other things would be just plain awful. Namely, erections. I mean, maybe they wouldn't be awful in certain situations, but I'd read Judy Blume's *Then Again, Maybe I Won't*. I knew all about how erections could happen totally out of a guy's control and in the most embarrassing of places. Like in math class, say, when you've just been called to the board to work out an equation.

When it came to erections, I was definitely glad to be a girl. I was glad to be a girl most of the time, actually, though

I suspected I'd always be fascinated by the squillions of boy/girl differences out there.

This morning, as I silently got dressed while Cinnamon and Dinah slept blissfully on, I found myself contemplating hair. Plenty of guys had long hair, but the majority had normal, short *boy* hair. As I put on Bo's baseball cap and pulled my own hair through the hole in the back, I thought about how those short-haired boys never got to experience the comforting jounce of a ponytail. I loved the feel of a jouncy ponytail. It just made me happy.

On my way downstairs I made a pit stop at the bathroom, where I did *not* pee standing up, thanks very much. I didn't squat, either. I was so not a squatter. But when it came time to flush, I had a small crisis of conscience. Or of prudishness? Because there was a framed sign above the toilet, and it was needlepointed, and it said, IF IT'S YELLOW, LET IT MELLOW. IF IT'S BROWN, FLUSH IT DOWN. And there were butterflies and sweet little flowers.

Last night, Dinah had gone into the bathroom, promptly reemerged, and with tightly knitted lips, dragged me in and said, "Look."

She pointed at the needlepoint sign. I read the curlique letters, and my eyebrows shot up.

"What does that *mean*?" she said, but the panic in her tone suggested she knew full well.

I could either giggle or be mortified. I wasn't yet sure which was going to win out. "Um . . . well . . ."

"Cinna*mon*!" Dinah bleated. "Get in here right now please!"

She wandered in, brushing her hair. "Yeah?"

For the second time, Dinah pointed. She was like one of those hound dogs that stood rigidly "at point" when they sniffed a rabbit. Dinah wasn't sniffing rabbit, however. The tingle in my own nostrils prompted a quick peek into the pot, where—gross!—the mellowing of somebody's yellow was already taking place.

"Whoa, ripe," Cinnamon said. She pushed past me and Dinah and flushed the toilet.

"Uh-oh, you naughty kitten, now you shall have no pie," I said. The giggling had won out, though the mortification hovered just below the surface.

"You didn't *read* it," Dinah said. She jabbed her finger, still in pointing position, at the needlepoint sign.

"If it's yellow, let it mellow," Cinnamon said. "If it's brown—" She broke off, overcome by chortles. "*Dude!* *Wrong*-ness! We're not supposed to flush when we pee?"

"Only if your pee, um, has a friend," I said.

Cinnamon pondered. "Well, when I take a crap—"

"*Please,*" Dinah begged, possessed by a rising hysteria.

Cinnamon eyed her to say *Wait your turn, young lady.* "When *I* take a crap, there is usually pee-age as well." She furrowed her brow. "In fact, I don't think I've ever just plainly crapped. I *do* plainly pee, though. Quite a lot, actually." She patted her stomach, presumably in the general vicinity of her bladder. Her air was that of a farm girl complacently admiring a flock of geese.

Dinah's chest heaved. "I *can't*. I can't go to the bathroom and just . . ."

"Leave it for all the world to enjoy?" I said.

She paled.

"Whose do you think that was that we just flushed?" Cinnamon said.

"Ryan's?" I said, hazarding a guess. "Out on the beach, he drank a *lot* of Mellow Yellow."

"You mean Mountain Dew," Dinah corrected me.

Mischief flashed in Cinnamon's eyes. "Actually, we just *think* it was Mountain Dew. For all we know, it *could* have been Mellow Yellow." She chortled. "Bottled at the source."

"Ew!" Dinah said.

"They're the same color," Cinnamon said. "Mountain Dew and Mellow Yellow *and*"—Cinnamon waggled her eyebrows at the commode—"the fine specimen we have here."

"I wonder if we'll all get to know each other by the color of our pee," I mused. "Like if I'll go to the bathroom and say, 'Why look, Brooklyn must have just stopped by.'"

Dinah, her eyes big and round, pushed us out.

"Don't forget—no flushing!" I called through the door.

"Unless you poop," Cinnamon said. Her voice reverberated in the hall. "Are you pooping in there, Dinah?"

The lock clicked.

Cinnamon and I grinned at each other.

"She's going to flush," Cinnamon said.

"I know—even if she doesn't poop."

"Go *away*!" Dinah cried.

"It's probably for environmental reasons," Cinnamon reflected. "You think that's the deal? Virginia wants us to be green?"

"Virginia wants us to be *yellow*," I clarified.

"I mean it!" Dinah said. "I can't do"—there was a pause loaded with frustration—"*any*thing with the two of you standing there!"

"You can't pee *or* poop?" Cinnamon queried, just to make sure anyone within hearing range understood. "Are you constipated, Dinah?"

Down the hall, a door opened, and footsteps sounded. Footsteps which were coming our way.

"Oh no," Cinnamon said. We huddled close. I clutched the sleeve of Cinnamon's shirt.

"Here," Ryan said, tossing us a small box. Cinnamon fumbled, but managed to catch it, which impressed me mightily. If it had come my way? It would have hit my body and ricocheted to the floor. "Dem marshmallows can gum up the works."

Cinnamon blinked. Other than that, her face was motionless and betrayed very little.

"Um . . . thanks?" I said.

"Duffenetly," Ryan said, all Mafia-like. He sauntered back down the hall. "Night, ladies."

As soon as he was out of sight, we looked at the box. DULCOLAX STOOL SOFTENER, it said. GENTLE, SOFTENING RELIEF.

"*Why?!*" I whispered, meaning *Why would Ryan have such a thing?*

"Winnie?" Dinah said from within the bathroom. "Cinnamon?"

In a hushed, almost reverential tone, Cinnamon read the fine print. "It doesn't make you go, it makes it easier to go." She lifted her eyes to mine.

I took the box from her hand. I placed it outside the bathroom door and gave it a quick pat. "We'll just leave it here for her."

"Excellent idea."

Our whispers didn't sit well with Dinah, who said, "Who's out there? For *real*, y'all!"

Cinnamon tiptoed back to our room. I followed. Two minutes later we heard the toilet flush (of course).

Cinnamon held up her index finger. "Wait for it . . ."

Seconds ticked by. Dinah was washing her hands. Dinah was drying her hands. Dinah was unlocking the door and stepping into the hall . . .

A yelp pierced the air, then cut off abruptly and was replaced by the pounding of feet on the stairs. She was flushed when she appeared in the doorway.

"You *guys*!" she exclaimed, giggling wildly.

She cocked her arm and let the box of stool softeners fly, aiming for some reason at *me* instead of Cinnamon. I squeaked and tried to shield myself, but she missed me by a mile.

That was last night. Now here it was the next morning, and the toilet was full of my pee. Anyone on this floor of the house—Cinnamon, Dinah, Mark, Ryan, Erika, and Brooklyn—could easily figure out that it was my pee, since I was the one on pre-sunrise turtle crawl duty.

Did I really want that? To let my pee "mellow," at the possible expense of my dignity?

But . . . it was a house rule. Virginia had taken the time to *needlepoint* it, for heaven's sake. And if I was all, *Ooo, I'm too un-wimpy to squat, squatting is for girly-girls who wrinkle their noses and never go barefoot and worry about their hair getting windblown* . . . Well, if I was bold enough to be a seat-sitter, shouldn't I be willing to throw dignity out the window and follow the when-to-flush rule?

It was a test of character, that's what it was. So . . . *fine.* I pulled back my hand from the toilet's handle. *I did not flush.* It was hard, but I did it, and as I washed up, I very briefly identified with my own urine, idling brazenly in the pot.

I am Winnie's pee! I thought. *Hear me roar!*

It was times like these when I wondered if everyone really was as strange as I was, or if I was just a special case.

I went downstairs and found Alphonse in the kitchen, rinsing out a glass. He had his long hair held back, I noticed, but I wasn't sure it would classify as a ponytail. Even if it did, I *knew* it didn't jounce, because his dreads were so thick. I liked the leather cord he used instead of an elastic.

"I made you some peanut butter toast," he said. He went to the toaster oven and opened it. "You want?"

"Sure," I said, although my stomach wasn't awake yet. "Thanks."

"Good protein boost."

"Okay. Uh . . . cool."

Nobody else was up. Outside the big kitchen picture window, the marsh was dark and ghostly looking, thanks to a low ribbon of fog. Alligator eyes, half-submerged, could be watching me and I wouldn't even know it.

"You can eat it on the way," Alphonse said. "Let's go."

I followed him through the back of the kitchen, which connected to the green staircase, which, like the blue staircase, led both up and down. Going up would take us first to a screened-in porch, then to the level where the den was, and finally to the Crow's Nest. Going down, as Alphonse now did, took us to the bathhouse, where people could shower and change after coming in from the beach. Cutting through the bathhouse was another way to get outside.

"So . . . what do we do?" I asked Alphonse, after we took the short trail to the beach.

"Well, first we take a moment to enjoy," he said in a tone just sanctimonious enough to rub me the wrong way.

Oh, please, I thought. *You've been here, what? One whole week longer than I have? That doesn't make you Mr. Ocean-Appreciator-Extraordinaire.*

But it *was* lovely. The first rays of the sun were creeping over the horizon, way out at the impossible-to-discern end of the ocean. Seagulls swooped through the sky, crying *"Ahh-ahh!"* in lonely bird voices. The surf advanced. The surf retreated. The foamy dregs of the waves reminded me of lace.

"Nice, isn't it?" Alphonse said.

"Yeah," I said.

Not another human was visible in either direction. It felt like we were the only people in the world.

Alphonse started walking, heading north toward the undeveloped stretch of beach I'd spotted from the Crow's Nest.

"When turtles lay their eggs, they're more likely to do it away from the houses," he explained. He pointed to the dunes, where a strip of fluorescent orange tape fluttered in the breeze. "See up there? That's a nest we've already marked."

"Can we go look?" I said. "Is that allowed?"

He veered right. I followed him up into the brambles. We reached the slim wooden stake marked with the orange tape, and he knelt beside it. I knelt, too, but all I saw was normal old . . . normalness. Sand, sticks, reeds. Bracken, which wasn't a word I used often (if I'd ever used it at all), but which seemed like the right term for what was before me.

"I don't see anything," I said.

Alphonse carefully dug down. The pale sand coated his

skin like cinnamon-sugar, and the muscles of his forearm were ropey and lean.

"There," he said, shifting his weight and shaking the sand from his arm. He lifted his head to see my reaction. Only he was so close, and his gaze so warm and steady, that instead of looking at the nest, I found myself sucked into his brown, brown eyes. It wasn't a boy-girl flirty moment. At least, I didn't think it was. Even though things between Lars and me were slightly . . . complicated, we were still together. We were *totally* together.

And yet, maybe guys and girls couldn't help it sometimes? Couldn't help the quickening heartbeats, or the way the air grew charged, as if molecules of me were bridging the gap to Alphonse, while molecules of him did the same thing in reverse? Like circus fleas, or static electricity. Or maybe just biology.

I tore my eyes from his. I looked down, and in the sand I saw a hundred eggs, maybe more, all the size of Ping-Pong balls.

"Whoa," I said. "There's so many," I said.

"A mama sea turtle can hold five hundred eggs inside her," Alphonse said. "That's called a clutch. She lays them in batches of a hundred or so. She lays them in different spots to increase their chances of survival."

"Why does that help?"

Alphonse shrugged. "A fox could find the nest, or a raccoon. Even a dog'll dig up a nest for the fun of it. A dog won't eat the eggs, but it could crush them, or leave them exposed to predators."

"So it's like hiding treasure," I said. "Hide it in lots of different spots, and it's less likely to all get found."

"Yeah." He lifted an egg from the nest. It wasn't oval like a chicken's egg, but perfectly round. Its shell was the color of cream. Alphonse brushed off most of the sand and held it out to me.

I was nervous, but I cupped my palms and accepted it so very carefully. A teeny life was in my hands. A teeny, growing, unborn sea turtle.

"It's warm," I marveled.

"The sand acts as insulation," Alphonse explained.

I lifted the egg to my ear. I listened.

Alphonse regarded me as if I were odd, but amusing. "Hear anything?"

I adopted a teeny turtle voice and made the egg talk. *"Put me back! I miss my brothers and sisters!"* Then I placed the egg with the others. I helped Alphonse cover them up with sand.

"I get how marking the nest protects it from people, and maybe dogs if their owners are with them," I said. "How does it help with raccoons and foxes?"

"It doesn't," Alphonse said, rising to his feet. "That's why Erika's making cages."

I stood up and brushed the sand off my shorts. "You put the cages over the nests?"

"Yeah. They're made out of metal, and we plant them deep enough that a fox can't dig under it."

"So this nest'll be safe? Once a cage is over it?"

He started down the dune. "Safer than it would have been."

"That's awesome," I said. I took skittering steps behind him, hopping over sticks and brambles. "I mean, that's *a lot* of turtles."

"Do you know how many'll survive to adulthood?"

"Uh . . ." I'd assumed all of them would, if they didn't get eaten or crushed while they were still in their eggs. But his tone suggested otherwise. "Seventy-five?"

"Guess again."

"Fifty?"

We cleared the dune, and walking grew easier.

"Two," Alphonse said.

"*Two?* Out of a hundred babies, only two will survive?"

"And that's if we're lucky. Could be one, could be zero."

Watching Alphonse by the nest, it was clear he cared about the turtles. I sensed he enjoyed being the bearer of this bad news, though.

"Why?" I demanded. "What happens to the other ninety-eight?"

"The hatchlings are born with a built-in mapping system. They know to follow the moon to the water. But if there's another source of light, they could head for that instead of the moon."

"Oh yeah," I said.

"Or a predator could get them as they make their way across the sand. Seagulls will swoop down and get them, too."

I winced. What a terrible way to go, snatched up and carried off before you were a day old.

"And the turtles that *do* make it to the water . . ." Alphonse shrugged. "A lot of them will end up as shark food."

"*Shark* food!" I shuddered. "DeBordieu has sharks?!"

"Uh, yeah," he said, as if I were being stupid. "It's the ocean."

"I don't like sharks," I stated. "Sharks are mean."

He shook his head, smiling. He was acting totally condescending, and it made him so much less cute.

Well. That wasn't true; it actually didn't take away from his cuteness at all. But it did make me appreciate Lars, who would never make fun of me for saying sharks were mean.

"My boyfriend's going to flip out," I said. "He already wants me to come home. And when he hears there's sharks? That I'll be *swimming* with *sharks*?!" I let out a low whistle to say those sharks better watch out—and then felt immediately fake-ish, like I was playing a role and not being the real me.

Maybe I just wanted to get the boyfriend bit out in the open?

I slid my eyes sideways to see how Alphonse was taking it.

"If I had a girlfriend, I'd want her to do more than sit around and look pretty," he said.

What?! I made a face, which—if he chose to notice—

would tell him how ridiculous his comment was. Like Lars just wanted me to sit around and look pretty. What*ever*.

Wait. Was Alphonse saying he thought I was pretty?

"If *I* had a girlfriend . . ." he went on. He paused, glancing at me. Then he gazed deliberately into the distance and kicked a shell.

Oh good grief. Another difference between boys and girls was how boys operated under the misapprehension that the start-a-sentence-but-not-finish-it ploy was, like, clever and cool. Alphonse wanted me to beg and plead and care soooooo much about this hypothetical girlfriend of his, but I was *not* going to give him that satisfaction.

So I gazed deliberately into the distance, too. *La la la, gazing into the distance, thinking deep thoughts . . .*

"If you had a girlfriend, *what*?" I demanded.

Alphonse smiled smugly. "She wouldn't be the type of girl who was afraid of sharks, that's all."

Nych, nych, nych, I responded silently. What I said out loud, was, "How lovely for you."

He laughed a clean, happy laugh, and just like that, I liked him again. But not as a boy! Just as a person!!!! Or, hey—as a new friend, which meant I could cross off another item on my list. *Sweet.*

"Well, good thing we're not going out," I told my new friend. "Because if we were, you'd have to dump me. I'm even afraid of *land* sharks."

"Land sharks," he repeated.

"Yup. Security guards, too."

He cocked one eyebrow, that smile of his tugging at his lips. "Am I missing something?"

"Uh, *yeah*," I said, using the same tone he used when I asked if DeBordieu had sharks. I spread my arms and held out my hands, palms up. *"Me."*

"You? How?"

I looked mysterious (or tried to) and stayed mum. Either he'd figure it out or he wouldn't, and it didn't really matter, since I wasn't sure what I meant, anyway. It danced somewhere along the lines of how he was missing out on fabulous me because of his decree not to date girls who refused to swim with sharks. Or something.

Of course, I also meant it hypothetically

I already had a boyfriend.

Be Completely Spazzy

J UNE TURNED INTO JULY, and my skin turned the warm brown of maple syrup. Even Dinah got tan lines, though they developed so gradually, I couldn't have said when. We operated on "beach time," as Virginia called it, which meant not worrying about boring details like what day it was, or even what time it was. Getting up early to scout for turtle crawls was the only activity done on schedule, as it had to be done by sunup.

I learned the strangest thing ever, though. I (dare I say it?) was a morning person. I liked the stillness of dawn. I liked the peace and quiet. So I stayed on crawl patrol. It suited me.

Cinnamon turned out to have a knack for building cages, and she and Erika became pretty good friends. And yes, Erika *was* gay, Cinnamon confirmed. She had a girlfriend back home she was always talking about.

"And her girlfriend is *pretty*," Cinnamon told me and Dinah as we rode borrowed bikes to the gatehouse one hot Saturday in July. The grizzled old guard had called to say he had something for Virginia, and we'd volunteered to go pick it up. "Like, *really* pretty. Girly pretty, with makeup and everything."

"So Erika's, like, the guy?" I said. "And her girlfriend's the girl?"

"Except they're both girls," Dinah said.

"Right," I said. I swung my handlebars to the right and then to the left, tracing lazy S's on the asphalt road. "What do y'all think about that?"

"About what?" Cinnamon said.

"About . . . I don't know. About them being gay."

"Hmm," Dinah mused. "I don't think it's *gross* or anything. Do y'all?"

"No," Cinnamon said with attitude. "Why would I think it was gross? In fact, why would I care, period? I don't care who Erika goes out with."

"You cared enough to tell us how pretty she is," I pointed out.

"Oh," Cinnamon said. First she looked pissed at being caught out . . . and then she laughed. "I did, didn't I?"

"I don't think it's gross, either," I said. "I do think it's *interesting*, but I think all relationships are interesting." I paused. "Like you and James, for example."

Cinnamon turned red, and Dinah and I shared an amused glance. All we had to do was *mention* James, and right on cue Cinnamon would turn red. Our tough-as-nails Cinnamon had been slayed by sweet, skinny James.

"Don't you start on James," she threatened. She pedaled faster.

I sped up to keep even. "I can't help it. You two are so cute together."

"You know how I feel about that word, Winnie. Don't you use that word—I mean it."

"But you *are* cute, how you're always holding hands and gazing adoringly at each other. Cute cute cutie cute."

"Remember that very first day?" Dinah said. Her sentences came out choppy, punctuated by huffs of exertion. "When James complimented your flip-flops?"

Cinnamon turned a brighter shade of red and stood up to pump. She was giggling helplessly, however, because that's what James did to her. I thought it was great. James was far nicer than Bryce, and he'd managed to do what no one else could. After three weeks in James's company, she was *finally* off her Black Widow kick.

"Slow down, lady!" I called.

Her words floated over her shoulder. "Will you change the subject?"

"Hmmm . . . maybe?"

She worked those quads and didn't let up.

Dinah, who was dying, called, "Yes!"—pant, pant—"We promise!"

Cinnamon stopped her manic pedaling and coasted. I caught up first and coasted alongside her.

"Hi!" I said cheerfully.

She pretend-scowled, but her twitching lips betrayed her.

"For reals, you and James are adorable," I told her. I glanced behind me to see how close Dinah was. "But I'll stop talking about it *for now*—if you'll help me put Dinah in the hot seat, eh?"

"Thank *god*," Cinnamon said. "And yes, please. With my whole heart, I beg you."

Dinah reached us, and we rode along peacefully for a minute or so. *Tra-la-la.* Dinah caught her breath.

Then, with the innocence of a daisy, I said, "You know who else is a cutie?"

"Who?" Cinnamon said, equally daisy-esque.

"That guy who hardly ever talks," I said. I scrunched my forehead. "Shiloh, is it?"

Dinah grew immediately flustered. *"Guys."*

"It's *Milo*," Cinnamon corrected. "And he talks—just not to us."

"Really?" I said. "Then to *who*?"

"Please don't," Dinah begged. "If you talk about this, I'm going to wreck."

I glanced at her to see how pink she was. On a scale of one to ten, she was an eleven.

"He doesn't even like me," she went on.

"Sure he does," Cinnamon said. "Why else would he keep signing up for bumper sticker duty?"

"Because he likes bumper stickers?"

"Or because he likes *you*," I said.

She rode over a rock that was directly in front of her, sending her front tire wobbling all over the place.

"Whoa there, Romeo," Cinnamon cautioned.

"You mean Juliet," I said. "Milo is Romeo."

"Mile-ee-o," Cinnamon said, trying it out.

Dinah moaned. "He's so smart, y'all. And funny. I know y'all haven't seen that side of him, but he is. Did I tell you about his online fund-raiser?"

"Yes," Cinnamon and I chorused.

"Where he challenged people to participate in his first annual Oatmeal Cream Pie Eat-Off?"

"Ye-e-es!"

"And Milo ate—"

"Two dozen oatmeal cream pies," Cinnamon and I recited in unison. "And he vlogged it on Blog.TV, even the part where he threw up, inspiring his viewers to donate over *two hundred dollars*—"

"To the no-kill animal shelter in his town," Dinah finished. She sighed rapturously. "Because he loves animals. Just like me."

"You two are a match made in heaven, and I'm not even lying," Cinnamon said.

Dinah thought so, too. It was written all over her face.

"He's gotten handsomer since we got here," I said. "I think the sun has helped his skin, don't you?"

"I don't care about his skin," Dinah said.

I *hmmm*-ed, because I didn't believe her. Milo's skin *was* looking better, but in all honesty, his acne was still pretty bad.

"I *don't*," Dinah said, sounding mad. "I don't care about superficial stuff like that."

"Okay, okay," I said. "Sorry."

She glanced at me to say *Fine, but don't mention Milo's skin again.*

I kept thinking about it, though. Did Dinah truly not care, or did she just like Milo enough to look past it?

If I had bad skin, *I* would care. Did that make me superficial?

If we were all blind, it would be a different story. And maybe blind people were less superficial for that very reason. Also, people in wheelchairs and people who were missing limbs, like that famous surfer girl who got her arm chomped off by a shark. That must have been so scary for her, though I read an article about her in *People*, and it seemed as if she'd gone on with her life just fine.

Sometimes I thought, *If I'm going to lose my arm—if it's written in the cards that it's going to happen one day—then let it happen now so that I can go ahead and start being self-actualized.*

But imagining losing an arm made it hard to breathe, especially on this beautiful hot day, on this clunky loaner bicycle, which I probably wouldn't be riding if I only had one arm. I was decent at riding one-handed for brief spurts of time, but not forever and ever, amen.

I sent the universe an amended message, closing my eyes just long enough for the words to go through. *Never mind!* I prayed. *Pay no attention to the superficial girl behind the curtain—she actually* does *want to keep both arms!*

"Win! Head's up!" Cinnamon called.

"Whoa," I said, opening my eyes and swerving to avoid the **Please Do Not Feed or Molest the Alligators** sign. The DeBordieu roads didn't have curbs, and I'd ridden off the pavement without realizing it.

"That sign's coming home with me, you know," Cinnamon said.

"That sign is private property," Dinah scolded.

"Yes, but it says *not to molest the alligators*," Cinnamon said. "That kills me."

"The alligators'll kill you if they see you stealing their sign," Dinah said.

"Wah, wah, wah," Cinnamon said good-naturedly. "Dinah, you worry too much about those gators."

"I worry just the right amount," Dinah retorted. "They will *eat* you, Cinnamon. They'll eat you quick as a wink if you give them the chance—just like they ate that poor man's dog."

Two days ago, an old guy let his Yorkie go sniffing around in the marsh, and the Yorkie never returned.

"The gators see dogs and cats as snacks," Virginia had said, shaking her head. "Renters are always learning that the hard way."

"Look, there's the gatehouse," Cinnamon said. "Race ya."

She took off at a clip. Neither Dinah nor I gave chase, choosing instead to watch her lean into the wind and pump.

"Yes!" she cried when she got there first. She thrust

her fist up high. "Whaddaya think of that, suckers?" She glanced around, breathing hard and gloating. When she realized she was alone, she put on her brakes, straddled her bike, and looked over her shoulder.

"Heyyyy!" she objected.

I smiled at Dinah. She smiled back.

"I do think Milo likes you," I told her. "You just have to get him alone so that he can act on it before it's too late."

"But what if he doesn't?" Dinah implored. "What if I give him all sorts of hints, and he still doesn't act on it?"

Hmm.

"Kiss him," I said impulsively. Last year, before Lars and I had our first kiss, Dinah and Cinnamon had teased me without mercy. "Do it!" they urged, and, "You *know* you want to." And from Cinnamon alone, "Just jump his bones, Winnie. Sheesh."

"Seriously, Dinah," I said. "Just, the next time you're alone, just grab his shoulders, lean in, and plant one on him."

"Winnie!" Dinah said, blushing like crazy and looking around to make sure Milo wasn't floating along behind us or hiding beneath a particularly large rock.

"Hurry up, you lazy-booties!" Cinnamon bellowed. "Put the pedal to the metal!"

"Hey, Cin, I need you to weigh in on something," I called. "I told Dinah she should—"

"Winnie!" Dinah squeaked.

"What?" I said.

There was panic in her eyes. "Don't you remember what

it was like before Lars kissed you? How nervous you were?"
She dropped her voice, because we were almost to the gatehouse. "Please don't give Cinnamon any ideas, because she'll
bring it up in front of Milo. You *know* she will."

I grimaced. She had a point.

"Didn't quite catch that," Cinnamon said as we coasted
up to her. "What do you want me to weigh in on?"

"Nothing," Dinah said quickly.

Cinnamon turned to me, raising her eyebrows.

"It was crazy talk," I said. "Don't worry about it."

"But I love crazy talk, and I am worrying about it," Cinnamon said. "Spill."

"Well, if you *really* want to know . . ."

"Winnie," Dinah begged.

"I do," Cinnamon said.

I swung my leg over the seat of my bike and hopped off.
"You can't be all *Cinnamon* about it. You have to be chill."

Cinnamon made the sign of the cross. "Swear to Bob."

"Who's Bob?"

"I dunno. But I swear on his name that I'll be chillier
than an icicle."

Dinah interrupted. "Shouldn't we get Virginia's package? She's probably wondering where we are."

"True," I said. I walked my bike into the shade, swung
off it, and put down the kickstand. "I'll get it."

"Whoa there, Sally," Cinnamon said, dismounting at
lightning speed and sidling in front of me. "Not until you
tell me what Dinah said."

"Cinnamon, you are so nosy." I twisted my arm, freeing myself and capturing her wrist in one smooth move. "All Dinah said was that she could beat you if she tried."

Cinnamon frowned.

"In a bike race. Actually, she said she could *easily* beat you, without even half trying, because you're a big weenie-butt. I think those were her exact words—right, Dinah?"

"Exsqueeze me?" Cinnamon said.

"Go, Dinah!" I cried. "While you've got a head start!"

Dinah *eek*-ed and leaped into action, taking awkward hitch-steps to turn her bike around.

Cinnamon struggled to get away from me.

"Hurry, Dinah!" I yelled, giggling. "I can't hold her much longer!"

The gatehouse door creaked open. "Girls?" said the guard. "Y'all got some sorta problem?"

"No, sir," I said as Cinnamon twisted her arm like a snake. "We're just here to pick up a package. For Virginia MacKinnon?"

"Oh, thas right," he said in his thick drawl. "Th'missus saved some chicken necks on account'a she knows how Virginny 'preesheeates 'em."

"I'm sorry . . . what?"

"Ah reckon they're for you kids. Hold on one second."

He shuffled back into the gatehouse.

"Did he say *chicken necks*?" I asked Cinnamon.

"Yep," Cinnamon said, wrenching free. She loped to her bike.

"Hey, wait—where are you going?"

She threw her leg over the frame. "See you back at the house, *sucka*! I've got a race to win!"

She pedaled hard, closing the distance between her and Dinah.

The security guard returned with a plastic grocery bag. A *dripping* plastic grocery bag, with lumpy things weighing down the bottom. The smell was awful. I wrinkled my nose.

"Stinks to high heaven, don't it?" the guard said. "Them necks've started to rot is why. Jes the way Virginny likes 'em."

He thrust out the bag. My stomach roiled, but I took it. A drop of . . . *something* sploshed onto the toe of my sneaker, making a dark spot.

The guard shielded his eyes and looked down the road. "What happened t'yer friends?"

Another drop of disgustingness dribbled from the bag.

"Well"—I checked his name tag—"*Earl*, they are bad, bad, bad-bad girls, and it appears that they have left."

Earl squinted at me. "Stuck you with all them chicken necks, dint they?"

"They sure dint," I said. I shook my head. "I mean *did*. They most surely and sadly did."

The chicken necks were for going crabbing, Virginny said. I mean, *Virginia*. She stored them overnight in a cooler, and then, the next day, hauled twine, stakes, nets, and a five-gallon bucket onto the deck and called everyone to join her. Cinnamon wasn't around—she'd gone swimming with James—and Alphonse and Erika were out checking cages, but the rest of us got comfy in the deck chairs and listened up.

"Tie the raw chicken to the string," she said. She lifted the string to show us. "Then tie the other end to a stake." She lifted a stake. "Then throw the baited end into the water and stick the stake in the ground. Then you wait. That's all there is to it."

"What do you mean?" Brooklyn asked. She chomped on a piece of gum.

"What do you mean, what do I mean?" Virginia said.

"You said, 'Then you wait.' For what?"

"Till you catch a crab," Virginia explained. "When you see a line go taut, you slowly pull it in and net the crab. And tonight, we eat them."

Brooklyn made a face. "Will they still have raw chicken in them?"

"I'm sorry?" Virginia said.

"If *they* eat the raw chicken, and then we eat *them* . . ."

"I wouldn't worry about it, Brooklyn," Virginia said.

"Can't raw chicken give you salmonella?" Dinah whispered to me.

"It's not just raw," I whispered back. "It's rotten. You should smell it."

Dinah blanched.

"Guys," Virginia said. She regarded us as if we were a

bunch of city slickers. "We'll cook the crabs. You won't get salmonella."

"We'd still be eating rotten chicken," Brooklyn pointed out. "Even if it's cooked."

"Stop worrying about the chicken," Virginia said. "If there's anything to worry about, it's the alligators—which, actually, you do need to keep an eye out for any time you go crabbing."

"Alligators?" Dinah repeated, her voice ratcheting up a notch.

"Bet they go for that raw meat," Ryan said.

"Duffenetly," Mark agreed. "Dem gators love dat stuff."

Ryan shoved him. "Oh, yeah? How would you know?"

Mark shoved him back. "How would *you*?"

Virginia smiled the smile of a preschool teacher trying to make her students stop whomping each other with blocks. "Alligators will occasionally come up on land if they smell the chicken. If they do, abandon your line and get away *fast*."

Dinah gawked, and her expression was so horrified that I had to laugh.

"Winnie, it's not funny!" she said, hitting me. "Has that ever really happened to you, Virginia?"

"Yeah, how big's the biggest one you ever saw?" Mark asked.

"The biggest alligator I've seen here at DeBordieu? Fifteen feet long, probably. It was just slowly crossing the road." Virginia turned to Dinah. "But the biggest one to ever come after my crab bait . . . oh, it couldn't have been more than eight feet at most."

"Is that supposed to be comforting?" Dinah said, her voice going high and squeaky.

Ryan and Mark cracked up, and I giggled, too. This was not to say that I wasn't equally petrified at the thought of a one-on-one with *any* size alligator, because I was.

Milo, however, locked eyes with Dinah from across the deck and sent his silent support. My laughter dried right up, that's how surprised I was. And delighted. And when Dinah smiled gratefully at him, I thought, *Awwwww!!!*

"It's rare that they'll come up on shore," Virginia said, not yet realizing that nothing she was going to say was going to calm Dinah down. Virginia and Dinah were constitutionally different, that's all there was to it. Raw chicken necks and living, breathing alligators were manageable within Virginia's practical view of the world, while Dinah's comfort zone pretty much ended at kittens.

"Usually you see their eyes coming, or their jaws snapping, and you get out of there," Virginia went on. "Then wait for the alligator to move away from your gear so you can return and pack up. At that point you might as well call it a day, because all the crabs'll be hiding, anyway."

"Uh-huh," Dinah said weakly.

Virginia gestured at the gear. "So, who's going to go get dinner?"

Brooklyn stood up and said, "I'll pass, thanks. I'm too

young to die." She strolled into the house. The screen door banged behind her.

"If we do the catching, does that mean someone else'll cook?" Ryan asked.

"Sure," Virginia said. "Anyone who goes crabbing is released from dinner detail *and* cleanup."

Ryan's hand was up before she'd finished. "Me! Pick me!"

"Dude," Mark said to Ryan. "You and me's got a date with Lia, or did you forget?" Lia was a young intern working with the park rangers, and he and Ryan thought she was the bomb. Only, they said *da bahm.*

"Oh *yeah*," Ryan said. "She's gonna take us to the point in her four-wheeler. Someone called in a dead turtle, and Lia needs a couple'a strong guys to haul it in for her."

"And Ryan's such a pal, he volunteered to go anyway," Mark said.

Ryan slapped Mark's head. "Oh-ho. Always the wisecracker, ain'cha?"

Virginia turned to Milo, Dinah, and me. "How about you three?"

"Uh . . ." I said, stalling. Crabbing sounded fun, despite the threat of alligators. But while the logical part of me knew there was no way on God's green earth that Dinah was going to volunteer, I had to let the situation play out *just in case.* Because if Milo said yes, and Dinah said yes . . . How fantabulously romantic would that be?!

Maybe Milo was thinking along those same lines,

because he gulped and said, "I'll give it a shot." His gaze flickered to Dinah, and I pinched Dinah's bare leg.

"Ow!" she said.

"I, um, need to take a nap," I said, my voice coming out louder than I intended. I abruptly stood up. "But you go, Dinah. Really."

She glared at me so hard that her eyeballs bulged.

"Okay, well, bye!" I said. "Bring home lots of crabs!"

Once in the kitchen, I pressed up against the wall and peeked out the window. Dinah was on her feet, and she was green in the gills, but Virginia was handing her the net—*and she was taking it.*

"Yes!" I cheered.

"You're weird," Brooklyn said, and I jumped. She was perched on one of the bar stools, lazily eating chips.

I opened my mouth, then closed it. I flashed her a smile. "Yeah," I said. "I know."

And Have It Come True
(my prediction, that is!!!!! squeee!!!!)

OFF THE GREEN STAIRWELL, between the first floor where the kitchen was and the second floor where the red and blue bedrooms were, was a screened-in porch with the most awesome hammock EVER.

It was a Pawleys Island Hammock, and it had been made in a hammock shop thirty miles up the coast. Its thick cotton cords were supercomfy, and there were wooden rods at each end that the ropes were looped through, and that kept the hammock all stretched out and lovely and meant that you didn't turn into a caterpillar in a cocoon the second you flopped into it. There was a yummy pillow to rest your head on; it was strapped in place, so it stayed exactly where it was supposed to. A "hammock-pull" dangled from a nearby hook; you could reach up, grab the knotted cord, and give a tug whenever you wanted the hammock to swing side to side. On the porch wall, Virginia had even thought to build in a small shelf, just the right size for a single glass of lemonade.

Cinnamon, Dinah, and I could all three fit on the hammock if we squished, which we often did. It was our favorite chill-out spot . . . well, other than the Crow's Nest and the L-shaped sofas in the main room and the window seat up in the den. (Okay, fine. The MacKinnon-Karrer house had many excellent chill-out spots.) But the hammock was a special favorite, and we'd come up with the brilliant idea that far far off in the future, when we got married, we'd give each other rope hammocks just like this one as wedding presents. We swore to it and everything.

The hammock was where I went after I spied on Dinah and Milo long enough to confirm that they had officially headed off on their crabbing adventure. I was worried Dinah would pull a last second wimp-out, but she didn't. She marched bravely forth, transferring the crabbing gear into the golf cart Virginia owned. (The golf cart was how we got around the island if Virginia wasn't available to drive us, and it was made of awesome. I'd lobbied to add "golf cart" to our personal BFF wedding registry, but the vote didn't go through. I blamed Dinah and Cinnamon.)

Anyway, the golf cart lived behind the house, and by crossing to the window at the back of the kitchen, I'd been able to look down on Dinah and Milo as they loaded up the lines, stakes, bait, and bucket. Then Dinah had climbed onto the small vinyl front seat beside Milo. She let him drive. The golf cart jumped forward when he pressed the accelerator, and she grabbed his arm for balance.

"Why are you so fascinated by your friend and that guy?" Brooklyn had asked, still eating her chips.

"I don't know," I replied, not taking the time to give a real answer. "I just am."

I watched until the golf cart was out of sight. Then I came up here, to the porch. I swayed on the hammock and let my thoughts float as they pleased.

They landed, eventually, on Lars.

I missed him—and yet, I didn't. I missed his touch, his easy grin, the way his hazel eyes darkened when we kissed. I missed lacing my fingers through his, and how our hands had learned over time to fit together just right, with his thumb folding over mine. Thinking about that gave me a physical pang, especially when held up against Cinnamon's and Dinah's tingly new-crush energy. New-crush energy was fun, very much so. But sharing a history with someone was even better . . .

. . . wasn't it?

What I missed most, I decided, was being *known* by Lars. Known in a way that mattered, and was real, and that twined through both of us. After all, the deeper the roots, the higher the reach, right? That's what it said on a framed poster that hung in the Starbucks I went to, back in Atlanta. The poster showed a tree with white flowers and red fruit and green leaves, and the branches were engraved with phrases like "a place for you and me" and "the promise of a glance."

I liked that poster, but I also knew it was cheesy—or at least that it was cheesy to see it in a Starbucks and have, like, an emotional response to it. How many Starbucks, scattered all over the world, displayed that exact piece of "art" over on the wall by the whole bean coffees?

Except couldn't cheesy quotes be both cheesy *and* true?

Yes.

Was it possible my thoughts had flown to that poster not because of its content, but because of a less pleasant association?

Well, maybe. It was possible, *I suppose.*

And did it go back to my birthday, and Lars's gift to me, and the awful possibility that Lars didn't know me as well as I thought?

Um. No comment.

And that was why I missed him in such an aching way, because the ache stemmed from more than being physically apart.

In fact, the ache might not go away even if Lars were right here next to me. Even if I could snap my fingers and make Lars miraculously appear, there was a chance—a strong chance—I would *still* feel lonely . . . which was incredibly depressing to consider.

Because I wanted to be known, but wasn't. Not in a way that mattered, and was real, and that twined through both of us.

I groaned, and not two feet away, someone said, "*Now* what?"

I bolted upright, making the hammock rock herky-jerkily. "Brooklyn!" I cried when I saw who it was. "Holy *crap*, you gave me a heart attack!"

She regarded me impassively from the director's chair where she sat.

"How long have you been there?" I demanded. I felt caught out, and I wanted to blame someone—mainly *her*. "And . . . where are your chips?"

She rubbed the bit of skin between her eye and the bridge of her nose, her expression indicating that my "where are your chips?" accusation sounded as pathetic to her as it did to me.

"You grunted," Brooklyn stated. "Why?"

None of your beeswax, I considered responding. *And it wasn't a grunt. It was a groan.*

But I changed my mind. Maybe it was the feeling of being weightless. Maybe it was the odd freedom of knowing that Brooklyn and I were still basically strangers, and that after another week, we would probably never cross paths again. She didn't know Lars and wasn't ever going to meet him. So what the heck?

"It's my boyfriend," I confessed. "We're having . . . problems."

"He's stepping out on you?" Brooklyn said.

"What? No."

"You stepping out on him?"

"Are you kidding?" What a crazy thing to even consider. We were talking about *me* here. Winnie Perry. I wasn't a stepping-out sort of girl. Anyway, who would I step out *with*?

I snuck a glance at her. Did she think there was someone I might conceivably be stepping out with? Not that I used that expression in normal life. At Westminster, kids said "cheating on." As in, Bryce cheated on Cinnamon. Like that.

"So you're not," Brooklyn said.

"Brooklyn, do I look like the kind of girl who would step out on her guy?"

Okay, that sounded really weird, my brain said to me. It was as if I were street-talking for Brooklyn's benefit—and no doubt doing it wrong.

Brooklyn, who was wearing another of her tube tops—today's was hot pink—rolled her eyes.

"What?" I said.

"I've seen you and you-know-who," she said. "I've seen the looks he gives you."

I was mortified by my suddenly racing pulse, but I did *not* let my voice shake—I think—when I said, "I have no idea who you're talking about."

She arched her eyebrows.

"No, seriously. Who are you talking about?"

She pushed herself up from the director's chair as if I were too wearisome to waste her time with.

I should have been glad she was dropping it. Instead I said, "Wait. You don't mean *Alphonse*, do you?" I even pushed out a laugh.

"Hot black guy with the dreads?" she said sarcastically. "The one you take those early morning walks with? *Yeah*, him."

This demanded further discussion.

"Sit," I said, gesturing like a dog trainer. Not that she was a dog. Nonetheless, she sat, and I wiggled into a wobbly cross-legged position on the hammock.

"Do you think *I* have cheating thoughts toward *him*?" I said, trying my best to ignore the tidal wave of embarrassment swelling within me. "Or that *he* has cheating thoughts toward *me*?"

"I think you both have cheating thoughts toward each other," she said, like *duh*.

"Really?" I said eagerly. I tried again. This time, I went for casual skepticism. "I mean . . . *really*?"

The look she gave me told me clearly that she considered me an idiot.

I needed to get off the subject of Alphonse and back to Lars. Lars, Lars, Lars, who was my guy, but who didn't always show it in the right way.

"Forget that," I said. "Just forget that entirely. The thing is, my boyfriend gave me a *gift certificate* for my birthday."

"Yeah? From where?" Brooklyn asked.

From *where*? I told her my boyfriend gave me a gift certificate for my birthday, and she wanted to know *from where*?

"Starbucks," I said. "But that's irrelevant."

"How much?"

"Well . . . twenty-five dollars."

"Sweet."

"*No*, not 'sweet.'" I flapped my hands impatiently. "A Starbucks card for your girlfriend's birthday? C'mon, that's a crap present and you know it."

"You don't want it? Give it to me."

"Ha ha. I already spent it."

She cocked her head. Her expression made my cheeks grow hot.

"Oh, shut up," I muttered.

"Listen," she said. "You want to know what my boyfriend gave me for my birthday? My *ex*-boyfriend, that is?"

Heck yeah, I did. I hoped it was so craptastic that it would make my Starbucks gift card look like a princess tiara. Like, if her ex gave her a mud flap with Yosemite Sam on it, then of course she'd see a Starbucks card as an acceptable gift. If her ex gave her a Yosemite Sam mud flap—a *mud flap*, when she wasn't even old enough to have her driver's license!—then I could stop feeling judged by her and get back to feeling sorry for myself.

"Sure," I said. "Hit me with it."

"A note scrawled on a Post-it. A breakup note, saying he was too young"—she brought out the quote fingers—"'to be saddled with such heavy crap.'"

"What heavy crap?" I said.

She twisted the corner of her mouth. "Darryl's a loser. My kid brother—Lucas—he's got CP. I take care of him a lot, that's all."

"CP, like . . . cerebral palsy?"

"Yeah. And my mom, she works the night shift at the Black-eyed Pea, so . . ." She lifted her fingers from the arm of her chair, then let them flutter back down. "Whatever. Like I said, Darryl's a loser."

Um, no, I'm *the loser,* I thought. I didn't know tons about cerebral palsy, but I'd seen kids who probably had CP. They were bound to wheelchairs, their hands curling in on themselves and their heads drooping on the fragile stems of their necks.

"I'm sorry," I said awkwardly.

She grew fierce. "Hey. Lucas is worth ten Darryls. Ten *hundred* Darryls. No, forget that—Darryl can fall off the planet, and no one would even care, least of all me. But Lucas?" Her mouth did something funny: not a tremble, not a scowl, but a tightening that was defiant and proud and . . . *adult.*

"Lucas is special," she said, jabbing her finger at me. The sparkly pink polish on her nail was chipped.

I nodded, choosing to believe her. Maybe needing to believe her.

She was so tiny. And she wore tube tops. Her pale tummy poofed out above the waist of her shorts, and she cared for her disabled kid brother while her mom worked at a chain restaurant that served, if I was remembering the right commercial, fried pickles and "cheese crunchers."

Brooklyn leaned forward and dug a slim plastic wallet from her back pocket. She was a lot more friendly now that we weren't talking about me. "Wanna see his picture?" She flipped open her wallet and held it out. "I take him to the portrait studio every three months. I have a punch card."

The photo showed a toddler—Lucas—standing in a

walker equipped with four wheels, a harness, and handgrips. Except he wasn't exactly standing. More like *leaning*, in a skewed-hip, propped-up sort of way. He was grinning, and his head tilted at an odd angle over his shoulder. Across the bottom of the picture was the word KMART in gold gilt lettering.

"He's adorable," I said. I ran numbers in my head, reviewing what I'd learned from Mom's baby books. "Is he . . . two?"

"Two-and-a-half," Brooklyn said.

"Is he, um, able to walk?" I said, struggling to sound as normal as I could. *Keepin' it real*, said a voice in my brain, but luckily, I managed to suppress it.

"Near enough." She looked at me sharply, like, *You gonna make something out of it?*

I handed the picture back to her. "I have a three-month-old sister," I told her. "Her name's Magnolia Grace."

"Aw, I like that," Brooklyn said. "Bet she's started laughing by now, huh? At three months, that's when you can make them laugh for real, not those fake gassy laughs."

I nodded, seeing baby Maggie in my mind. Her laughs were sweeter than gumdrops.

"You miss her?" Brooklyn asked.

"For sure," I said. I hesitated. "Do you miss Lucas? Who's taking care of him while you're here?" Then I realized how untactful that was and said, "Never mind."

"He's with my grammy," Brooklyn said. She turned

away, pretending to look out the window. "I'll see him in a week. No big."

I felt sad for her. I also felt uncomfortable, because not in a million years could I imagine *being* her. Having her life. Having baby Mags, or Ty, be disabled and strapped in a walker. I saw her tube top in a new light, like a flag waved bravely in the face of adversity.

"What made you decide to come to DeBordieu?" I asked. "Since it meant leaving Lucas, I mean."

"My grammy wanted me to just be a teenager for a month," she said, her voice barely there.

To lighten the mood, I said, "Well, sure makes my problems seem stupid, doesn't it?"

"Pretty much." She swiveled her head to regard me. "Does your boyfriend know you didn't like the gift card?"

"Um . . ."

"What'd you want him to give you? Jewelry? Perfume?"

"What? *No.*" I was *so* not a stupid girly-girl pouting because I didn't get a necklace with a chubby gold heart on it.

"Then what?" she pressed.

I scrubbed my face with my hand, then let my hand drop. "If you *have* to know," I said. "I wanted a cupcake, all right?"

"A cupcake?"

"A cupcake."

"A *cup*cake?"

"Yes, a cupcake! Can we move on?"

"Well, did you *tell* him you wanted a cupcake?" she asked. "Because he's not a mind reader, I'm guessing. Unless he works as a psychic in a carnival tent and you forgot to mention it."

I rolled my eyes. "No, he's not a mind reader."

"So what's the problem? Are you one of those shriveled violets who can't stand up for herself?"

I suspected she meant *shrinking* violet, and *please*, how ridiculous. "I think you have me confused with Dinah," I said.

"Dinah?" Brooklyn repeated. "Who right this minute's wrestling alligators in the swamp?"

I tried to laugh, but the laugh didn't even make it half-way out.

"And here you are, afraid to tell your boyfriend you want a cupcake." She pressed her hands against her pale thighs, flexing her wrists and bending her elbows in a way elbows weren't meant to be bent.

"Whoa," I said. "Are you double-jointed?"

She shook out her limbs and rotated her wrists, not bothering to answer.

"Listen," I said. "*You* didn't go crabbing, either. You said you were too young to die."

"Free piece of advice," she said. She stood and tugged at her tube top, which had ridden up. "You only live once."

"Gee, really?"

"Don't waste it being stupid." She fluffed her bangs and strode from the room.

Virginia found me later. I was this close to drowsing off when she jostled the hammock and said, "Dinner duty or cleanup—what's your poison?"

"Huh?" I said, blinking up at her.

"Dinah and Milo are going to be back with the crabs soon. Do you want to cook or clean up?"

"Oh," I said. "Cook. Only, I don't know how to cook crabs."

"Easiest thing in the world," Virginia said. "Clean the muck off them, fill a pot with boiling water—it's got to be boiling—and plop 'em in. Add the Old Bay, and you're done."

"What's Old Bay?"

"Seasoning. I'll put a bag on the counter. Maybe corn on the cob and salad to go with it?"

A *bang* sounded from the front of the house. A glance out the porch window told me it was Cinnamon and James returning from the beach.

"And tell those guys they're in charge of cleaning up," Virginia said.

I swiveled my legs off the hammock, slid my feet to the floor, and sat up. I yawned. "Okay, sure."

"Great," Virginia said. "I'm off to the aquarium, but I'll be back in an hour."

I nodded.

"Just be sure the water's *boiling* before you put in the crabs, got it?"

"What would happen if the water wasn't boiling? And wait—the crabs'll be dead by the time I get them, right?"

"Dead? No, they die when they hit the water."

Oh. I hadn't thought about the mechanics of it until now. Without thinking, I put my hand to my stomach. "Do they . . . feel it?"

"I hope not, but I suppose it's possible. You do have another option. You could stab an ice pick behind their eyes."

I found that option horrifying, and I suspect my expression showed it.

"Handle it as you choose," Virginia said. "I'm off."

I handled it by switching jobs. That's what I chose to do.

"You and James are supposed to cook dinner," I told Cinnamon after hunting her down in the kitchen. She was freshly scrubbed and slightly pink from her afternoon in the sun. Out in the driveway, a low hum and the clunk of gravel announced that Dinah and Milo had arrived.

"Great," Cinnamon said unenthusiastically. She sighed in resignation, then bellowed, "Ja-a-ames!"

"I'm right here," he said, behind her.

"Oops," she said, giggling. "Hey, we have to cook dinner."

"So I heard." He twined his fingers through hers, pulled her closer, and lightly kissed her lips. She giggled some more.

It was hard seeing Cinnamon be so lovey-dovey. She

wasn't doing anything wrong; I just felt twisty because of what was going on with Lars.

"You have to boil the crabs," I told them. "You have to make sure the water is actually boiling when you drop them in."

Cinnamon wrapped her arms around James's neck, touching her nose to his. "Won't that hurt them?"

"I hope not," I said. "Your other choice is to stab them with an ice pick."

"Winnie, gross."

Dinah and Milo entered the house through the basement.

"We have cra-abs!" Dinah called.

"TMI!" Cinnamon called back. James cracked up, and I would have, too, except I wasn't in the mood.

Dinah tromped up the stairs and plonked a five-gallon bucket on the counter. It was full to the top.

"Look how many!" she bragged.

"Dinah, that's awesome," I said. "Was it fun?"

"*So* fun," she said. She brushed past me on the way to the sink and whispered, "I kissed him!"

"What?! Dinah, omi*gosh*!"

She turned on the faucet. *"Shhh!"*

"We're not going to boil them *alive*," Cinnamon pronounced, still gazing at James.

"You have to. Virginia said." Milo came in looking v*ery* happy and *very* proud, and I cruised by the sink. To Dinah, I whispered, "For real? You kissed him?"

She leaned closer, eyes shining. "Actually, *he* kissed *me*!"

I'd *known* this was going to happen. I'd known it from the very first day we got here—and *omigosh*, it really had! I was happy for Dinah—I *was*—but I felt a prick in my heart, too. I covered my feelings with a smile.

"Nice haul," James said to Milo. "You guys have fun?"

Milo's eyes flew to Dinah. "We saw an alligator," he said.

"But Milo threw a rock at it," she said proudly. "It hit him smack on his snout, and he ran off."

"Dude," James said.

"Ah-ha, I know," Cinnamon said. "We'll put them in cold water, then gradually heat the water up. Don't you think that would be better, Dinah?"

"Uh-huh," she said. She wasn't listening.

Cinnamon addressed the room in general. "Like how you get in the tub, and you *think* the water's hot, but really you can stand it so much hotter. You just have to get used to it first."

"But that doesn't apply to scalding yourself," I said. "If you heated the bathwater to boiling, you would feel it."

"Not necessarily," Cinnamon argued.

Dinah shut off the faucet and turned around. Across the room, Milo swallowed.

"Should we, uh, go unload the rest of the stuff?" he said.

"Okay," she agreed. They clattered joyfully back down the stairs.

Cinnamon broke free from James and strode to the bucket of crabs. "Hey, sweet little crabbies," she cooed. "Time for your bathie-wathie, crabbies."

"Cinnamon . . ."

"What?!" she snapped. *"God,* Winnie."

All I wanted was to tell her that it really did matter, the boiling water part. But her tone, and the exasperated way she was looking at me . . .

It made me mad, and tight, and because of those bad feelings, I said, "Fine. Nothing."

James slipped his arms around her from behind and rested his chin on top of her head.

"You can leave," Cinnamon informed me.

"Oh, can I?" I said.

"Yes," she said. "We'll call you when it's time."

Fifteen minutes later, she did exactly that. I was already on my way back to the kitchen when I heard her, because my conscience, which had been wrestling with my grumpiness ever since I left, had finally come out on top. I couldn't let Cinnamon hurt those crabs. I might be pissed at *her*, but I couldn't take it out on the poor, innocent crabs.

From the middle of the staircase, I heard, *"Ahhhhh! Help, help! OMIGOD THEY'RE CLIMBING OUT OF THE POT!!!"*

I rushed the rest of the way. The crabs were scrabbling up and over the top of the pot, while Cinnamon, who was up on her toes, flapped her hands and shrieked as James lunged about, trying to catch the crabs. The water in the pot was lightly steaming, and as the last crab flung itself to freedom—*forgive me!*— I pressed my hands to my mouth to smother a laugh.

"Omigosh," I managed to say. "You were supposed to *boil* the water first, remember?"

One crab click-clacked across the floor and over Cinnamon's bare foot. She screamed.

James scooped up a crab on a mad dash for the living room. Its legs flailed. "Cinnamon, bring me the bucket!" he said.

"Winnie, bring him the bucket!" she screeched.

But I couldn't. The crabs were too scuttle-y and gross, and plus, I was laughing too hard. I had never in my life seen Cinnamon reduced to a girly-girl screecher.

"Run, little crabs!" I said. "Run for your lives!"

"Get it off me, get-it-off-me, *getitoffme*!" Cinnamon squealed, hopping around like a crazed booly-booly dancer. Swinging from her cutoffs, its crusher claw affixed to the frayed denim, was a humongous crab. Its hard shell was grayish-green; it had way more legs than seemed necessary; and horrible thin antennae protruded from his head, with nubblets that were possibly eyeballs bobbing from the tips.

I sank helplessly to the floor—then sprang right back up

as a stampede of crabs made a break for it less than a foot away.

"James!" Cinnamon wailed. When she moved, the crab on her cutoffs swung back and forth. I thought of my grandmother's curtains, brown and orange with pom-pom balls dangling from the trim.

"He likes you!" I said through mad laughter. "You are his savior!"

"Get it *off*!" she said. "It's yucky!"

"Did you know that once a crab imprints on you, he follows you everywhere?"

The crab must have heard me, because he floundered his crusty legs, scrambling for purchase on her smooth thigh.

"I'm going to faint," she said, and if James hadn't dashed to catch her, she might have. From her prone position on the floor, the crabs would have borne her away, lifting her high and proclaiming her Queen of Crustaceans.

I went to her and shook the leg of her shorts, dislodging the monster crab. I jumped back as it hit the ground. Cinnamon looked at me greenly.

"Remember the very first day we were here, when you hid under my bed?" I said. I was making this up, this cobbled-together motivation that hid the uglier truth of my jealousy. But the crabs were safe, and I felt better . . . and Cinnamon *did* have it coming to her.

"And you jumped out and said 'boo,'?" I shook my head. "I almost *died*, that's how scared I was."

"I didn't say 'boo,' and you didn't almost die."

"Well, now we're even."

Dinner was delicious, consisting of corn, salad, and buttered slices of bread. Virginia also put a jar of peanut butter in the middle of the table.

"I can't believe you boiled the corn alive," I said to Cinnamon as I took a warm, salty bite. *Mmm*, I loved corn on the cob.

Ryan guffawed. "And think of all the wheat you murdered to make the bread."

"Ha ha," Cinnamon said. "The bread is store-bought, doofus."

"Ah, but you condoned it," I said. "Every time you eat a piece of bread, you're saying it's all right to chop down those poor stalks of wheat and . . . husk them or whatever." I had no idea what you did with wheat, really, to turn it into bread. I crunched off another bite of corn.

"You guys are, too, then," Cinnamon said. She nodded to include the table at large. "Every single one of you who has bread is condoning the murder of innocent grains of wheat."

"I, for one, am glad you let the crabs go," Dinah said. She sat next to Milo, and I could almost swear their knees were pressing up together beneath the table. "Even though I'm the one who caught them—"

"Yes, Dinah," we all chorused. We'd heard many times the story of how she'd braved the alligator-infested marsh.

"Well, *Milo* and I," she self-corrected, giving Milo a dreamy look.

"Yes, Dinah," we chorused.

Milo's acne-scarred skin turned redder than usual. Dinah sighed happily. "Even though Milo and I are the ones who caught the crabs—all twenty-five of them, did I mention that? Twenty-five crabs?"

"Yes, Dinah!" we caroled.

"And Milo!" I added.

Dinah smiled. "I was just going to say that even though we caught the crabs, I, personally, am glad you didn't kill them, Cinnamon."

Cinnamon gave a slight bow. *"Thank* you."

"I agree," said tube-top Brooklyn. "It's mean. Some of them probably have babies to take care of."

"Aw, *geez,*" Mark scoffed. "Babies? Who cares about crab *babies*?"

"Anyone with a heart," I responded. Later, I would catch Cinnamon and Dinah up on all I'd found out about Brooklyn. For now, I wadded up a piece of bread and lobbed it at Mark. I caught Brooklyn's eye, and she hesitated, then shot me a smile.

"You shouldn't eat an animal you've met," Dinah said.

"A crab isn't an animal," Ryan said. "It's a crustacean."

"But it's okay to eat an animal you haven't met?" Alphonse pressed. "Like a McDonald's hamburger?"

"A McDonald's hamburger isn't an animal, either," Ryan said. Mark joined in for the follow-up: "It's a McDonald's hamburger." Cracking up, the two of them slapped palms.

Lifting her chin, Dinah said, "Actually, I'm considering becoming a vegetarian."

"You go, girl," I said, gesturing with my corn. I didn't believe her—she liked Chick-fil-A too much to go to such an extreme—but I gave her points for saying something, *any*thing, to Alphonse, who had a knack for winning most arguments he took on.

I mulled over Dinah's new feistiness, wondering if somewhere in the world, a previously self-assured girl had suddenly lost her spunk. I was thinking about the whole yin-yang concept, I suppose. Like a quote I'd once seen: "For every well-balanced person in the world, there is an equal and opposite person with a huge fanny." (Now *there* was an excellent Starbucks quote for you. It was just begging to be made into inspirational framed art.)

You're avoiding the question, my brain broke in.

Oh, plop. I was. Because when it came down to the nitty-gritty, maybe what I was really wondering was this: If Dinah was no longer the shriveled violet of our group, where did that leave me?

Don't Die

GOOD-BYES WERE NEVER FUN, and I knew saying good-bye
to my DeBordieu buds was going to be especially hard.
When Brooklyn decided to leave early, I got to do a trial run,
kinda. I was sad to see her go, but glad for her, since it was
what she wanted.

When her mom arrived to pick her up, we all walked
outside with her. She tossed her bag into the trunk of her
mom's beat-up car, and then she leaned halfway into the
backseat and emerged with her little brother, Lucas. Her
face was lit up. She looked happier than I'd ever seen.

"This is Alphonse," she told Lucas, "and this is Mark,
and this is Ryan."

Ryan let out a low whistle. "Her brother's handicapped,
huh?"

I stepped backward onto his toe.

"Ow!" he said.

Brooklyn made the rounds, lifting Lucas's wrist and
making him wave at all of us. When she got to me, my heart
seized. I reached out and touched his chubby foot.

"Hey, big guy," I said, suddenly and desperately missing
teensy baby Maggie.

Brooklyn shifted Lucas to her other hip with practiced ease. "All right, well . . . bye," she said to all of us.

"Bye," we said back.

"We'll miss you," Virginia said.

Brooklyn opened her mouth like she was going to say something. Then she changed her mind. She climbed into the backseat, got Lucas strapped in, and fastened her seat belt beside him.

"Bye!" I called as Brooklyn's mom drove away. "Bye-eee!"

It was the beginning of the end. It made my stomach knot up.

"Only four more days till the rest of us have to go, too," Cinnamon wailed that evening, falling backward onto her rainbow-quilted bed and gazing tragically at the sloped ceiling. "What am I going to do? I'm going to miss James *so much*!"

"What about me?" Dinah cried. "You've at least had a boyfriend before, but—"

"Bryce does *not* count as a boyfriend," Cinnamon interjected.

"Yes, he does," I said. "You kissed him in the cloakroom at Becca's Bat Mitzvah."

"I'm erasing him from my mind," Cinnamon proclaimed. She swiped her hand above her in the air. "*Swoop.* Gone. And why? Because nobody can hold a candle to James." She groan-moaned. "What am I going to *do*?!"

Dinah, realizing she wasn't going to get much of anything from Cinnamon, turned to me. "Winnie, I don't know how you do it. Don't you miss Lars so much?"

I winced, kind of, and slightly raised my shoulders. It could have been interpreted any number of ways.

"You're so brave," Dinah said. She looked at me but didn't see me. "You're just. So. *Brave*."

Another moan came from Cinnamon's prone form. Next, she would probably rend her garments and gird herself with sackcloth—*if* she could hunt down any sackcloth.

On Wednesday, Cinnamon moped ghoulishly down the halls. I trailed behind her, because it was entertaining in a macabre sort of way.

"Three more days," she intoned, sticking her head into Ryan and Mark's bedroom.

She found Erika in the den, reading a paperback on the window seat.

"Three more days," Cinnamon informed her.

"I know," Erika said. "Go away."

On Thursday: *"Two more daaaaays."*

On Friday, with feeling, and as if she were trapped in a drainpipe: *"Only one mooooore daaaaaay!"*

"You are going to drive me to an early grave!" I told her, grabbing her by the shoulders and shaking her. "Stop focusing on the bad part! Enjoy the good!"

"Like me and James having to do the long-distance

thing?" she said. "Like having to go back to sucky Atlanta, city of suckville, land of no James?"

It was predawn. We were standing in the stairwell. I was about to head out for my last-ever early morning crawl patrol, since tomorrow our parents were coming to pick us up. Tomorrow morning was earmarked for packing and taking the sheets off our beds and stuff like that.

Cinnamon shouldn't have even been awake . . . except, she'd never gone to bed. She and James had cuddled on the living room's L-shaped sofas *all night long.*

"We didn't *do* anything," she'd told me when we ran into each other in the stairwell. "We just snuggled. And talked." She'd looked at me plaintively. "I can talk to him about anything, Winnie."

"You can talk to me about anything," I replied.

"It's different when it's your boyfriend," she said. "*You* know."

I did know. Girl buds were essential. Girl buds made the world go 'round. But boyfriends *were* different. It wasn't that they were better, because I loved Cinnamon and Dinah with all my heart.

A boyfriend, however, didn't borrow your hairbrush; he stroked your hair instead. And a boyfriend didn't stick his hand in your face and say, "Paint my nails." He wove his fingers through yours and gazed at you in that melt-y way.

Except Lars hadn't gazed at me in that melt-y way in weeks. That was because we'd been apart, of course . . . only, he hadn't talked to me on the phone in that melt-y way in a while, either. Things had been weird. One way I knew they were weird was because I *did* miss him, but not so desperately that I couldn't wait to see him.

When we did finally see each other, what if things weren't good anymore? What if we weren't *us*?

You're laying here feeling sorry for yourself, afraid to tell your boyfriend you want a cupcake. That's what Brooklyn said that day on the porch. And yes, she used poor grammar—if she went to Westminster, she'd know that a person "lies"; a chicken "lays"—but that didn't mean she wasn't onto something.

A person lies . . . was I lying to myself about boys and sadness and snuggling and Lars?

A chicken lays . . . was I a chicken for not just talking to him about it? For being too wimpy to lay my stupid issues out in the open?

Omigod, I was both.

Crap.

I was a lying chicken.

I shook my head to clear it. My hands were still gripping Cinnamon's shoulders, and she was just . . . letting them. Letting *me*, as my hands were not some separate entity, gallivanting off and gripping things of their own volition.

She was one step below me, so I shuffled clockwise one-hundred-and-eighty degrees. Now she stood where I used to be, and vice-versa.

"Go to bed," I instructed, pushing her toward our attic room. "You need sleep, or you will have horrible purple circles under your eyes, and James will think you're ugly."

"No, he won't."

"You're right. He won't."

"He thinks I'm beautiful. He said so. He calls me his beautiful Cinnabuns."

Cinnabuns? Awww. My heart grew heavy with the sweet-goofiness of it, like the sweet-goofiness I once had with Lars.

"You *are* beautiful," I said. "But if you don't get at least a little rest, you'll be worthless at the bonfire."

At sunset, we were all going to meet on the beach. We'd cook hot dogs and marshmallows and foil-wrapped packets of corn and potatoes, though not necessarily in that order. We'd have to put out the fire once it got dark, because of DeBordieu's beachfront lighting ordinance, but there'd be plenty of Mountain Dew to keep everyone going. I had a feeling the party would last late into the night.

Cinnamon swayed. Weariness was kicking in; she had to struggle to keep her eyelids in their open and upright position.

"But it's our last full day," she said. "I don't want to miss any of it."

"It's going to be okay, I promise." A cloud of melancholy settled over me. *"Go."*

Alphonse and I didn't speak as we patrolled the dunes. Moisture hung in the silvery air; I could smell the salt and the brine as I breathed. I wanted this scent to cling to me forever. I wanted it to stay in my hair and soak into my clothes, strong enough to overpower Mom's dryer sheets once I got back home. I wanted to bottle it up and use it as a body lotion. I would smear it all over me and be a mermaid, only with strong, tan legs.

I must have sighed, because Alphonse turned and looked at me, a question in his eyes.

I gave him a half-smile and shook my head. *It's nothing.*

He nodded. *Okay. (If you say so.)*

I clasped my hands behind my back, kicking the sand as we strolled along. A breeze whispered over my skin. I loved the way it lifted my hair and kept it aloft. Strands would touch down, tickling my upper back, and then they'd flutter up again.

People all through time have felt the wind in their hair, I thought. *I am one of them . . . and here I am, right now, walking along the shore. This will always be part of me, even after I leave.*

And then Alphonse's fingers were on my arm, on the bare skin of my upper arm, and the pressure he exerted said, *Be still. Be quiet.* We already were being quiet, but the sudden tension of his body language told me to *stay* quiet and not blurt, "What? What's going on?"

I straightened my spine as I, too, went on high alert. My arms fell to my sides, and Alphonse took my hand. *Whoa, holy pickle crap, Alphonse was holding my hand. Alphonse was holding my hand?!*

His grip was strong. His skin was warm. My hand felt small in his, just as it did when Lars was the one on the other end of the hand-holding. These thoughts flared in my mind—the spurt of flame as a match is struck—and would have been extinguished, *should* have been extinguished, except Alphonse didn't let go. He stepped closer so that we were side by side, our shoulders touching. He stared intently at a scraggly scrub bush.

"Do you see?" he whispered.

"See what?" I could feel the heat of his body, and it made it hard to focus.

He pointed, his muscled brown arm extending straight and true across the line of my vision. Only his arm wasn't what I was supposed to be looking at! I was supposed to look *past* his arm, *past* his pointing finger, to whatever he was pointing *at*.

Get it together, Winnie! I told myself.

I pulled my hand free of his, hugged my ribs, and tucked my fists in tight by my sides. *Then* I looked where he was pointing.

"Oh," I said. My breath whooshed out of me. I swallowed, got some of it back, and said it again: *"Oh."*

I moved silently over the packed sand. He followed. Inside my chest was a balloon, but not a human-made one with its yucky rubber smell. The feeling expanding inside me was awe and amazement and fragile, fearful hope for tiny creatures so new to the world.

There were zillions of them streaming from the nest.

They climbed over broken eggshells. They used their brothers and sisters as stepping stools. Dozens were at the water's edge; dozens more were close behind. And probably lots of them were already in the water, taking their first swimmy, splashy strokes (and hopefully not being gobbled up by sharks).

"Do you know how rare this is?" Alphonse said. "To see a clutch of eggs hatch?"

I didn't know the scientific probability of it, no. I didn't need to. All I needed to know was that each baby turtle was the size of my thumb, with adorable flippers and an intricately patterned shell, and that we were witnessing something sacred. Knowing this had nothing to do with textbooks or research. It came simply from being graced with a soul.

The baby turtles headed from the nest to the sea in a stumbling, tumbling flow. A turtle highway. One little guy—or gal—fell headfirst into the sand and got trampled by the next couple of turtles to come along. Its flippers got buried, and it couldn't undig itself.

"Ohhh," I said, moving to help it.

Alphonse put his hand on my arm for the second time. "You can't. They have to get to the water by themselves."

"But what if they can't?"

"They have to," he said. "That's how they build up their strength to swim."

I didn't argue, and I didn't help the stranded turtle. But in my head, the question didn't go away: *What if they can't?*

Alphonse gestured with his chin. "Look. He's okay."

Sure enough, he'd freed his front flippers and was pulling himself from the small hole. He flapped his back flippers, giving a funny wiggle to shake the sand off, and my ribs loosened.

"They remind me of the baby spiders in *Charlotte's Web*," I said softly. "When they came pouring out of Charlotte's egg sac." I glanced at Alphonse. "Did you see that movie?"

"I read the *book*," he said, his tone indicating how much better he was than me. Alphonse was gorgeous, and for the most part he was pretty cool. But sometimes he acted like he was better than everybody else.

Maybe he realized it, because he added, sheepishly, "*And* I saw the movie. The original animated version, not the ridiculous Dakota Fanning one."

"It wasn't ridiculous," I said. I'd seen it with Ty, and I'd cried at the ending. "The original was better, though."

"Well, of course," Alphonse said.

This time, as I rolled my eyes, I laughed. Not loud enough to startle the turtles, but enough to make Alphonse frown. I didn't care. He needed to know how superior he sounded.

We watched the hatchlings. They were so tiny and perfect. I knew, intellectually, that some would get snatched by hungry seagulls or eaten by prowling fish. The weakest of the turtles might not even make it out of the nest. All of that would happen whether I wanted it to or not; my wishes had absolutely nothing to do with it.

But some of them would make it. They would paddle into the sea, and grow big and strong, and one day—if they were girl turtles—they'd come back to this very beach and lay their own eggs. They could live, if they were fortunate, to be *a hundred years old*. Some of the itsy-bitsy turtles waddling so determinedly through the sand could outlive me.

"Should we go to the house and get the others?" I asked. I didn't want to leave, but I didn't want to be selfish. They should get to see, too.

"It would take too long," Alphonse said. "The nest is almost empty."

He was right. The baby turtles had been at it all night, waking up brand-new to the world. It was so amazing—and not just the turtles, but *all* of the incredible events that took place *every single day*. Every single minute. Every single second.

And me? I was one girl, contained inside this one body, soaking up as much of the world as I could . . . which, based on how huge the world was, was practically nothing.

It didn't make me feel small, though.

It made me feel grateful—and also as if I needed to *evolve*, kinda. Life was too short to get hung up on the stupid stuff. I sat down, taking care to disturb as little sand as possible. Alphonse followed suit. He leaned back on his elbows, which put his forearms within inches of me, and which might or might not have been intentional. Energy hummed between us, and I accepted the fact that this was how it was going to be. Whatever it was we shared . . . there it was. It wasn't going away.

I *had* to call Lars, and I had to do it now. Or at least now-ish. Yes, I'd see him in the flesh tomorrow (if it wasn't too late after our six-hour drive back to Atlanta) and if I didn't see him tomorrow, I'd see him for sure on Sunday. I *could* wait and talk to him in person.

But though part of me wanted to wait, I sensed that my desire to put it off was a big fat red flag telling me I shouldn't. I needed to step up, or man up, or girl up, whatever.

I needed to call Lars.

While Dinah and Cinnamon and the others ate breakfast, I situated myself cross-legged on my bed and held my iPhone in my lap. I looked at it. I pushed the button to wake up the screen; I slid the SLIDE TO UNLOCK arrow. I went to FAVORITES and gazed at Lars's name just sitting there, looking so familiar. But I didn't put the call through. Not yet. Instead, I pulled up the picture I'd put on his contact page.

I'd taken it at my house, one night when he'd come over to watch a movie. Only we never got around to watching it, even though it was a total "guy" movie that he'd picked and brought over, and which promised all sorts of car chases and CIA stuff and people getting shot at. But we got to talking, and it was such a good conversation that we just kept *on* talking, even when I said, "Um, if we're going to watch the movie, we better start it *now*."

"We can watch it another night," he'd said. "I mean . . . if that's cool with you?"

He'd given me such tender glance that my heart swelled, and I thought, *Oh, you dear boy.*

And then, because I was a spaz, I got all jittery-nervous. It scared me to feel so close to him, I guess, when we weren't even touching. So I'd defused the moment by reaching for my iPhone and taking his picture.

"Smile!" I'd said.

But he already *was* smiling. Not a toothy "smile!" smile, just an I'm-here-and-I-like-you smile. *I'm here, and I like you, and you don't have to run away from our closeness, but you can if you want—and you know what, Win? I'll* still *like you.*

His hazel eyes were warm and trusting. His head was sideways, propped in his palm in a way that pushed his cheek up in a slightly squishy way that was completely adorable. So why did looking at him make my chest hurt?

The ON function timed out, and the screen of my phone went black. *Bye-bye, Lars. Hello, darkness.*

I closed my eyes. *You have* got *to get over yourself,* I commanded.

Right, then. I pushed the ON button—again. I unlocked the screen—again. This time, I went to the FAVORITES page and tapped his name. A message flashed on top of the screen: CALLING MOBILE.

I brought the phone to my ear. What if he wasn't there?

Would that be good or bad? Did I want him to answer, or would it maybe be better to get his voice mail? I could leave a nice message. I could be bright and chirpy and say—

"Winnie. Wow."

I drew my crossed legs more closely in, because that wasn't what I would say. That's what Lars would say. That's what Lars *did* say, his voice alive and real even though he was miles and miles away.

"Hi," I said.

"Hi," he said.

Was I making it up, or did he sound weird? And the way he first answered: *Winnie. Wow.* When used nonironically, "wow" was a great word. But when used any other way? Not so wow.

I didn't know what to do—or say. It was as if I'd gone gluey inside, and the only part unaffected was my rapidly beating heart. Oh, and my sweat glands. I was stinky all of a sudden. Gross.

"Um . . . hi," I said. I winced. I already said that, didn't I?

"What's up," he said. There was no question mark implied at the end; he was doing the guy-flatline thing of saying "what's up," but not actually meaning it.

He *definitely* sounded weird.

"I got to see some baby turtles today," I said tentatively. "Tons of them. *Hundreds* of them." I shifted my position. "They were hatching. Um, from their eggs."

"Cool."

"It's really rare to get to see something like that. It was . . . pretty amazing."

"That's great, Winnie," Lars said, and I bowed my head. He *did* think it was great, I suspected, but what I heard in his voice was that even so, he was having to make an effort to be happy for me.

I was hurting him.

He was hurting me.

This sucked.

You could call it quits and walk away, a whisper said inside me. *Could be the kindest thing to do. . . .*

But, no. To break up with Lars would be . . . would be like dying inside. I gripped the phone.

"Lars—" I said.

At the same time, he said, "Winnie—"

I made a noise that someone might have called a laugh, I suppose. "Sorry. You go."

"That's all right," he said. "You first."

"No, you."

"No, *you.*"

Oka-a-a-ay, this was going nowhere fast. *Don't be a shriveled violet,* I coached myself. *You only live once. Don't waste it being stupid.*

"Lars?"

He hesitated. I thought I heard him swallow. "Yes?"

"There's something I need to tell you. It's, um, stupid, but I need to say it."

He waited.

"It's kind of been on my mind for a while."

He still didn't say anything. It was freaky to be having this conversation without seeing him.

"It's just . . . like I said, it's *stupid*, but . . ."

"Just say it, Winnie," he said gruffly.

I felt scolded. I also felt feverish, and I knew I *had* to say it, or I would throw up or faint, or both. "On my birthday— you gave me a Starbucks card." My voice hitched, *not* on purpose. "And it made me feel bad. That's all."

There was silence on Lars's end . . . and then he laughed. He *laughed*! I'd opened my heart to him, I told him what I'd been holding in all this time, and he laughed?!

I hunched over, wrapping one arm around my ribs and pressing my phone to my ear. "Stop laughing," I said.

"That's what you needed to tell me?" he said. He sounded downright *jolly*, and it pissed me off.

"Yes, and *stop laughing*. I *told* you it was stupid . . . but now you're making me feel worse."

"I can't believe you've been mad this whole time over a Starbucks card," he said.

"So you *knew* I was mad? Since when?"

"Mad, cold, whatever." He laughed again. "Why didn't you tell me?"

"Why didn't you *ask*?" I said. Flecks danced in front of my eyes. My breaths were shallow and fast. "Since apparently I've been such a drag to be around."

"Win, you're not here. You haven't been a drag to be around, because you *aren't* around."

"You were the one who originally wasn't going to be around! It's not my fault your mom's fellowship got canceled."

"I never said it was. Listen, Win . . . this is stupid."

"Duh! I said it was stupid from the beginning!" *And you don't get to call me* Win *while things aren't good between us,* Larson*!*

"Calm down," he said, which—big surprise—didn't turn my hurt feelings into a cloud of butterflies that disappeared merrily into the sky. "What *did* you want for your birthday?"

"I don't want to tell you anymore," I said.

"Come on, I won't laugh."

I tightened my jaw. This was a no-win situation. I couldn't *not* tell him, not after making such a drama out of it. But if I *did* tell him, he'd think it was dumb. Which it was, and which I fully admitted! And maybe he wouldn't laugh out loud, but secretly he would think I was "being a girl." He might even think it was *cute*, and if he said anything— anything at all—that smacked of, "Oh, poor Winnie, let me pat you on the head," I would fling my phone at him all the way from South Carolina and hope it struck him right between the eyes.

"I have to go," I said. "They're waiting on me for breakfast." Not true, but he didn't know better.

"Win," he coaxed.

"Forget it. It doesn't matter, okay?"

He sighed. And then, *because he was an idiot*, he took my words at face value. "I can't wait to see you," he said in his thinking-about-kissing voice. "I miss being able to hold you."

And I miss being held, I thought. A lump formed in my throat because it was all so wrong. A kiss *wouldn't* make everything better. Neither would a hug.

"I wanted a cupcake," I said. "From Sugar Sweet Sunshine."

"Sugar sweet . . . huh?"

"And you *knew* I did, or you should have known, because I only dropped five thousand hints." Tears welled in my eyes. "But, no. You thought, 'Oh yeah, it's my girlfriend's birthday. Hey, I know—I'll give her a stupid piece of plastic.'"

"A stupid piece of plastic," he repeated.

"Pretty much," I whispered. It was awful, the grayness pressing in on me on this beautiful, sky-blue day at the beach. My last beautiful, sky-blue day at the beach.

I lowered my phone and hit END CALL.

Figure Out Who I Am . . . ?

BABY TURTLES AND THEIR UNCERTAIN FUTURES—that's what I thought about on and off throughout the rest of the day. And Lars. Of course Lars. Except thinking about him made my stomach hurt, so I tried not to.

It was my last day at the beach. I didn't want to waste it.

Last walk to the point, last search for sand dollars, last porpoise-sighting, last swim. So many "lasts"—and others, possibly, that I didn't even notice as they happened. (Lars and I . . . had we kissed for the last time? Life wasn't supposed to happen like that. Big things, important things—a person should know when they happen.)

Don't cry, I ordered myself as I showered off in the bathhouse. I didn't know for sure that Lars and I had broken up; I didn't even know for sure if I wanted us to. And maybe—I wasn't sure—but maybe I'd been unfair to him? When we talked, and I got my feelings hurt, and kind of . . . hung up on him?

Oh, go ahead if you have to, I told myself as tears mixed with the water from the showerhead. And if I had to cry, the shower was a better place than most.

But up in my room, getting ready for the cookout with Dinah and Cinnamon, I held it together. I didn't tell them about Lars. Why should I put a damper on their good time, or make them feel as if they had to take care of me? I could take care of myself. I'd be fine. So I smiled and said thanks when Dinah complimented my yellow sundress with the blackbirds on it.

"Ty packed it for me," I said. I blinked a few times. "Isn't that so cute and so *Ty*?"

Dinah tilted her head. "You miss him, huh? Oh, *sweetie*."

She moved to hug me, but I stepped away. If she hugged me for missing Ty, when actually I was missing Lars (or something), then I would lose it.

No losing it. Cookout. Fun. That was the plan.

"You'll see him tomorrow," Dinah said, confused.

"I know. I'm fine." I tried the whole smile thing again. "Want me to do your hair?"

The cookout was lovely. It really was. There was something about staring into a fire that smoothed my mood, and when the bonfire was on the beach, as this one was, it was magical. The ocean, the sand, the twilighting sky . . . it was the perfect backdrop for the pop and crackle of the fire. The flames looked like they were dancing. They flickered and swayed, and each flame burned with so many colors. I would hate to fall into a fire, or be burned at the stake, but I could stare at one forever.

"You didn't eat your hot dog," someone said. *Alphonse.*

He stood above me, and his bronze skin glowed. If there were such a thing as Greek gods anymore, he would be one, except he'd be Jamaican. A Jamaican Greek god. The day I'd first met him, he hadn't been wearing a shirt, and he wasn't wearing a shirt now. Only his long surfer trunks.

"Not hungry?" he said.

"Huh?" *Oh, right. Hot dog.* I lifted my paper plate from my lap, and together we regarded my charred hot dog with its bubbling black blisters.

Alphonse furrowed his brow. "Utter failure, huh?"

I laughed ruefully. "Epic."

He indicated the empty spot beside me. "May I?"

"Yeah, sure."

He sat down beside me, leaning back on his elbows and taking up space the way guys did. He smelled good, like salt.

The sun was almost down, and Virginia said it was time to douse the fire, so Mark and Ryan went at it with two-liter bottles of Mountain Dew. Swear to God, they had an endless supply—and judging by how hyper they were, they'd poured as much into their mouths as they were now pouring on the fire.

"You think maybe water would work better?" Virginia suggested.

"No way," Ryan said, circling the fire like a deranged cannibal and spraying Mountain Dew in exuberant arcs. "Dis is da bahm!"

"Duffenetly," Mark said. "Youse guys gotta try it!" He tried to get everyone up. Cinnamon and James were easy sells; so was Erika. Dinah and Milo glanced at each other, and then made the exact same Oh-why-not expressions.

Milo was wearing a T-shirt that said, HARVARD—BECAUSE NOT EVERYONE CAN GET INTO MIT. It was so dorky that it was beyond dorky. It was so dorky that it went around the bend and was somehow cool, at least on Milo. Or maybe I just liked him for making Dinah so happy.

"Winnie," Mark coaxed, holding out a Mountain Dew bottle and waggling his eyebrows. "You know you want to."

I crinkled my nose. "Nah, I'm okay."

"Oh, come *on*," he said, as if he couldn't believe my lameness. He turned to Alphonse. "Alphonse. Buddy. It's Mellow-Yellow-licious."

Alphonse glanced at me, which I saw out of the corner of my eye. I'd returned to staring at the fire, drawing my legs to my chest, and resting my chin on my knees.

"I'll pass," he told Mark.

Mark started to give him a hard time, then changed his mind. He looked from Alphonse to me and chuckled. He held up his hands, palms out. "All right, man. All right."

By the fire, Cinnamon shook a bottle of Mountain Dew as if her life depended on it.

"This one's for the guppy!" she shouted, untwisting the cap to unleash a fizzing spray.

"I think she means the Gipper," Alphonse commented.

"I don't think she knows what she means," I replied. "And I have never understood what 'the Gipper' is." I looked at him from under my bangs, which were clumpier than normal in the moist ocean air. "What *is* the Gipper?"

"Football," he said. "Notre Dame."

Uh-huh. And I *still* didn't understand what the Gipper was. I sighed.

"What's wrong?" Alphonse asked.

I hesitated. Was there an answer to that question? An answer I could give to Alphonse, at any rate?

Before I could put any thoughts into words, the maniacs around the dying fire started belting out a mambo-cha-cha song I recognized from the radio station my mom listend to. Or rather, the guy maniacs sang the mambo-cha-cha song. The girl maniacs giggled.

"A little bit of Erika in my life," they crooned. "A little bit of Cinnamon by my side. A little bit of Dinah in the sun. A little bit of Winnie all night long."

Normally, I'd have been giggling, too. They were attempting a sideways sway that involved leaning at the waist and snapping to the beat. Not that they were *on* the beat, but they were trying.

But tonight . . .

It wasn't happening for me, that's all. I felt like a buzzkill, sitting stony-faced while everyone else was enjoying themselves. Forget that—I *was* a buzzkill. Even in my pretty sundress, I was a buzzkill.

"Wanna get out of here?" Alphonse asked.

"And go where?" I asked.

"I don't care. Down to the water?"

I didn't know if I should. Alphonse wasn't doing anything weird, or wrong. But a muscle in his jaw twitched, and I knew that his offer wasn't as casual as he wanted it to seem. And being aware of that meant that I couldn't respond casually back. That crazy electricity was jittering between us again.

Was it awful that one boy could make my heart pound, while another boy—who wasn't even here—could take that same heart and squeeze it till it bruised?

"I'm not asking you to marry me," Alphonse said. "Just if you want to go down to the water."

My cheeks got hot. I was glad it was dark.

I rose to my feet and tugged at my sundress to make it hang right. Alphonse noticed; I could *feel* him notice. My heart beat faster.

I walked to the water's edge. The waves washed over my feet, and I curled my toes in the wet sand. I wrapped my arms around my ribs.

Alphonse came up beside me, and I felt a little like saying, "Hey! *Mister!* Who gave you permission to stand so close?"

I hugged myself tighter and tried to breathe. But I felt dizzy, like there was all this pressure on me to . . . well, I didn't *know*, that was the problem. Or maybe I did know? Maybe *that* was the problem?

"Winnie, look at me," Alphonse said.

I swallowed.

"*Winnie.*" He touched my shoulder and turned me to face him. "I want to kiss you." He drew his eyebrows together as if he couldn't figure me out—which, *sheesh*, made two of us. "Can I?"

My heart was pounding so hard I thought I might be sick. Different impulses competed inside me, and I had a surreal vision of myself with a tiny angel hovering at one ear and a tiny devil at the other.

No, the angel said.

Why not? the devil said. *You only live once.*

But it would be wrong.

So?

So it would be WRONG. I would be cheating. On Lars.

Yeah, but who's going to tell? Tomorrow you leave. You'll never see Alphonse again.

He touched my face, and the particles and electrons between us knocked into each other and hummed. The little hairs on the back of my neck stood up.

You know you want to, the devil voice cajoled.

Except . . . did I? Did I *really*?

Alphonse was gorgeous. *Check.*

He was a cool guy, despite his occasional bouts of arrogance. *Check.*

He was inches away, and he smelled of summer and the sea and bonfire smoke, and—miraculously? incomprehensibly?—*he wanted to kiss me.* The intoxication of knowing that, from *seeing* it in the intensity of his gaze . . . it was a pretty powerful—a *very* powerful—drug.

And yet . . .

Alphonse wanted to kiss me, but did *I* want to kiss *him*, this cool and gorgeous boy who wasn't Lars???

No, I said to myself. Or possibly I said it out loud. Did I say it out loud?

Confusion passed like a shadow across Alphonse's features. He shook it off. His hand moved to the back of my head, and he leaned in.

"No," I said, stepping away.

Alphonse's arm fell to his side. "No . . . I can't kiss you?"

It was a weird moment, and I felt bad.

At the same time, I found myself able to stand a little taller. "No," I said with conviction.

"I thought you wanted me to."

"I know. I'm sorry."

"But if you're *sorry . . .*" He looked not at me, but just over my shoulder. His frustration was obvious. "I don't get it."

I didn't blame him. Was there a way to explain that while my body *did* want to kiss him, my heart knew it would be wrong? Not wrong as in right and wrong, *and now hold out your palm, young lady, so I can slap it with a ruler.* That was part of it, but not the whole tamale.

The whole tamale resided in my soul, I think. Although what was a soul, anyway? I imagined my soul as residing in my heart—which complicated the argument of "my body says yes, my heart says no," since my heart was *part* of my body. It was an organ. It beat inside my chest.

But sometimes my heart made bad choices just like my body did. Exhibit A: the way I handled my conversation with Lars this morning, which I was regretting more and more.

Still, if I had to listen to one over the other, my body or my heart, it was a no-brainer. I had to go with my heart, and my heart said, "This boy in front of you? He isn't *Lars*."

Alphonse exhaled, and I realized I'd been making him wait. And for what? Nothing, unless he could magically read my mind and divine for himself that really and truly, it wasn't him. It was me.

I tried to get him to look at me. I tried to will my thoughts from my brain into his. But the set of his jaw told me loud and clear, it wasn't happening.

"Whatever," he said, holding out his palms. "I'm going back up to the others."

A sudden realization made me dizzy. A realization so obvious that I felt like the biggest idiot in the world for not grasping it sooner.

"I *said* I'm heading back up," Alphonse repeated with enough pout to suggest that I could still make him change his mind.

"Um, okay," I said distracted. Now that I'd been hit with this new way of looking at things, I had to follow it to its bitter end.

I mean, God. I'd wanted Alphonse to *magically read my mind*? People couldn't magically read other people's minds. Maybe, possibly, some people could, if ESP existed. But I didn't have ESP, and clearly Alphonse didn't, either. And guess what? *Lars didn't either.* If he did, he'd have done party tricks for me for sure, asking me to think of a number and then wowing me time and time again by saying, "Three!" Or, "Six hundred fifty-two and three-fourths, ha *ha*! Thought you got me, didn't you?"

If he had ESP, he'd have given me that stupid cupcake I'd become so fixated on. He'd have given it to me on my birthday, easy-peasy-lemon-squeezie, and we'd have been *la la la, look at us, aren't we happy*!

But he didn't have ESP, and he wasn't psychic, and even if he was, it wasn't as if my thoughts and feelings were so crystal clear that he'd have been able to read them like an instruction manual.

Geez Louise, if even *I* didn't know what I wanted, how could I expect Lars to?

Maybe being known by someone, *really* being known by someone, wasn't a party trick like ESP. Maybe it was about opening your heart to that person, consciously and on purpose. And that meant the flip side was also true: to know someone in return required conscious effort, too. *Ag.* And, like, willingness to try . . . even when it was hard.

"All right," Alphonse said, startling me because I thought he'd already gone. "See ya."

"Uh-huh, see ya."

His Adam's apple jerked, and I berated myself for being such a lousy human being. He was kind of a victim of my freakishness, when it came down to it.

"I'll be up soon," I said in a more even tone. Not flirty—
no more flirty—but as one friend to another. Well, *ish*.

Alphonse's posture loosened, as if I'd given him
permission to reclaim his dignity. He smiled wryly and
headed back up toward the blackened bonfire.

My thoughts returned to Lars. For the zillionth time, I
replayed our phone conversation, and I burned with shame
at the memory of how he'd laughed at me. I finally came
clean about the stupid cupcake, and what did he do? He
laughed.

But . . . possibly . . . ag. I hated being wrong, I really
did. Even more, I hated being *in* the wrong. *Lars thought
you were going to break up with him,* I admitted to myself. *He
laughed because he was relieved, you numbskull.*

It might possibly have had to do with the, um,
ridiculousness of holding onto a grudge for so long. Over a
cupcake.

I might *possibly* have laughed, too, if I were him.

I faced the ocean, heaviness weighing me down like
rocks. Like Virginia Woolf, the writer who loaded her
pockets with stones and walked into the sea—that was how
I felt. (Though I would never, ever, ever do something like
that. Never.)

But I was seeing something with increasingly
uncomfortable clarity . . . and, it wasn't pretty.

When it came to me and Lars, I'd been a big baby. *There.*
And I'd probably known it for a long time, in the deepest,
truest part of myself.

I hadn't been a baby every single minute of every single day—and for sure Lars could have handled certain situations better, himself. But take the night of the penguin, for example. I'd been pissy that he wouldn't dump Bryce for me, but was I willing to dump Cinnamon and Dinah for him? Uh, *no*.

Big whiner baby.

When he told me about going to Germany, I blew up at first, and then got sullen. And then—poof! big smile!—I pretended in the very next moment like all was hunky-dory. We both knew it wasn't, but instead of talking about it, we went along *tra-la-la* as if it was. Only since we were both faking, it was a tainted, sloggy *tra-la-la*. More like a *tra-la-lump*.

I gazed at the inky water, surrendering to the hypnotic *swoosh* of the waves. A path of moonlight stretched from the shore to the horizon. Somewhere, baby sea turtles were following that path, listening only to the message in their hearts: *head toward the light, bitsy hatchlings. Head for the light!*

Farther up the beach, I heard Cinnamon shriek.

"Yes!" she cried. "Omigod, we have to do it *this very second*. The sign is mine!"

She *had* to be talking about the "do not feed or molest the alligators" sign. It was destined to be hers; I'd known it from the beginning.

Cinnamon and the sign, Dinah's first kiss . . . God, I'd

known so many things from the beginning. So why, when it came to my own life, was I so slow?

Voices drifted toward me: Dinah, trying to talk Cinnamon out of her plan; Ryan or Mark calling out for more Mountain Dew; Alphonse saying gruffly, "Yeah, she's down there."

The "she" he was referring to was me, and despite my gloom, I was glad someone cared. And now that person was coming to check on me. I could hear the squeak of footfalls on the sand. I was glad for that, too—even though the only person I really wanted to see was Lars. I wanted to make things right with him. I *needed* to make things right with him.

A terrible thought stopped my heart from beating: *What if it was too late?*

The footsteps grew louder, and if I hadn't been struck immobile by the fear of losing Lars, I would have turned around to see who it was. But all I could do was stand there, frozen, until I was released by the warmth of an arm slipping around my waist, pulling me close.

My heart whammed back into action, crazy fast and trying impossibly to leap from my chest . . . because I *knew* that arm! The smell of Mennen deodorant filled my nose, and I felt faint . . . because I knew that smell! I *loved* that smell!

I twisted around and melted into Lars's embrace. I hugged him *so* hard, my Lars, and sobs burbled up. They burbled and turned to laughter, and I craned my head to see his sweet, wonderful face. Somehow I managed to say, "Why are you here? *How* are you here?"

He grinned.

"My brother drove me," he said. "He has a buddy in Myrtle Beach. He's going to hang with him tonight."

"And you're going to hang . . . with me?" My eyes were so wide that I could feel my eyebrows way up past my bangs. I was smiling so hard that my cheeks felt like cherries.

"Yep," he said, loving every second of my reaction. "I called your parents, and they said Jake can drive you home tomorrow."

"Really?"

"Really. Cinnamon and Dinah, too, since we're already here."

"Omigosh, I can't be*lieve* this. I am so happy. I am so so so so happy!" I squeezed him tight, pressing my face into his shirt and breathing in deep. My lungs expanded to about three times their normal size.

But even though I was hugging him with everything I had, he was hugging me back with just his one arm.

"Why are you only hugging me with one arm?" I asked goofily. "I'm so not down with this one-arm hugging business! I want the full caboodle!"

I fumbled behind me for his other arm so that I could plant it in its proper position. I found his forearm, but what was . . . ?

His hand had something in it. That's why it wasn't free for hugging. And the thing he was holding? A box. A small, cardboard bakery box, tied with a pink curlique ribbon. A sticker on the top said SUGAR SWEET SUNSHINE.

"Lars!" I exclaimed, filling that single word with the uncomplicated gratitude of a puppy dog with oversized manga puppy dog eyes. And my oversized puppy dog eyes would look wet, and have twinkle stars in them, and be super-duper adorable—but not as adorable as Lars, *who brought me a cupcake.* Because of course that was what was in the box. I didn't have to open it to know.

"I was such a jerk," I confessed. "It's like . . . okay, I've been thinking about it a lot."

"I have, too," he said. "A Starbucks card—it *was* kind of lame."

"Yeah, but how could you know that? You picked it out on purpose because you thought I'd like it, right? It wasn't like you suddenly at the last minute said, 'Oh, crap, I've gotta get Winnie a birthday present.'" I felt a brief stab of doubt. "Um . . . did you?"

He shook his head. "I picked the one with the beach scene, because of how much you love the beach."

"And I was totally rude."

"But I could have done better."

"But I could have let you know how I felt. And see, that's what I realized. I thought that you should just magically know what I wanted, and if you didn't, that meant you didn't know *me.*"

"When actually"—he half-laughed—"I just didn't know what you wanted."

I half-laughed, too. I was embarrassed, but so so happy. "And I didn't know how to tell you."

He handed me the bakery box. I took it, but didn't open it. I wasn't ready to stop the hugging.

"It's a cupcake," he said.

"Cool."

"It's chocolate with chocolate frosting. And they put a candle in it for me."

"Is the candle pink?"

"Pink and white striped. Does that work?"

I hugged him tight and told the universe *thank you, thank you, thank you* for letting me have this wonderful boy in my life. I could have ruined it, and I felt a brief, dark tremor at just how close I came.

Lars pulled back and looked down at me. I lifted my head, and our eyes locked. We stayed like that for a long time, just soaking each other in.

Then we kissed. We did that for a long time, too.

That night, we decided to sleep on the beach: me and Lars, Dinah and Milo, Cinnamon and James. It wasn't all that comfortable, but the stars were amazing. God's jewelry box, Virginia said. Distant bright glimmers in a sky as inky-dark as the ocean. Plus, speaking of the ocean, the *swush* of the waves was better by far than Dinah's sound machine, which she used back in Atlanta.

I might have to buy a sound machine myself, though. The one Dinah had made a pretty good "waves" track. I'd kinda like to keep falling asleep to the sound of waves, even back home.

Home.

Lars took off his long-sleeved flannel shirt (he was wearing a T-shirt underneath it) and let me use it as a blanket. It smelled like him and, after the others had drifted off, I held it close and thought about tomorrow. I'd have to say good-bye to so many things: DeBordieu, the beach house, Virginia, all my new summer friends who'd probably slip quietly from my life, despite the promises I bet we'd make to keep in touch.

Or maybe they wouldn't. Who knew? Dinah and Cinnamon had already invited Milo and James to come to Atlanta and go to Six Flags before school started, and they both said they would. I'd be up for an end-of-the-summer Six Flags blowout, as long as Lars was by my side. We could ride the Scream Machine. We could share a kiss on the tippy-top of the Great Gasp.

But tomorrow we'd drive back to Atlanta, and if Cinnamon had her way (and she almost always did), we'd stop at the halfway point for burritos from Taco Bell. And then she would get gas, and she would find herself hilarious, while the rest of us rolled down the windows and gagged.

When I got home, there would be hugging galore, and Mom and Dad would *ooo* and *ahh* over the pictures on my iPhone. I'd suggest that getting a beach house of our own would be a supergood idea, and Dad would say, "How about a new lawn mower instead?" I would say, "Ha ha ha," and Mom would say, *"Joel."*

There would be Sandra-ish-ness, and maybe Bo would stop by to say hey. And of course Ty would have all sorts of stories about the inventions he'd designed and the "water feature" he'd constructed for our backyard, made entirely out of multicolored plastic straws, aluminum foil, and Mom's baking bowls. (Mom had told me about the water feature already, last week when I called to check in. But I'd let Ty tell me fresh.)

As for teensy baby Maggie, sheesh, she was probably driving by now. She could take me for a spin!

Beside me, Lars microsnored: not loud and chainsaw-y, but just audible enough to be endearing. I yawned and snuggled up next to him, knowing that I needed to get some rest, too. Anyway, cute as snoring-Lars was, I was not Edward, and he was not Bella. (Thank God.)

I loved the guy, but I didn't need to watch him sleep.

Peace Out

COMING BACK TO ATLANTA was like unraveling a sweet roll and plucking off bites and popping them one after the next into my mouth until my taste buds sang.

Teensy baby Maggie? Had a tooth!!!!! Her very first!!!!

"It broke through her gums, and so we immediately told *all* the grandparents and aunts and uncles," Dad said.

"But not me?" I said indignantly.

Dad squeezed me. He was sitting beside me on the sofa, his arm around me as I held my baby sister. "Well, hold on, it gets complicated," he said.

"Yeah," Sandra said, leaning between us from behind. "Because before calling you, Dad had to tell *all* the neighbors."

"It was smack in the middle of the day," Dad protested. "I knew your schedule by then. I wanted to talk to you in person, not leave a voice mail."

"So he filled the hours by also telling the dude at the grocery store," Sandra said. "And the dude at the drugstore, and that creepy lady with the mustache who works at the dry cleaners."

"Sandra, be nice," Mom said. She had her legs tucked

up under her on the purple armchair, and she looked way more well-rested than before I'd left. In addition to having grown a tooth, Maggie was now sleeping through the night. *Go, baby Mags!*

"Is 'truthful' not nice?" Sandra protested. "I think the 'dry cleaning' bit"—she made exaggerated air quotes—"is a front for a crime ring. That's what I think."

"A crime ring?" Ty said, his eyes lighting up. He was sitting on my other side and giving me a foot rub, that good boy. Though it was more like a foot pummel. "What kind of crime ring?"

"No crime ring," Mom said.

"But all those chemicals," Sandra said. "And that smell. She's covering something up for sure—maybe a dead body."

"*No*, Ty," Mom said. "Do not go repeating that." But her lips twitched, and Sandra (who would be leaving for college soon! *ack*!) grinned.

"Ahem," Dad said. "The tooth?"

I'd been sitting quietly, just soaking my goofy family in, but I roused myself and said, "Yes, Dad. Pray continue."

"The tooth emerged, like a great white whale," he said. "We alerted the press."

"All except *me*!" I said.

"And then the tooth *went back under*—"

"Also like a great white whale," Sandra interjected.

Ty dove his hand down. "*Whoosh*. Back to the depths!"

"Huh?" I said. "Her tooth went *back into her gums*? That is just weird."

"It finally came back again," Sandra said. "Just not until Dad had to eat crow with Grandmom and Granddad and everyone who wanted proof of this alleged 'tooth.'" She made more air quotes, and I giggled.

"So we waited this time," Dad said, giving me a noogie. "We wanted you to see it for yourself."

"Then let me see, baby," I said to Mags. I turned her in my arms and wedged my finger into her mouth. She gurgled happily and chomped down.

"I can feel it!" I cried.

"That's my girl," Dad said proudly. I didn't know if he meant me or Maggie, not that it mattered.

It was good to be home.

But there were sadnesses, too, since life wasn't made up only of happy things. The last month of summer turned into the last week of summer, and one muggy Saturday morning, Dad helped Sandra load her stuff into the trunk of his Honda. Freshmen at Middlebury weren't allowed to have cars, so Dad was going to drive her to Vermont and get her settled.

Sandra was the second person out of her group of friends to leave for college, and her remaining best buds came to the house to tell her good-bye. I watched from the back door. And then, when they left, Bo pushed off the side of the house from where he'd been waiting. He held her tight and rubbed small circles on her back . . . except what good was his comfort when he was the one she was going to miss most of all?

I shouldn't have watched, but I couldn't help myself, until Dad came in all sweaty and said, "Let's give them some privacy, huh?"

"But—"

"Come on and sit down with me," he said. "I could use a break."

When I didn't budge, he placed his hand on my shoulder and steered me, still resisting, to the kitchen table. A lump formed in my throat.

"I don't want her to go," I said.

"I know," he said.

"I'm going to miss her!"

"I know."

I looked into his eyes, which were teary just like my own. He pulled me into a hug and held me tighter than normal.

"We're all going to miss her," Dad said. "But that's just the way it is. That's the way it should be."

He and Sandra left an hour later. They pulled away, and Mom and Ty and Maggie and I waved and waved, and afterward, it was awful to see her golf-ball-yellow Bimmer parked lifeless in the garage. At the same time, it was reassuring. It meant she'd be coming back.

Then the last week of summer turned into the last day
of summer, and the last day of summer was also—freaky,
freaky—*the last day before high school.*

Ahhhh!

I went from jumpy-stomach scared one second to excited
the next, and my brain *would not shut up.*

Holy crap, I am so not ready for this, I thought, trying not
to hyperventilate over grades and extracurriculars and permanent records, and the knowledge that how I did in high
school would determine what college I went to. And after
college came *life*, and, like, choosing a purpose for my entire
existence, and holy crap, I was *so* not ready for that!

But on the other hand . . . *ooo, what to wear, what to wear?*
And all the people I'd meet, and the cool classes I could
take, and just being in *high school* instead of junior high. It
was a much realer feeling, somehow. Like—*ag*, but true—*I
was growing up.* I *was*, and there was nothing anyone could
do to stop me. Beneath the fear, I was pretty stoked.

And then, out of nowhere, Amanda called. *Amanda*, my
old best friend. When we were ten, we thought we'd grow up
together and be old ladies together. We totally planned it out:
We'd live in a huge house with wood floors, and we'd wear
our gray hair in braids, and we'd roller skate in swooping
circles around the living room. It was a done deal . . .

. . . and then it wasn't.

And then, five thousand years later, an unknown
number flashed on my iPhone. I knew from the area code
that it was an Atlanta number, so I answered.

And it was Amanda.

"Sorry to bother you," she said. Her voice was halting, yet familiar enough to make the blood rush from my head.

I sat down on my bed. "No problem," I said dumbly. "What's up?" *And who'd you get my number from? And you're probably calling from your cell phone, huh? Because I still know your home number. I'll probably know it when I'm forty, or even when I'm eighty.*

(But will I wear my gray hair in braids?)

"Nothing," she said. "Anyway, I'm sure you're busy." I heard her swallow, and it was her nervous swallow, and I knew she was upset. And it was so frickin' weird to be talking to her out of the blue and to *know* that.

"Amanda," I said, "what's wrong?"

She started crying. My throat closed.

"Sweet Pea died," she said. "She got hit by a car."

"Oh, A*man*da!"

Sweet Pea was Amanda's cat, and also my cat's adoptive cat sister. Only now Sweet Pea was . . . *dead*?

On reflex, I scanned my room, and my rib cage loosened when I spotted Sweetie Pie in her customary spot on my computer chair. Then it tightened right back up again with sorrow and guilt.

"When?" I asked Amanda. "To*day*?"

"I found her when I got"—she gulped—"when I got home from Gail's. And . . . and whoever hit her hadn't even *moved* her." Her crying sounds stretched into keening. "Can you come help me, Winnie? Puh-puh-*please*?"

I couldn't speak. My heart raced, and I felt sweaty, but in a cold way that made me dizzy. *And Sweet Pea was dead, and poor Amanda found her . . .*

"Never mind," Amanda said. She pulled herself together, and *wham*, her weakness was gone, shoved deep down inside her, the door slammed shut. "I'm fine. Really."

"No, you're not," I fumbled. "And of course I can come. I'll be right there."

"Seriously, Winnie, I'm fine," she insisted. "I'm sorry to bother you. I was feeling . . . *you* know . . . but I'm better now." She let out a small self-deprecatory laugh. "Just a minor freak-out, I swear. Um . . . thanks *so* much for listening."

Maybe I would have believed her if I were someone else and not her best friend from years and years ago.

"I'll be there in ten minutes," I told her.

She'd put Sweet Pea in a box. A Fendi shoe box, to be exact, and I knew just which shoes had been in it . . . well, unless Amanda had tons of Fendi shoes and not just the one pair of suede platform pumps I'd noticed her wearing last year. They were crazy, those pumps. The spiked heels were six inches tall at least, but the toe parts were thick and round and chunky, and the whole package was swampy brown with black trim, if I was remembering correctly. So while it looked like the type of shoe only a New York fashion model would wear, it also had a slight grunge factor, or an alternative factor, or *something*, and Amanda had found a way to pair those pumps with a retro babydoll dress and somehow avoid the dress code police.

It was a cool look, and I'd wondered, at the time, if I could pull such a look off. (I couldn't.) I also wondered how much a pair of shoes like that cost, and if I could even afford them. (Later, I Googled them. I couldn't.)

But no Fendi pumps lay in the shoe box today. Only Sweet Pea, who was no longer Sweet Pea but a limp ball of fur. It seemed horribly and wrenchingly wrong that a body could exist without a soul, because what was in front of me . . . it *wasn't* Sweet Pea.

"Amanda . . ." I said. I lifted my eyes from Sweet Pea's body to Amanda's tearstained face. "I am *so* sorry."

She nodded. Her hair was short—her beautiful blond hair, and not just short but *way* short—and her eyes were puffy. Green eyeliner dribbled down. "I hid the spot . . . you know." She sniffled. "Where the blood is."

"Yeah," I said softly. "Do you think she . . . died immediately?" As soon as the words were out of my mouth, I regretted them, because how would Amanda know? And if she hadn't died immediately, was that really something to dwell on?

"I'm pretty sure," Amanda said.

"Me too," I said. "I think, um . . . yeah."

"I thought we could bury her in the backyard," she said. She gazed at me from under her choppy bangs, which, come to think of it, were a paler blond than her hair used to be.

They were practically white, or maybe the right word was "platinum." She squinched one eye, perhaps to put a little distance between us. "I mean . . . if you . . . ?"

"Of course," I said.

She nodded again, and sniffled again, and swiped her hand beneath her nose. Then she lifted the box with Sweet Pea's body in it and went around the side of her house.

I followed, feeling as if I were stepping back in time. I knew these magnolia trees; Amanda and I used to make boats out of the broad, green leaves. We'd float them in the gutter after a rainstorm. And I knew this wrought iron gate that separated the front yard from the back. I knew how to jingle-jangle the latch to make it squeak open, and so I stepped forward and did it, since Amanda had her hands full. She gave me a small smile.

In the backyard, I was hit by so many memories that I felt as if I were in the company of ghosts. The gnarled dogwood with one branch sticking straight out—Amanda and I dangled from that branch for *hours*, trying to get up enough nerve to "fall" and break our arms. The concrete stepping-stone inlaid with fragments of brightly colored glass, which Amanda had made from a kit one year. "I love you, Mom and Dad!" it said in little kid finger painting. The clump of honeysuckle growing at the far edge of the yard, where a wasp had flown up inside Amanda's shirt and stung her three times before I figured out what was going on and wrestled her shirt over her head.

Afterward, we'd quarreled about it.

"It was a bumblebee," Amanda insisted. "They sting the worst, and I could feel its fuzziness."

"No, it was a wasp," I argued. "Bumblebees die after one sting, and this one stung you *three separate times.* The proof is in the pudding."

I wondered, now, if Amanda had been mad at me for ripping her shirt off right there in the open. We were only ten and had nothing to be embarrassed about. But Amanda began caring about that stuff earlier than I did—not that I knew it then. Maybe she felt embarrassed, in addition to being angry and in pain. Maybe she poured all of those emotions into our stupid bumblebee/wasp squabble.

Standing here four years later, I almost asked her. I almost said, "Hey . . . remember the time that wasp stung you?"

But I decided it wasn't appropriate. Plus, what if she just blinked at me?

The old Amanda, if asked about that wasp, would have shoved me and said, "*Bumblebee,* you mean. And of course I remember. I almost died."

She didn't, though. Almost die. Two years later, I'd get stung thirty-two times by a swarm of yellow jackets, and I wouldn't die, either.

It made me feel ancient.

"You think . . . oh, I don't know." Amanda kicked a patch of ground with the toe of her sneaker. "Here?"

"Sure," I said. She's chosen a spot beneath the dogwood

tree. "Sweet Pea would like it. All the birds and everything."

Amanda started crying anew, because Sweet Pea loved chasing birds. *Used* to love chasing birds.

"God, Amanda, I'm sorry," I said, feeling like an idiot for saying the wrong thing once again. "I'm making everything worse, aren't I?"

"What? No!" she said, and her reply was so vehement that I believed her. "You came. You're here." She gestured around. "Do you see anyone else lined up to help me bury her?"

I blinked. Had she asked any of her other friends to come over? If so, surely no one would have actually said no. Would they have?

Amanda sucked in a shuddery breath. She carefully set Sweet Pea down and said, "I'll get a shovel. Be right back."

She left, and I scratched my head. My eyes went to Sweet Pea, then just as quickly away.

I had to do something, so I got down on my knees and picked clovers from the grass. I wove them into a tiny garland, which I placed on Sweet Pea's head like a fairy crown.

"Be well, wherever you are," I said. "Watch the birds, listen to their songs, and know that you will be missed."

Amanda knelt beside me. I hadn't realized she'd returned, and my face flamed. But Amanda put down the shovel and took my hand. With her other hand, she stroked Sweet Pea's lifeless body.

"Go on," she said.

"Um . . . you were a good cat," I said, faltering.

Amanda made a chokey sound, which made *me* make a chokey sound. My eyes filled with tears.

"Better than good," she whispered. "The best."

I stayed for a while, afterward, and we drank Clementine Izzes and talked. I told her I liked her haircut, which I did, after I'd had time to get used to it.

"Gail thinks it's retarded," Amanda said.

"What? Not at all, and I hate it when people say that." I thought about Brooklyn's baby brother in his walker. "People don't choose to be retarded. It just . . . happens. It shouldn't be used as an insult, just like 'gay' shouldn't be used as an insult."

Amanda neither agreed nor disagreed, and I worried she thought I was slamming her when my intent was to slam Gail.

"She says it makes my eyes look too big," she said, looking at me with blue eyes that *were* almost impossibly huge.

I *pfff*-ed. "She's jealous. Since when did big eyes become a bad thing?" I cocked my head, considering her quirky blond tufts. "Anyway, you look like a forest sprite, or an elf."

She laughed. "Only you, Winnie."

"Only me what?"

"Would say someone looked like a forest sprite and mean it as a compliment."

I smiled as if I understood, but how could comparing someone to a forest sprite *not* be a compliment? I would love to look like a forest sprite. Or an elf.

She said nice things about how tan I was, and I said, "You should see Cinnamon. Omigod, she is so dark." Then I worried I'd hurt her feelings by bringing up Cinnamon, or made things weird somehow. Then I told myself, *Winnie, stop being a spaz. Things already are weird, and plus, the two of you do have different friends. It's not a secret, and it's not something you need to hide. And plus, if things are ever to get un-weird, you've got to just relax.*

So I asked how Gail was, and Malena, and Amanda said the two of them spent all summer in synchronized swimming camp.

"Reeeaally," I said, drawing out the *e* sound.

"They wore flowered swim caps and matching teal swimsuits," Amanda said.

"Like the Aqua Girls!" I giggled, flashing on our short-lived club from sixth grade. "We had to wear teal for that, remember?"

"Oh, God," she said, rolling her eyes. "But for synchronized swimming, it's even worse. They had to wear *nose plugs.*"

"No way."

"Way."

I took a swig of my Izze, loving the image of Gail and Malena wearing nose plugs. But I didn't want to be a brat, so I said, "That's hilarious . . . but kinda cool, I guess." I envisioned rows of girls doing fancy things with their arms while egg-beater-ing their legs beneath the water. "Very old-school glamorous."

"I guess," Amanda said.

"How about Aubrey?" I asked, referring to her goth friend. Maybe Amanda was tighter with her these days than Gail and Malena.

"Aubrey?" Amanda repeated.

"Yeah, Aubrey. How's she doing?"

Amanda drew her eyebrows together as if trying to establish whether or not I was kidding. "Winnie . . . Aubrey moved to Alaska."

"A*las*ka? For real? When did that happen?"

"At the beginning of June. She e-mailed once, then"— she did a magician's *snap*—"nothing. Nada. Guess she's communing with the moose."

"Or with Karen," I said. Karen went to elementary school with us, and then, like Aubrey, disappeared into thin air when her dad got a new job—also in Alaska, of all things. "Remember Karen?"

Amanda blinked. "Omigod. I haven't thought about Karen in . . ." She drew her thumb to her mouth. "She *did* move to Alaska, didn't she?"

"We brought up the moose with her, too, before she left. She cried and said she didn't want to make friends with any moose—or maybe she said *mooses*. She said she just wanted Louise."

Amanda whistled. "I'm kind of . . ." She shook her head. "You're kind of blowing my mind here, Winnie. Don't you think it's bizarre that Karen and Aubrey would *both* move to Alaska?"

"Well, sure," I said. "But no more bizarre than life in general, you know?"

"Maybe," she said. She eyed me. "*No*, I think it's pretty bizarre."

"You could e-mail Aubrey and give her Karen's name," I suggested.

"I could," she said dubiously.

I watched her face. "You're not going to."

First she looked guilty. Then she laughed. "Y-y-yeah, I'd say there's about . . . hmmm . . . a point-five percent chance I'll be e-mailing Aubrey about Karen. I don't even remember Karen's last name, do you?"

I did. It was Hughes. But I saw no need to say so. "Alaska's a pretty big state," I agreed. "Lots of people, not to mention all those moose."

Amanda put down her Izze bottle. "You're funny, Winnie," she said, as if it were a revelation. But it wasn't. I'd always been funny. She'd simply forgotten, just as she'd forgotten Karen's last name.

"I'm charming and delightful, too," I said lightly.

"You are," she granted. She furrowed her brow. "Why did we . . . ?" She broke off.

"Why did we what?" I said. We were entering dangerous

territory—except, didn't the real danger lie in tiptoeing carefully away? We were blood sisters, after all. Amanda's blood flowed in mine, and mine in hers.

"Why did we stop being friends?" I said.

She didn't answer, so I gave it a stab.

"I guess we just . . . grew in different directions," I said. I was trying to be honest, but it came out sounding awfully *how-to-raise-your-teenager*-y. "I didn't want us to, though."

"Me, neither," she said.

I raised my eyebrows, and spots of color rose in her cheeks.

"Well, maybe a little, I did," she admitted.

I blushed, too, because she *had* wanted to grow in a different direction than me. She'd gone from being my best friend to being embarrassed for me, because I wasn't into makeup and bras and stuff. And then, not long after, to being embarrassed *of* me.

Wood sprite, I thought, and this time it stung.

"But I think you picked better," she said. "Your friends . . . they're *realer*, I think. Than mine."

It must have cost her something to say that. How could it not have? And I agreed, not point-five percent, but one hundred percent. Dinah and Cinnamon *were* realer than Malena and Gail and Aubrey.

"Well, you might be right," I said at last.

"You *know* I am," she said.

"Okay, fine. You are." *But I'm proud of you for stepping out of the land of stupid tiptoeing,* I added in my head.

She smiled ruefully.

"Amanda, you can be friends with us, too," I said, leaning forward. Though as I heard the words come out of my mouth, I wondered, *Really? Can she? What if Dinah and Cinnamon have something to say about this?*

A fierce voice spoke up inside me, startling me and making me realize that my younger self was still very much alive.

Now you listen, the voice said. *If she wants to be your friend, you will make it happen.*

"That's nice," Amanda said, as if I were throwing her a bone and both of us knew it.

"No," I said in a tone that left zero room for doubt. "Really."

My younger self loved Amanda, despite it all. And as it turned out, my nearly fourteen-and-a-half-year-old self did, too.

So . . . and then . . . yeah. I left Amanda's, and night fell, and the moon rose. The crazy, beautiful moon. I opened my blinds before climbing into bed, and then I curled up under the covers and gave myself over to it. My thoughts loosened as I grew drowsy, and for once, I didn't rein them in. I just said . . . *go*, and they did: to the beach, to heaven, to all the people scattered all over this crazy, beautiful world. And not just people, but cats, too. And dogs, and howling coyotes, and cows with mad jumping skills. Porpoises. Sea turtles. Brooklyn and Lucas. Alphonse with his broad shoulders. Pingy.

And in my dream (I think it was a dream), there was an old lady with long gray braids. She was roller-skating around me, and I told her to stop, but she wouldn't. She just laughed. At first I was put out, but then I laughed, too.

"You did it, you know," she said.

"Did what?" I said, taking awkward, rotating steps to keep her in sight.

She smiled in a knowing way.

"*Oh!*" I said. "My list!" I did a mental review, putting check marks by all the things I'd accomplished on my To-Do-Before-High-School list. And what do you know? I'd done them all, every single one of them. "You're right, I did!"

"That's not what I mean," the old lady said. She skated past me, spreading her arms and lifting one leg in a show-off pose.

"Stop that," I said. "Could you just be still? Just for one second?"

She sprang into the air, did a half-twist, and landed on her other leg so that she was now gliding backward. "You didn't need that list," she said. "You never needed that list."

"Oh, like you're the great expert," I said. I should have been embarrassed at talking to an old lady like that, but I felt like I knew her. Like she could take it.

"I *can* take it," the old lady said. "You can, too."

"Huh?"

She grinned and skated off, and thank God, because I was growing dizzy. The world was spinning, and my thoughts were spinning, and they floated by me in actual words, like this:

> *your whole life brought you here, not just the last*
> > *half a year*
> *and you've done a pretty good job, really*
> *better than Amanda, right?*
> *not to be rude . . .*

How weird, how amazingly cool, to dream in words. My whole life was a book, and I could flip back or jump forward . . . or just be where I was. Be *who* I was. Was that what that nutty old lady was trying to tell me?

Everything I'd ever done—the days I'd lived through, the years I'd racked up, the birthdays I'd celebrated—all of those moments had brought me forward to *here*. And all I'd had to do, really, was be me.

I liked being me. In fact, I *loved* being me . . . just as I loved the moon, which was still shining through my open window, giving me such topsy-turvy dreams. Yet in China, the moon had already set and the sun was high in the sky.

Was it tomorrow in China, or yesterday? And how could that be, anyway? Wasn't today just plain today?

Didn't matter. Chinese girls would head to Chinese high school, some for their very first day, and for some, the sky would be full of marshmallows . . .

. . . or rather, *clouds*. Silly brain. Though sometimes clouds looked like marshmallows. Sometimes they looked like pirate ships. Sometimes puffy hearts.

Then I was a butterfly, and my wings were made from

Lars's soft flannel shirt, which I never gave back after he let me borrow it at the beach. I flew out my window— *whoosh*—and into the dark night, which smelled like lilacs. Streetlights lit up as I passed, but the moon was brighter than all of them, glowing like Brooklyn's pale tummy. Like teensy baby Maggie's first tooth and a shooting-star kiss and Amanda's white-blond pixie cut, perfect for her delicate features.

When I grew tired, I let the wind carry me, and I bobbed on its currents like a porpoise riding the waves. I almost caught a glimpse of Dinah when I passed her house, but she rolled over, and anyway, the curtains were drawn in her purple bedroom.

No matter. I'd see her soon enough, and Cinnamon, too. I'd even see Amanda, because if our paths didn't cross, I'd make them cross. When our eyes met, I'd say "hey," and she'd say "hey" back. I knew it deep in my butterfly soul.

I flew to the moon itself, and when I got there, I was giddy. *Oh,* I thought. *This is why the coyotes howl: They want to gobble it up, this yummy pale pie.*

The next thing I knew, it was morning. Mom fixed me a bowl of cereal, but I was too nervous to eat, even though the Cheerios looked so cheerful in the white milk. Their round-ness reminded me of something. I couldn't figure out what.

And the *next* next thing I knew, Dad was dropping me off at Westminster. Not at the junior high building, but at the entrance to Campbell Hall, where the high school girls had homeroom.

"Bye, princess," Dad said, leaning over and kissing the top of my head. "Have a great day."

"Okey-doke," I said, as if this were so normal, pulling up to Campbell Hall and starting ninth grade. I was glad it was Dad, and not Mom, who'd brought me, because Mom would have known how un-normal it was. She would have said something about it, trying to be all Mom-supportive, and her remark would have had the exact opposite effect than she intended.

But here I was, and there was nothing to do but get out of the car. Anyway, there was Cinnamon, sitting on the front steps of the building, and yep, there was Dinah, too, climbing up to join her. They exchanged words, excited, and Dinah plopped down beside her. Their heads turned toward me.

"Winster!" Cinnamon summoned. "Come on!"

Oh, my friends, I thought, feeling a swell of love. I climbed out of the car, and I swayed, maybe out of dizziness or maybe because it was finally here, this day I'd been waiting for forever.

Except, I hadn't just waited, had I? I'd done *a lot* in my fourteenth year so far. There'd been good times and bad times, silly times and sad times. Baby sea turtle times— *yay*! And rotten chicken-neck times—*gross*.

And my friends, and Lars, and an extremely delicious chocolate cupcake with chocolate frosting.

All that, and I was only at the halfway point. Who knew what waited around the corner?

Behind me, Dad was pulling away. Other cars pulled up, and other girls got out. Voices filled the air, colliding and bouncing off each other. One girl giggled anxiously. Another greeted a friend with delight.

"Winnie, are you okay?" Dinah called, half-rising from the steps. Cinnamon pulled her back down.

"Of course she's okay," she said. "She's just slow."

Am I? I thought. Hmm. *Sometimes yes, sometimes no. But, hey—I made it, didn't I?*

Cinnamon cupped her hands around her mouth. "Winnie! Babe! Places to go, people to meet—what are you waiting for?!"

Nothing, I realized.

"Chill!" I yelled, startling the girls nearby. "Oh. Um, sorry," I told them.

"No big," one of them replied. She scuttled away quickly nonetheless.

Cinnamon and Dinah were laughing at me. I could tell. The morning sun was behind them, making them glow, as I headed up to join them.

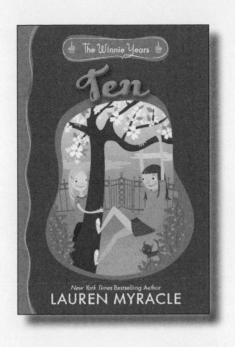

Winnie Perry is turning ten and ten is BIG: it means double-digits, more responsibility, and being an almost-middle-schooler. And with best friend, Amanda, by her side, Winnie plans on enjoying every last second of their last year in elementary school.

978-0-525-42356-0

"Lighthearted and well-observed...sure to strike a familiar chord with girls on the brink of adolescence."

—*Publishers Weekly*

978-0-14-240346-4